I0672096

DAKOTA'S DIARY

M.T. CONNOLLY

♣ ╠ THE ROCK HILL COMPANY ╣ ♣

Copyright © 2012 by M.T. Connolly

All rights reserved

Library of Congress Control Number: 2012919557

Published in the United States of America
By
Rock Hill Publishing
a division of
The Rock Hill Company, Inc.

In conjunction with

CreateSpace
of Amazon

For Information about permission to reproduce selections from
this book, write to Permissions, Rock Hill Publishing .
40 Clough Road, Dedham, MA. 02026
therockhillcompany@gmail.com

ISBN-13: 978-0-9857371-1-5
ISBN-10: 0985737115

Book Design By Llyonnoc

DAKOTA'S DIARY

The Story of the
Fruit of the Poisonous Tree

And the Lord God said, *It is* not good man should be alone: I will make him an help meet for him.

And the rib, which the Lord God had taken from man, made he a woman, and brought her unto the man.

And the woman said unto the serpent, We may eat of the fruit of the trees of the garden: But of the fruit of the tree which *is* in the midst of the garden, God hath said, Ye shall not eat of it, neither shall ye touch it, lest ye die.

And when the woman saw that the tree *was* good for food, and that it *was* pleasant to the eyes, and a tree to be desired to make *one* wise, she took of the fruit thereof, and did eat; and gave also unto her husband with her, and he did eat.

And the eyes of them both were opened

And the Lord God called unto Adam . . . Hast thou eaten of the tree, whereof I commanded thee that thou shouldest not eat?

And the man said, The woman, whom thou gavest to be with me, she gave me of the tree, and I did eat.

And the Lord God said unto the woman, What is this that thou has done? And the woman said, The serpent beguiled me, and I did eat.

GENESIS　　　CHAPTER II AND III

The Story of Pandora's Curiosity

The first mortals lived on earth in a state of perfect innocence and bliss. Man was content. Jupiter ascribed a good part of this beatific condition to the gift [of fire] conferred by Prometheus He was greatly displeased and sought to devise a means to punish mankind for accepting the heavenly fire.

He assembled the gods on Mount Olympus in a solemn council, they decided to create woman; and as soon as she had been artfully fashioned, each one endowed her with some special charm, to make her more attractive.

They decreed she should be called Pandora. She was given to Epimetheus as a gift from heaven. The first days of their union were spent in blissful wanderings.

One evening while dancing on the green, Mercury appeared carrying a heavy huge box. He asked if he could deposit it with them for a time. He left it in their house to return for it later. Pandora speculated with feminine curiosity upon what was in the box.

Epimetheus told her that her curiosity was unseemly but he left her alone in the house. Pandora set to work attempting to untie the intricate knot in the golden cord that kept the box shut. When she did a voice inside begged her, "Pandora, dear Pandora, have pity upon us! Open, open, we beseech you!"

She lifted the lid slightly. Jupiter had malignantly crammed into this box all the diseases, sorrows, vices, and crimes that afflict poor humanity and they flew out and evil entered into the world.

MYTHS OF GREECE AND ROME   H.A. GUERBER

INTRODUCTORY NOTE:

I've had this thick spiral five-subject notebook in my possession for a while now. I found it one morning about nine-thirty at a Starbucks on Second Avenue in New York City between Seventy-Fifth and Seventy-Sixth Streets. I went in to have a coffee and sat at the table with my computer to catch up with my emails on the internet. I noticed it on the seat next to me. I was there fifteen minutes or so and no one came to retrieve it.

I picked it up and looked in it. I was hoping that perhaps it was blank. If that was the case it would be unlikely anyone would come back for it. I'd be in luck because I was planning to buy one. I opened it and saw it was filled with writing in a beautiful long hand. I flipped through the pages reading a little bit here and there. It was about 80 to 85% full. I knew then a lot of work had gone into it so I didn't want to put it back on the chair, fearing it may be picked up by an irresponsible person and just tossed into the trash.

I carried it over to the counter and spoke to the woman behind it. I told her I found it on the seat and asked her if she'd hold it in case someone came in looking for it. She refused. The policy of the store was not to allow employees to take the responsibility for handling personal effects of other persons. I asked her if she would take my name and cell number and if anyone came in looking for it to give it to them. She said that she would, but that she was only working until noon.

I asked her if she'd pass on the information to whoever came after her. She indicated she would but I wasn't confident that she'd do it. Later that afternoon I went back there. I asked if anyone had come in looking for a notebook they had left behind that morning. I was answered with blank stares. I explained the situation. It was the first time they heard of it. I gave them my information and left.

This went on for a few days with me reminding the counter help that I had found the notebook and giving them my number. I also made up some notices and put them in a few stores in the area. I went on Craigslist and posted the information.

I never disclosed the color of the notebook cover or its size so that some person who did not own it would try to claim it. That was my way of making sure that the right owner got it back. I also planned on asking any claimant for a handwriting sample since the person who wrote in the book had such a beautiful, distinctive hand.

To make a long story short, no one ever claimed the notebook. I did everything I could think of doing to find its real owner, but to no avail. Up to that point, I had not read it, other than when I first picked it up and scanned through it. I figured it was none of my business. But as time passed and I received no inquiries, I thought that perhaps a clue to its ownership could be found in its pages. I read the book, hoping I could identify the woman; yes, from the handwriting I concluded it was a woman, whose handwriting was in the book. She called herself Dakota, but I don't know if that is her name or not since at some point she seems to indicate that it isn't.

There's a lot of information in those pages. If what is written is true, I realized that a great miscarriage of justice may have occurred somewhere in the United States. Because of that, I engaged a person to type up the notes. I am distributing them as widely as I can through the internet for all to see. I have the original notebook locked up in a safe deposit box here in the city.

I feel like I am breaking the woman's confidence and intruding into her personal life, but considering the information she put forth, I really feel that I have no choice. She herself wrote that if her information came in another's hand, it could not be kept a secret, even if that person were a priest or psychiatrist. She expected that once someone else knew about what she had done, he or she would be compelled to do something about it.

The real problem I have is I don't know if the woman was telling a story about what actually had happened or if she just made up a story. If what she wrote is true, I hope to God that those who suffered at her hands can use this to get their lives back in order. Also, if what she wrote is true, I'm wondering whether something happened to her.

What follows is what was written in the spiral notebook I found. I call it Dakota's Diary.

1

SATURDAY NIGHT: AROUND ELEVEN

A long time ago, I heard a song that starts off: "My story is much too sad to be told." It's been years since I heard it. But lately I find myself silently singing that lugubrious refrain over and over again. I'm wondering why I'm continually doing this. Do I think it applies to me? I assume I must, or at least my subconscious does. Why else would I always be humming those words if I didn't?

I suppose the saddest tale is that of Eve. She and Adam were frolicking in the Garden of Eden without a care in the world and suddenly they lost it all because she succumbed and took Adam with her. I've often been amused that Eve took the rap for the fall but then again it was a man who wrote about it, so what should I expect. But the thing is Eve's story was told. The question remains then, what is it about my story that makes it too sad to be told?

In a sense mine is like Eve's. I also took a bite of the fruit of the poisonous tree but I wasn't living in the lap of luxury at the time. But the person who I was at that time at least I liked. Now, lately, or probably for a much longer time than I choose to admit when I look into the mirror at her I see looking back at me, a jaded, bitter and implacable stranger who has taken up living with me. She's morose and unsmiling. She brings an icy chill to my soul when I see her. She casts a gloom over me, darkens my surroundings, and makes me despair of going through the day. I don't like looking at her anymore. In truth I despise her.

It wasn't always like that. For most of my life she exuded joie de vivre, flashed a brilliant smile whenever she appeared, and happily sent me out to face the hardships of the day. I loved her. I gleefully ran to see her each morning. I thrived in her company always acting the spry innocent colt in spring time.

But now it is hard to remember those days or believe that was once the case. That must be why I'm thinking what I'm thinking. What could be sadder than to find yourself forever imprisoned with someone you hate with no chance of divorce? I'm stuck. I can't go to court and have a judge separate me from myself. I can't reassign my life. Is that why the song keeps coming up and whispering to me, "too sad to be told, too sad to be told" over and over again?

What was it I once learned? Yes, that was it, we were taught to love our neighbor as ourselves. Good advice, I suppose. But what are we taught to do if we hate ourselves. Should we hate our neighbors? Maybe that's why I'm tormented by those words from the song. I sometimes wonder if it's too sad to be told perhaps it's too sad to be lived any longer.

I've thought of getting professional help. What's the use? I don't believe that stuff works. No one I know has really been helped by it, not that any of them really have real problems. Yet each continues her weekly trek to the shrink of her choice on an endless merry-go-round coming back to the same spot with every seven day turn. I've always thought those visits were nothing more than buying an hour of uncritical friendship, an hour in which one could hold a sympathetic ear into which to pour problems or as the old spiritual would have it, "to lay my troubles down."

You know I recently read a New York Times article. I think it was in that paper. I'm not absolutely sure. Anyway, the article was about high-priced professional women offering sexual delights who charged hundreds of dollars an hour. These high-priced prostitutes said that around twenty percent of their customers did not want sex. They paid these high prices just to talk to a woman. They paid for the use of their full body but only occupied their ears.

Maybe having a sympathetic listener is worth the price. You know if by telling one your troubles you're better able to walk over the depleted uranium cluster bomb strewed field of life then maybe it's worth it. Who am I, a person imprisoned with one I hate, to tell you not to do it. I try not to judge others, accepting the idea of different strokes for different folks.

Here's my problem. Even if I believed a friendly ear into which I could pour my burdens was available to me and by doing that I would lift some of my cares off my shoulders, I couldn't use it. Given what I've done, I'd never trust another person with my secrets. I believe there is no such thing as a secret, once it is told to another person. I know for absolute certainty there is no person who could keep my secrets to herself. Yes, herself, because I would not even conceive of disclosing them to a man. She'd just have to tell. If she had any common decency, she'd have to shout it out for all the world to know.

That's just how I think. If you don't agree, that's fine, but you don't know my story. I'll tell you this. You could never convince me otherwise that someone could keep my secret.

Lately. I've have occasional flashes of thought that it may be best to eliminate that horrid person in the mirror. I don't think I'm quite at a critical point where I will. Although

I've read when one reaches that point one usually doesn't know it.

As I said, I'm thinking to maybe call it quits if I'm convinced that is the only way out. Deep down I know I won't because it'll take a little more courage than I now have. But I think if things keep like they are I can gin up my fortitude if need be. But I don't have to decide that at this moment. I have not totally given up on the idea that somewhere deep inside me that other person who used to sing to me, and dance me around the room and cheer me up still lives and will come back. Maybe I'm kidding myself. I hope not.

Listen! Did you hear me? I'm doing it again. I'm humming the words of the song. I told you. It has become more and more frequent. Bizarre, isn't it, my subconscious pounding away at my nerves like that when I'm trying to work my way through this.

Wait a minute, maybe it's doing it for a reason and it's not strange. Maybe I'm looking at this the wrong way. I've been thinking of the impossibility of telling my story to another person, you know like a priest or a psychologist, which to me is a dreadful prospect, especially a priest, a man. But I just realized there's another way to tell a story. Suppose I write it down in the spiral notebook I have over there. I'll be telling it to the notebook. Then I won't have to worry about telling it to anyone who may betray me or harass me by telling me I have an obligation to fess up.

If I tell it, and face it squarely, I'll at least make that song go away since I would have told my story in spite of its sadness. Ha! Take that, unconscious! Not only will the song disappear, but it may help bring back the other face to my mirror, the one I love.

It's worth trying. It will delay the looming alternative for a bit, anyway. Why not try it?

These were my thoughts earlier tonight. That's why I'm putting this story down in this notebook. I'm not writing this because I want to go over this. I'd prefer never to think of what I've done. I'd leave it alone if I could, but I can't since I sense that I'm really beginning to lose it. I'm hoping to use this notebook as one would a psychiatrist. I'll lay out what's troubling me by talking to the notebook. I'm hoping if I can do this I'll begin to see things from a different perspective or understand better why I did what I did. You know with a greater understanding I'll go back, climbing into the shoes I wore at that time and perhaps I'll see that my actions were justified and not horrendous. Maybe I'll be able to build my life again.

I'll make the notebook into a person. I'll call her Naria. That was the name of an old friend I used to have who loved to listen to me. I'll write as if I'm talking to her, like I'm already doing.

It was Tom who first suggested it. Who's Tom? He was my helpmeet — that's an old fashion term for husband. Juliet of the Shakespearian tale could not hold a candle to the love I had for Tom; I was so much in love with him at that time. I'll tell you that had he suggested we both take cyanide and end our lives in a loving embrace; I would have done it without batting an eye. I was so in love with him. But that's over now. Hah, there's no doubt about that.

When Tom mentioned it, I thought it was in jest. I laughed and said, "Sure Tom, that's a great idea. Can you see me of all people doing that?"

I followed up on it by making some allusions to myself engaging in that trade. We laughed about it. I didn't give it another thought afterwards believing it was some silly banter that we'd sometimes engaged in which sometimes turned Tom on.

We had been going through some tough times. Even so, there were limits I always thought to what one would do to pull through. The following few days after he brought up the topic I got up as usual and went off to work. Dear faithful Tom also continued as I believed to go out and spend the day looking for a job. It was that time of year when everything is damp, gray and cold. The time when winter brought enough troubles so other troubles were best left outside to keep the home as one warm and bright sanctuary against the season's gloom.

A little over a week had passed when he brought it up again. He asked me if I'd been thinking about what he suggested. "Thinking about what?" I asked. You see I had forgotten his earlier suggestion in the week that passed. He said, "You know, you and the boss." I laughed, although I've got to admit that when he mentioned it I found myself a little uncomfortable, a little uncertain, like something I'd never felt with him before. You know I got like a little creepy-crawling feeling on my skin. I don't like thinking of it since it still gives me a funny feeling.

I laughed and said, "That's all I've been doing." He reacted unusually, you know, like he thought I was serious, and said, "Great, what did

9

you come up with?" I shook my head and told him I hadn't given it a second thought since the last time. I said I thought he was just joking around.

Then he goes something like, "Joking around. I couldn't have been more serious." When he said that, I waited for him to smile to indicate that he was still joking around. When he didn't smile but had that serious look on his face that I always couldn't stand, I remember thinking, "Wow." Yes, that's it. "Wow." Nothing more! My mind was blank. I did not know what to think other than that. I said nothing. He let it pass without another word.

That night though I thought about it a lot. What did it mean he was asking me to do this? Being blindly in love with him, I found it difficult to take his suggestion as abhorrent even though by any standard norm I should have found it degrading and repulsive. I guess that's what being madly in love does, it makes black seem like white. I spent a long bad night tossing and turning, even worse than those nights I spent as a kid waiting for Santa Claus. But it was a Friday, so the lack of sleep was not too detrimental since I did not work the next day. Sometimes, I wish I had.

At breakfast, I tried to pretend everything was as it had been. When I heard Tom stirring I made the coffee, eggs and toast. I put the jam he liked most on the table. When he came into the kitchen I poured his coffee. It was our usual weekend routine but spiced up by the special jam. When he came in, rather than taking a chair at the table, he leaned against the counter and said something to the effect, "You know Kota, you probably want to come up with some type of plan that we can discuss. It's really our only way out of this mess." If I had half a brain I would have told him a better way would be if he'd get a job, but then love and brains don't mix well.

He then went to the table and sat down. We ended up discussing it a bit. Yeah, I discussed it with him. He seemed, as strange as it seems, to want to go into how it could work and wanted to talk about some of the stuff I'd be doing – yuck! Even though he seemed serious about it, I still didn't feel he meant what he said. I still hoped it was just some new fetish he had come across that got him aroused, so I played along in his silly man game.

As we talked on I began to sense that it was more than an excitement thing. He was actually serious. I remember him telling me some really stupid stuff, I'm not quoting his exact words but something like, "You know Kota, sex is only one part of marriage, probably only a minor part. What's real in marriage is the overall relationship between two people. That is its essence. To say that sex is important is to demean the total marriage."

It was something like that. Not that what he was saying was something new except in the context of the time we were speaking. We had talked in the past how even though we had a wonderful sexual aspect to our marriage there was so much more to our relationship, blah, blah, blah. You know, the happiness in and of itself of just being able to be with someone you yearned to be with at all hours of the day and night. We'd talk about how if for some reason sex was extracted from our relationship then nothing would change. We'd still have the same wonderful relationship. But those talks were in the days when things were good. I know now one

11

can pretend they can do without something when they have plenty of it and don't have to do without like when your belly is full you can think dieting is easy.

As I said, those talks of "no sex in marriage but still great marriage" happened during the good time before we move back to the Boston area. I don't think we once mentioned it after we moved back and our struggles began until Tom brought it up that morning. That, coupled with the subject that led up to it, caused me to become more and more discombobulated. Yes, discombobulated. I learned that word early on in high school. I often used it when thinking about myself to describe the uncomfortable and confusing situations I used to find myself in during those days. I thought I had grown out of the times of discombobulation but at that moment they came flying back with a vengeance.

One thing I recall him saying, that I can repeat almost verbatim is: "Kota, one can have sex with anyone, but that doesn't mean you want to marry that person." From that he jumped into saying "The sexual component of marriage was the agreement to have sex only with the other person." Then he said: "It was an agreement between two people. That agreement, like any agreement, could be modified with the consent of both parties especially if by doing that it would lead to bettering the marriage condition." Whenever he talked like that, I rued the day that I suggested to him that he attend Fordham Law School at nights. Even though he lasted a little over half way through his first year, he did take a course in contracts. You've all heard the expression that a little knowledge is dangerous. Tom certainly proved that adage to be true.

12

During breakfast he showered me with all that type talk. Just before he left to go to the gym, another part of what had become our Saturday routine, even though there was no evidence it seemed to do him any good, he said to me: "I expect you'll come through for me. Come up with a plan."

He was just beginning his day. He skipped out gaily after a hearty breakfast. My day seemed to have fallen off a cliff. I sat down. I tried to figure out what he was saying. I really was confused. On one hand what he said made sense, on the other it was sheer nonsense. I became frightened. I had an eerie feeling that I was married to a stranger.

Sitting there having a cold coffee it really hit home to me that we'd not talked much about anything like that since we'd returned to Boston. We'd just existed in the same space. The talk about sex made me focus on Tom's lack of interest in having sexual activity with me. I sensed this before this time. I had attributed it to our period of involuntary separation and now to our living conditions and accepted it. Oh, yeah, and I believed his grouchiness around me was because he'd go out looking for a job everyday without luck.

As you'd expect, I also blamed myself. The eight-to-five work day plus the two hour or so daily commute, not to mention the lousy weather and shabby living conditions tore into my amorous desires. I felt that as long as Tom was unemployed and we depended on my meager earnings, sex would not be a major subject in our lives as it had been. I figured that there was little hope things were going to change much anytime soon so I tried not to think of it.

I sat there at the kitchen table and cried for a bit. I probably sobbed, since looking back; I remember my insides writhed uncomfortably causing me some discomfort later. I forced myself to face up to the situation. Tom was desirous that I take this path and he was urging me and anxious for me to do it. He was telling me that if I loved him, which I absolutely did, I'd not hesitate for one moment to go ahead and do it especially since I'd be showing my love for him if I did. All that was left was for me to decide if I consented to his proposition.

What was it he said, if the two parties to agreement consent, the terms of the agreement could be changed. What was my choice? Continue to do what I was doing and watch as Tom slowly slipped away from me and take my marriage with him; or, to take a bold step, no matter how gross it may seem to me, to move us closer and out of our impoverished bondage.

For me, all that was important in the world was Tom. I'd do what he wanted. I'd come up with a plan and present it to him. My feelings had to be put aside. What counted was what Tom wanted. What mattered was our marriage. Yes, that was it, the sacred marriage.

I'm tired now. I can't write any longer. I'll go on in the morning. I do feel better having got some of that off my back. It's like I had someone with me for a visit. I feel less lonely. These Saturday nights at home alone can be tough.

SUNDAY MORNING: HAVING COFFEE

When I put Naria away I felt I'd actually been talking with a person. Lying in bed before falling off to sleep I wondered whether when I woke up I'd feel like going on with this or whether what I had been doing was just a way I'd used to slip through an evening pretending someone had come over, a way to chase away the Saturday night blues. Those doldrums usually never bothered me Sunday morning.

When I did wake, I found myself looking forward to continuing the conversation with Naria. I was glad she was still close by. It was like when I was young and woke up happily knowing I was going to see a very dear friend first thing in the morning. So here I am sipping a warm cup of coffee with Naria in front of me, patiently waiting to go on.

As I said, before he left Tom made his position clear. He wanted me to come up with a plan. Ever wanting to please Tom and after my crying jag, I put my qualms aside and quickly set about to work on it. I thought he'd come back early to see what I'd done. As it turned out, I had all day Saturday to work on it. Tom didn't come home until late. He told me that after the gym he wanted to spend some time thinking about things so he went to have a few beers at a local bar. He'd been doing this for several Saturdays.

His all-day outings seemed to cheer him up, or better yet, saved me from the drone of the TV, especially those endless repetitious football commercials, so I put up with spending Saturdays by myself. I was sacrificing for Tom. How noble! But as I mentioned, since he gave me this project to do, I thought that day it would be different.

When he came in I told him I had been thinking about what he said all day and I had come up with a plan. He said he was too tired to talk about it then. He suggested we do it in the morning. He went off to bed. I watched TV and went to bed after Saturday Night Live. Funny, I still remember watching that but forget what it was about.

The next morning over breakfast I brought up the matter and asked him if he wanted to hear the plan. He seemed indifferent to it. His mind seemed to be on something else. He said he'd listen to it when he got back from the gym. He finished eating and promised to be back right after he finished there. He got back around three or four. It wasn't as promised but it wasn't at midnight so I said nothing. I was tired of our arguments over this. They came down to his complaining that I was always bitching about what he did, always on his back watching his every step and that he never has a moment to himself, you know, things like that. Most times I tethered my tongue, but sometimes I'd get so frustrated it just ran loose.

He came into the kitchen and asked me what I had come up with. I told him. When he heard me out he enthused, "Dammit, I think it may work!" He jumped up from his chair at the kitchen table. His face bore a smile indicating his subtle satisfaction. He leaned forward over the table, his hands gripping the edge, and looked into my eyes. "Dammit, it will! It will work! Then we'll be free!"

I sat quietly. I'm sure my eyes sparkled with determination and gleamed with pleasure and spoke of my emotions as I stared back into

16

my Tom's face. I was deeply pleased that he did not recoil from my plan. You see, I thought I had truly put aside my doubts about Tom's suggestion and had become a true believer in what I developed. At least at that moment I thought I had. Yet his enthusiasm surprised me, or maybe scared me. I don't know what. His reaction was what I had ardently sought once I planned it out. Yet, even though I had become a great advocate of it in my mind and firmly believed in it I knew within me there one tiny sliver clinging to the hope that he was joking and would now tell me that he appreciated my idea but none of it was necessary.

You see, I was seriously conflicted. I had gone from repulsion at the idea, to wanting to do it, but still I clung to some reservations. It's like you've seen those TV programs where people rebel at thought of eating some gross buggy leggy hairy insects but are told if they refuse they'll be unable to win the money. You see their deep aversion temporarily molt away and they go through with it and you know full well they'll be mentally tortured by what they did later. That was me.

Tom's enthusiasm, which I had not seen for months, buoyed my spirits, and my reservations were put aside. I thought "Maybe the months of frustration, being unable to get a decent job forced him to this point. Maybe believing in a system that doesn't respond as expected relieves one of the duties to respond to the system as expected." I was always rationalizing Tom's actions.

He turned and walked the two or three strides that separated the table from the kitchen counter. He stood over the sink looking out the window. I went up behind him and put my hands on his shoulders and likewise looked out the window.

For several gloomy days, the drizzle caused by a northeasterly wind blowing in from the raw Atlantic had made the day light hardly more perceptible than the dusk. As I looked out I could see the dull daylight had blended into the short dusk and would quickly slip into the early darkness of a New England winter. Across the alleyway from our kitchen window, I saw the glow from a television's light dancing on our neighbor's ancient well-washed lace curtains that provided protection from prying eyes. Without ever having seen into the room, I knew that was the second floor rear bedroom in the neighboring three-decker. All of the three-deckers on the street seemed to have been cloned from one forebear. On occasion I would think that unlike the residents the homes were of different colors.

I could feel the tension in his body concentrated in the tightness of his shoulders. I gently began to massage them. I turned my attention from outside the window to him and studied his hair. Raven black, straight, glossy; a gift to him from an unknown ancestor, most likely from Asia or a Native American, who imparted this long hidden trait into the family's blood-line. It hid itself well until bestowing itself onto and revealing its existence with the appearance of baby Thomas. As I tenderly kneaded his shoulders, he continued as if oblivious to my touch, looking out into the night.

I sensed he was again reassessing my proposal. "Maybe he's thinking he jumped too soon and is trying to figure out how to back out," I thought, noting his failure to respond to my touches. Realizing I was proffering little relief, I released my grasp and ambled back to the table.

I took a cigarette from the community pack, lit it, and sat down.

I thought, "If he'll go along with this, then I'll give up this filthy habit. What do you mean if? He has to go along with it! What choice has he? He knows we're both at our wits' end. Look at us, sitting in this dive and smoking cigarettes that we can't afford to buy. We're slowly sliding and sinking into a stupor – aimlessly following all the precepts we were taught as children and here's our reward: smokes and squalor." You see, I had become a real convert to my plan, my recognition of our desperation slowly expelling my remaining reservations.

Tom turned toward me. His ardor had noticeably lessened. He walked over to the table, picked up the cigarette pack, and sat down. He took out a cigarette, gave the tobacco end a couple of taps on the table, and proceeded to light it. "I know it will work, Kota, I know it but, is it – I don't know Kota, is it worth it?"

As I'm absolutely convincing myself that the plan is our only hope, Tom's going the other way and is doubting it. I know this sounds strange because I spoke of my hope he'd give me an indication he did not want to do it and we'd put it aside but now it seemed I was losing something I had been looking for, a way out. That's how messed up I had become. At that point I did not want to not go on with it. Seeing his vacillation reinforced in me the idea that his months of enforced idleness and the plethora of employer rejections had eroded his fiber and nerve.

I remembered when he was strong, financially and mentally. He seemed to be decisive and courageous. I thought if we were back then he would have agreed to do what I proposed without batting an eye yet ironically my proposal would have been unimaginable then.

He sat there with his head in his hands. I thought maybe I was deluding myself into thinking he ever wanted me to come up with a plan. I was ready to chuck it. But it wasn't so easy when I had concluded it was our only door to freedom.

"Is it worth it?" I replied. "Tom, look at us. What have we got?"

Tom shook his head and dejectedly looked at the table. At this moment he represented to me everything I despised, a failure who had given up trying. I shunted aside my ephemeral repulsion at his actions clutching for a way to understand his torment and weakness. It was almost impossible. After all, hadn't I suffered with him day by day, hand in hand, as we sunk into the abyss, yet I still had my strength? Why is he so weak?

"Tom," I said in a firm voice which compelled his attention. "All we've got of any note now is this dirty habit." I squashed out the cigarette in the dish which we used as an ashtray and pushed from me.

"That's not true, Kota. We've still got each other. I don't want to lose that! That's why I'm not sure, Kota. That's why I'm not sure." He buried his head in his hands, pressing his hair flat onto his head.

"Tom, you're right! We've got each other, but barely," I said back in a calm voice belying my inner turmoil. He did not chide me for using the modifier 'barely' as I expected. I remember thinking, "That's how bad it is. He acknowledges the tenuous hold we have on each other. He doesn't remonstrate."

I continued: "Tom, I want you more than barely! I want you more than anything! But not like this, Tom! Not like this! We're both out of our element here. You can't take two suburban college graduates and plunk them down into the middle of the poorest section of Dorchester and expect them to live happily ever after. Our problem is we've seen a better life. We've lived a better life. We deserve a better life. How can we survive in this pit knowing these things?"

"We'll do all right, Kota, just give us time," Tom said in a voice empty of conviction.

"Tom, Tom, Tom, stop fooling yourself," I quietly responded as I reached across the table and gently tugged at his wrist to get his attention. He looked up at me while at the same time removing his wrist from my hold. He didn't seem to want me touching him. I looked into his deep brown eyes. Eyes that glowed brown like a spit-shined tip of a Marine's shoe. I loved to stare into these trusting doe eyes which signaled the innermost thoughts of my husband. Now I was a little unnerved when I realized I had not looked deeply into them for a long while and now that I was doing it I didn't read doubt and festering fear as I expected from his words and actions but a sort of devious determination mixed with scorn.

I began to argue the necessity of what I found repulsive because I had convinced myself of the need of doing it but I felt empty inside after seeing his eyes. As I spoke I did not know whether my words fit my feelings or whether they were outright lies. "Tom, I love you. I love you more than my life. But I can't sit idly by, watching us destroy each other as we foolishly cling to our youthful ideals and our puritanical morals. We're close to losing everything,

21

including each other. There's no way out! Do you understand, Tom, there's no way out except this!"

"Kota, we can make it without that. I'll work at a fast food place or some other menial job, you know. With both of us working again, we can save and get out of here. You'll see . . . Dakota, you'll see, when I . . . ."

Tom stopped in the middle of the sentence. I could feel my ire rising as I sensed the absurdity of the situation. Tom pressed me to come up with a plan. I had recoiled against his suggestion. I had tormented myself over it. I finally forced myself to face it and to convince myself that I could suck it up for Tom. For Tom I could do what I previously thought was unthinkable. Now Tom was having second thoughts and retreating from my proposition. I was getting angry until I caught myself and realized, "Yes, yes, Tom's right. My plan is a way out, but it is the wrong way out."

I said, "All right, Tom. You're right. The plan's stupid. Let's drop it. All right! We'll forget all about it and go on. I'm sure we'll get a break soon. We've just got to be patient." Wow, did I feel relieved. It was even more than that. I felt I had been enslaved and had been set free. As much as I convinced myself I would wallow in the mud for his sake, now that Tom had doubts, his doubts were my keys to my freedom. I knew then that I'd only have done it if he insisted.

Just as I breathed in this new air after having extricated myself from my mental anguish Tom said, "No, no! You're right Kota. You have to do it. You can't back out."

I felt as if he had plunged a dagger into my chest. "Tom! I won't. It's wrong. I realize it now. You realize it. It's wrong. It'll lead to our damnation."

He softened his voice and answered, "It's not wrong, Kota. You must do it for me, Kota – for us – otherwise, think of our future if you don't – think of what we'll never have if you don't."

I said, with some sharpness in my voice, "Tom, I made the plan looking at our future. What did I see? You know, like someday we'll move from this three-decker to a two family house in another section of the city in what — in five, ten years. Then what, Tom? Then what? Another five, ten years with you working in some menial job that you hate and me continuing as a receptionist, we'll be able to afford a house. Not any house, Tom, but one back in this neighborhood. Then what, Tom? Oh, we may want to have a family - that'll be good - we'll have kids and bring them up in the city. We'll have a wonderful life, Tom, seeing our kids go off to the Boston schools to get a solid education in nothingness and learn to become like us great achievers. Then what, Tom? When we're in our sixties we can – we can probably . . . – Dammit - I'm not interested in that, Tom. Neither are you! You can't live that life. You know that, Tom. You can't do it. Even less than I can, Tom. That is what I thought, Tom. I thought we can't go on like this, so I came up with that sordid plan."

I lessened the hostility in my voice and changed its tone to that of a supplicant. "Tom, I'm an English major who minored in acting and I can't get a decent job because of the gap on my resume during our good years. So now I'm a half-assed secretary who can hardly type 30 words a minute with no shorthand. I'm making thirty-six thousand dollars a year. After the social security and medical insurance, I'm bringing in twenty eight or thirty thousand. Our rent for this dump is almost eighteen, our car insurance is near four, our cigarettes cost us about six or seven thousand, and the cell phones a couple of thousand before we lost their use. We have after that what? Maybe four thousand dollars if we're lucky. Before taxes and before eating, we've got four thousand dollars for the whole damn year. And, Tom, you know how much four thousand dollars is — that's a little less than eighty dollars a week, Tom, eighty dollars and I'm paying thirty of it to commute to work. Do you understand Tom? And I haven't begun to count clothes and the other necessities, Tom; I haven't even begun to count soap, shampoo, or even toilet paper because I have to pay the heat, the light, the water and the excise tax, and all those other fees. Before we can eat, Tom, we owe money! And we have the mountain of those credit card bills we've got to pay back. That's what motivated me into coming up with the plan. But I hate it. It's not the way out."

Tom never looked up. He gave no indication he had heard a word. "Maybe," I thought, "he's heard most of this lament so many times that it no longer has any effect on him. Maybe I'm talking to a shell, a hollow soul incapable of responding. Maybe, it's already too late, plan or no plan."

I got up and walked over to the stove and turned on the gas. It didn't catch and I had a momentary thought to just let the gas continue to come in to the place and put us out of our misery. But it passed, and I lit a match to ignite the burner, thankful that the gas had not been turned off by the gas company as threatened. When it burst into flame, I put the kettle over it. Over my shoulder I called: "Tom, if you'll join me I'll make tea or else I'll make instant coffee. I don't want to waste a tea bag."

"No thanks, Kota, have the tea. Don't worry about saving the bag for a second cup." He stood up and said, "That plan, Dakota. If I want, will you go through with it?"

"For you Tom, of course," I said. I walked over toward him, badly wanting a hug from him since I was an emotional wreck. He turned away, saying, "I'm going for a walk. I want to think about this."

I watched him turn his back on me and walk to the hallway closet. I always thought that three-deckers were modeled after trains with the long corridor running down the middle and the compartments off to the side. Tom pulled out his well worn top coat that reeked of impoverishment. After slipping it on, he covered his head with a beat up scally cap. He turned and threw me a kiss. That had been the closest I had come to a kiss from him in a while. He left through the front doorway.

I remember listening as his heavy booted steps made their way down the one flight to the front door. I put the tea bag back and took out the instant coffee. I put half a spoon in my cup and poured the boiling water onto it. Circumstances had taught me to like my coffee weak and black. I sat at the table and considered my plan. How did such a devious design develop in such a naïve mind? Where did the ideas come from? Had all those stories which my father told the family about his job and the cases which he was prosecuting which I half-heard sprung from some inner recess of my mind in this darkest of moments? Or, was it my inordinate interest in the detective mysteries which I took to reading to shut out the reminders of my fallen financial state that percolated the ideas I'd told to Tom. I mused over my proposal. I was convinced I could carry out my part as obnoxious as parts of it might be. But I was confused. Tom had pressed the idea on me. When I convinced myself to do it and told him he began to doubt. I backed out and then he pressed it on me again. I was beginning to confuse up with down. I'd lost all ideas of right from wrong. Didn't Tom tell me that both parties had to consent to any abrogation of a part of the original contract? Did that apply to the marriage vows?

"Either way," I thought. "It's the end of innocence. If he pushes me to do it, then maybe some day I'll recapture the joy I've lost, but I'll never feel clean. If he backs off again, will our marriage survive much longer under these conditions? Even now, it seems he can't bear to have me touch him. My mere presence seems unwanted other than as a waitress cooking and serving food. He hardly speaks to me preferring the mind-numbing television as his opiate when he's home which hasn't been too often lately. But when he is he's in front of the TV listening to its early morning blabbering through the afternoon soaps past the reality shows and on into the late night. He's mesmerized by the TV's incessant braying. Is it to escape what he calls my continual bitching? The whole thing's bound to end in a few more months when the men in white coats take one of us out of here screaming irrationally. There's no aperture through which we can squeeze ourselves out of this plight. Tom's bound to throw in the towel."

What about me? I couldn't bear a future consigned to the ranks of the helpless poor indentured to impoverishment. I knew I couldn't. I'd had enough of it. "Enough!" I thought. "Throw away your doubts and reservations. You got to agree. Go along with it. You have no choice and only one door through which to go. It may lead to Hell but can Hell be worse than what we're now living? Can Hell be worse than a life with no joy? Is it worse than a life in which you age and grow deeper in debt with each passing day with no sign of a respite? We've no place to run to. So what's left? Either we go with my proposal or we go our separate ways. I thought I might as well have died because I could not live without Tom.

I had been over and over these thoughts since I started to come up with the plan. I had convinced myself absolutely of the rightness of my decision. It's righteousness I had earlier questioned but I was surprised Tom did because he had demanded it of me. When I unveiled it to Tom, I had an absolute assuredness of the necessity of my proposal. Tom's initial reaction was positive. His sudden change to reflectivity and then to second-guessing I did not anticipate so even though I'd convinced myself it was the only way out I gave it up – felt relief – but then he changes and insists I not give it up. I should have picked up more on this and wondered whether he was playing a game. Why didn't his aversion to my touch make me pause and think? But, as I said, love loves to delude.

I sat waiting for him to return. The silence amplified my incessant feeling of hunger. The compensation for this continuing reminder was my thought that at least I still had my slim figure. No fear of losing that when you don't eat. I sometimes thought of writing a diet book. I had been on the perfect diet for over a year. It was simple. The Dakota Diet. You put a low mandatory ceiling on the money available for

27

food expenditures, force yourself to live within that limit, and confine your consumption of food to vegetables and chicken. Oh yes, for dessert, have some fruit plucked off the grocery store rack in the back which is the resting place for fruit about to depart from the ranks of the edible. The monetary limit should hover around twenty-five dollars a week.

I remember as I thought of my planned diet book my mind wandered to my neighbors. I had lived for almost a year in the poorest of neighborhoods and most of the people living around me were obese. What was it that made these people with so little money so overweight? I could only assume that they found as one of their only joys the ingestion of unhealthy snack type foods which were used not so much for nourishment but as a catharsis.

The noise from the opening front door in the downstairs vestibule changed my mind away from my ruminations on my hunger. Immediately upon hearing the first three steps ascending the stairway I knew it was Mr. Costello, the tenant who lived above us. The heavy clunking steps told of another afternoon spent sitting in J & K's barroom, having his beers and balls. He staggered on past my landing and dragged himself up one more flight to his floor. I listened as he opened his door and as his heavy feet carried him to the kitchen. I heard something drop onto the floor directly above my head. "He must have gone shopping for more liquor," I thought assuming he'd carried into the apartment with him whatever he had just dropped.

I hated that place. Having always lived in a single family home, I could not adjust to the continuing aural intrusions onto my privacy.

Nor did I accept the snooping of my neighbors who unceasingly gazed out through the slits between the drawn shades and the edge of the window.

Again the sound of the front door opening gathered my full attention to it for a clue to its source. Tom was home. His steps were as familiar to me as his face. I anxiously listened as they sounded, despite his galoshes, light and quick as he came toward our apartment. I thought it a good sign. He opened the door and came into the kitchen still wearing his overcoat. The ragged coat made him look every part the homeless but handsome street person.

I looked up at him with an inquiring smile. "I've thought it over, Kota. We've no choice. Everything I've tried - you've given me your full backing. I've tried, God knows I've tried everything I could to do to get things going again. But I've failed. It's all come to zip - zippo. Now, I'll let you have a chance. You know maybe this will work out all right."

He walked out of the room and hung his coat up in the closet. I waited for him to return without making a comment. I expected he'd have more to say. I wasn't disappointed. "Kota," he inquired in a pleading tone, "I'll give you a hundred percent backing but there's one caveat. I don't want to know what you're doing. I'll play my part to a tee. I know I can do it. But I don't want to know anything about your part other than when it's time for me to play my hand. Do you understand?"

I walked over to him and buried myself into his chest and held him around the waist feeling his body tense. His arms hung down at his side as if stuck there, afraid to touch me. I avoided looking into his eyes, as I normally would have done because I feared seeing what I saw before. Without raising my head I said: "I understand."

He replied in a tone of voice which I found eerily unfamiliar, "And Kota, be sure you do. It's going to be hard enough keeping the thoughts of this out of my imagination without having anything to incite them. When I was walking to the store, I let my mind focus deeply on your proposition to picture the activity you propose. I almost got sick thinking about it. My stomach physically retched. But I'll adjust to it as long as I don't know it's happening; do you understand, Kota, do you?"

"I do, Tom, I do."

There was no way I could have known it was all an act.

SUNDAY: LATE IN THE AFTERNOON

I've just woken up from a nap. I've made some tea. This uncritical ear of Naria is nice. I'm feeling better than I have for weeks. It's like I had a monkey on my back and she's jumped into this notebook.

Looking back I remember that I slept well that night. It's strange that I did given the momentous undertaking I was about to assume. Obviously I was missing all the caution signs as I blithely and blissfully accepted that my planned actions at my great sacrifice would demonstrate my enduring love to Tom and restore what we once had. I guess I assumed that mixing clean water with just a little dirty water I could still have clean water.

The first thought in my mind when I woke up was a sardonic, "Today is the first day of the rest of your life." I agree it's a meaningless expression but at that time I had to have some thought, foolish or not, to fit my circumstance. I had before me an episode which I was planning to freely enter that was fraught with jeopardy. I at least had enough sense to know that what I planned to do that day would impact my life as much as any other decision I would ever make. I rolled out of bed and stumbled from the bedroom into the morning darkness of my apartment.

Groping along the blackened corridor my feelings now soured by the frigid air I thought "Maybe it's the last day of the rest of your life? It could be! Who the hell knows? Who cares? It's all the same thing - platitudinal garbage. Why am I in such a foul mood? Dammit, I've got to get a night light. How much electricity would that waste?" It was not an auspicious way to start this infamous day.

31

My hands as surrogates for my eyes deftly led me to the light switch on the inside of the bathroom door. Shivering, I closed the heavy painted door behind me, not so much for privacy but in an attempt to preserve any warmth that would be garnered from the hot water I'd be running. The door didn't close; it stuck - stopped by the layers of paint and grime that caused it to grow over time by fractions of an inch.

The chipped porcelain shower handles complained as I urged them along seeking their permission to release the torrents of water which were hidden in the recesses and confined like prisoners behind their locks. Silently, I prayed that the landlord had paid the oilman so that I'd have hot water. The water pipes argued with the faucet handles before consenting to let the water pass.

At first it rained cold, but then the steam told me the oil bill was current. I adjusted the water's temperature and quickly slipped from my terry cloth night robe into the clutches of the steamy stream. It restored my soul and crushed spirits by driving away the icicles. On those mornings when the cold water didn't convert over to warm, what little strength I'd left in me would be sapped. Then I'd sullenly slink from the obnoxious spray and spend several minutes violently shivering as I attempted to bathe by washing with an ice cold face cloth while silently cursing Ian Fleming's James Bond who extolled the delights to be found in a cold shower. I knew he never lived in a partially heated flat during a Dorchester winter.

But that morning for a while I luxuriated in the swirling warm downpour and transported myself on a fleeting fantasy from my fallen state to a fairly land where cold was forbidden to enter. Wave after wave of welcomed warmth washed away my sullen spirits and downcast demeanor. Like a frozen embryo implanted into a womb, I was coming back to life. "Maybe it's not such a trite saying," I remember I thought as I leaned back under the shower to let the water chase the shampoo from my hair. "It just has to be modified a bit for my purposes. Today's the first day of the rest of my new life. It's a new beginning. It's the start of the long road back but at least it's a start. What's that other expression - the longest journey begins with one step. Again it's inane but applicable. God knows where my idea is going to take us but I know one thing for certain — when I'm through I'll never see the likes of this apartment again. I'll never freeze my buns off day after day trying to urge my body out to work. I'll be - shee - eeet."

My mental wanderings were truncated by a startling surge of frigid water tolling the end of my morning's reveries. I accompanied the "shee - eeet" with a lithe, lilting leap from the tub to the towel. Quickly drying myself, I remained wrapped in the towel. As I blow dried my faded streaked amber hair, I tried to remember how long it had been since I last went to my hairdresser, Laurette, for the treatment.

I couldn't afford her anymore at that time. We had become good friends during the period that I often thought of as my prior life, the time when Tom worked and I luxuriated in his earnings. I thought of the folk-lore that suggests a hairdresser knows everyone's secrets. Well, it was true in my case. Laurette knew of my agonized slide into penury probably more than anyone else. She was so nice easing my guilt during those tough times I was freeloading. She'd insist she'd get me back in spades when I

33

got back on my feet. Finally, I couldn't continue to accept her gift of her services so my hair's limpness, its wildness, its dullness, and its legions of split-ends bespoke of the length of time since I'd last accepted her beneficence.

After further ruining my once silky hair with the blow drier, to compensate for the rude shock given me by the rush of cold water, I let the warmth of the hot blown air snuggle between my towel and my skin and flow over my exposed shoulders. Satisfied I had maximized the pleasure to be gained in the now tepid air of the bathroom and realizing my sojourn in comfort had ended, I emboldened myself for the mad dash back through the clammy clutching coldness of the corridor to the closet containing my chilly clothes. Now everything would be run in double time. I knew the next time I'd have a chance to feel any warmth would be fifteen minutes from the start of my dash if the crowded T bus was heated.

Just as Tricky Dick knew that Pat's cloth coat provided scant comfort for her against a chill Washington, D.C., wind, so I also knew my coat would provide similar relief especially that day given my plans for my dress. I put on my best dress, one of the few articles that remained from that prior life – the time when Tom would call me, "a lady of leisure." Wasn't that all I ever wanted to be? Was that asking too much of life?

My dress was black chiffon and followed the contours of my body as if carved on me. It should, I had it tailored specifically for me. Ah, the joys of having too much money. That dress was Tom's favorite. When we first settled into the Dorchester apartment, he'd implore me to wear it. It was his night out when I did. He insisted that one of the few pleasures left for him

34

in life was seeing me slink and sway dressed in my finery. He'd tell me that just thinking of seeing me in the dress turned him on. But that was in the early days as I said.

I'd never worn that dress to work before. I'd never thought of wearing it to work until I was developing the planned escape from poverty. Maybe, I remember wondering at that time that may also have been one of the reasons Tom wanted to take the walk to think over my proposition. Would my action this day in wearing his dress to work deprive it of its allure for him? Was this one of those objects that incites pleasure for the viewer only when it is not shared? How could I ever know? I thought if wearing the dress in public for other eyes was to prove fatal to our future how much more would the rest of the plan?

I gently put my dress spike heels and the exquisite undergarments, items it seemed I hadn't worn for years, into the plastic Marshall's bag. Just before leaving, I glanced out the window at the battleship gray morning. To my dismay, I saw an icy rain was conspiring with the slush to insure that during my trip to the bus stop my ankle high boots would be rendered useless. I could anticipate the damp chill about to encapsulate my soon to be wetted feet. I would normally have been thankful that I kept the woolen socks at my office. But that day, the thought gave me scant comfort. No woolen socks today. Today I'd be dressed to the nines.

I eased my way out of the apartment as quietly as possible to avoid waking Tom. Once upon a time like in a fairy tale without fail each morning I'd rush to dress so as to spend any spare moments sitting next to him on the bed caressing his hair as he struggled against the weight of his sleep to keep me company. As days went on these trips became more and more infrequent. This felicitous moment came to an end almost without notice. I sensed I was becoming an irritant to him which showed in his irritation at my touch. My joy was his torment. Oh, how blind I was – bright neon signs were blinking at me saying he's gone from you but I pressed on with my eyes closed to their message. I must have sensed some of this because I had stopped going in to the bed after getting dressed but I remember reasoning that it was because I did not have the time.

I've heard stories from women who've told me that "out-of-the-blue" their husband or long term friend walked out on them. I think they were like me, then. The warning lights were flashing all around them but they ignored them. Nothing happens out-of-the-blue to people who are not blinded by their feelings or routine habits.

This fateful morning, I was sorely tempted to seek Tom's encouragement. I had an idea I'd rush in and retrieve a comforting and supporting hug that would give me the added strength I needed to go on. But I harnessed my desire by realizing if I disturbed him this morning, he'd wake to see me dressed as I was. I was a certain, as certain as the bone-deep cold I was beginning to feel, that if I did we'd end up in a fight over something that would crush my spirits believing Tom would rebel at what I was about to undertake because of his love for me.

I had committed myself to doing this for us. My commitment was fragile. I knew any hurtful eruption would shatter it. I thought of how desperate we were. I decided, "Better not disturb poor Tom. He loves me as much if not more than I love him. If he wakes, he'll stop me. I'm sure he feels horrible knowing the extent to which I'll be forced to abnegate my virtue to save our floundering marriage. Only Tom could understand my dread of opening the front door and stepping out into the cold air and freezing muck. He'll never let me undertake this detestable journey now that it is at hand." I should have mused, "How naïve I am to think that Tom would interfere with me debasing myself. Isn't it the goal of all who have debased themselves to make themselves feel better by debasing others? Doesn't vice vilify virtue and seek its destruction?" But at that time I could not have possibly thought that.

That day the damp coldness struck me particularly hard and it grabbed me quickly running its icy fingers sharply across my spine. I shivered uncontrollably as I stepped down the snow encrusted steps following the frozen footsteps of my predecessors. Leaning into the wind that went through my clothes as if they were not on me, I made my way to the corner. I tried to find firm footing to ford the slushy puddles that gathered in the gutters aside the curbstones. Seeing what looked like solid ground, I stepped out onto it. What appeared to be a solid sheet of snow failed me. I sensed my foot sinking into the slush. Firm footing was found six or so inches below. The slushy water happily poured into my boot. I felt the gushing lumpy chilling water filling it. It happened in a split second because I snapped my foot back from the depths but the damage had been done.

For an instant I wanted to throw myself onto the snow piles and cry. I really did. I felt so cold and awful. Almost irrationally, I steeled up my resolve to go on. I plunged my already sodden foot right back into the same puddle with an attitude of "Is that all you've got" and commenced my squishy walk to the bus stop. I brightened at the thought of my pathetic plight. I was shivering noticeably. Every step the icy water rolling around inside my boot added to my chill but increased my resolve.

"What's left to do but to laugh?" I reasoned as I sucked in a deep breath and tried to relax my sinews remembering that I was once told that by tightening up and restricting my blood's circulation I would add to my chilliness. "Dammit," I resolved within myself, "I can't get any colder. My feet can't get any wetter. Things just can't get any worse. Full steam ahead!" I deliberately plunged my somewhat dry other foot into the opposite puddle believing that it was bound to get drenched no matter what I did so that by plodding straight through the obstacles rather than tarrying to circumvent them, I'd get warmer sooner.

Standing at the bus stop, I stomped boldly to the "swish, swish, swish" of my sopping boots. I started smiling. My movement, the noise caused me to begin singing imbecilely to the merriment of my fellow sufferers, "I'm singing in the slush, just singing in the slush, what a glorious feeling, just singing in the slush . . . ." Only the young can twist Nature's perverse adversities into joyous adventures. The sullen, dour mood of the bystanders was stymied by my actions and they found comfort by reluctantly joining in my merriment by encouraging my madness which momentarily took their minds off their miseries of being trapped in a New England winter. A line of laughing loons clambered aboard the well-heated bus and quickly settled into their normal stoic states. I also assumed a veil of silence, sauntered to a vacant seat at its rear, and beseeched its warmth to caress me.

It never did. The cold winter fingers did not lift from my body until I discarded my boots at the office, slipped into my woolen socks, and had sipped my way through a cup of hot soup. I'd never been so cold for so long. I wondered from what deep reserve I summonsed the will and gaiety which brought me relatively unscathed to the office. Reflecting back it was the idea that love conquers everything idea, what's an ice storm in the face of fervid love.

Fortunately I had arrived early, so I could warm up in the kitchen. Having done so, I moved into the woman's lounge. There, I transformed myself from the cute, singing, cold commuter to an alluring warm woman.

I strutted to my desk to the silent envious stares of my surprised fellow staff members. I fiddled and faddled with some of my unimportant chores while I waited for my boss Roger Hunt to arrive. I knew he was coming when I heard his empty, hurried greeting to the secretaries whom he passed on his way to the office, I rose from my seat and stood looking at a file in such a manner that his rush to his office would be obstructed by my presence.

I was a receptionist in Roger Hunt's inner office. When he approached reading through some papers he hrumped his usual morning greeting at me but my position caused him to slow as he attempted to pass. I replied: "Good morning Mr. Hunt, could I have a word with you?

"I'm tied up right now, Dakota," he answered without glancing up and trying to move past me.

"But Mr. Hunt, I'll only need a minute or two." Not used to being contradicted, he looked up. "Look Dakota," he started to say in his usual severe, scolding voice as he examined me. His words slowed, "I said . . . I'm very busy this, I'm . . . ." He paused.

His eyes caressed my chiffon dress and moved lustfully along its lines pausing for a moment at my hips and then down to my shapely oft-admired calves. He slowly moved them back up again, trying to look through my dress and back to my smiling face. "Well, Dakota," he murmured in a pleasant voice oozing delight, without taking his eyes from my boobs for a second, a tone of voice a stranger to me, "I suppose I have some time I can spend with you. Step in, young lady, step in."

I passed by him and felt a gentle touch on my shoulder and stoically accepted the revolting slide of his hand down over my spine, from which the frigid fingers of Jack Frost had so recently departed, and across my buns. I'd have much preferred the deepest coldness of Jack's touch to the present indignity. "Hang in there, kid," I thought. "Hang in there."

SUNDAY EVENING: AROUND EIGHT

When I first walked out on that snowy day and traipsed my way through the snow, sleet and slippery slush in my one good dress on my way to my job at Hunt Enterprises, I had two goals in mind. I wanted to set up Roger as quickly as possible and get on with my life with Tom. I figured incorrectly, as it turned out that it would be simple. I had an inchoate idea as to how I would do this. I planned to lure Roger into some type of sexual conduct toward me. I'd known from the office gossip that he had an interest in women, or, as the guys would say, "He had an eye for the skirts." I figured he'd be an easy catch and once I hooked him I'd somehow tell him that unless he paid me a large sum of money I'd go public with the matter. I'd been reading about all those sexual harassment suits and cases and how the companies made large financial settlements on the women who were victimized by the office environment.

It seemed so simple when I finally adjusted my feelings to Tom's suggestion weighing, as I said, my repulsion to the idea against losing Tom. I was a little unsettled by Tom's attitude. He urged me to do it, then his seeming reluctance, and then pushing it again. His wanting to talk about it in the beginning and then telling me he did not want to hear anything about it. Maybe I remember thinking that because of our difficult living conditions it was hard for him to figure out what he wanted and the sooner I got going the sooner Tom would become the old Tom.

When he came back that night from his nightly stroll and told me that he'd go along as long as we didn't talk about what was going on. That was fine with me. I could joke about it before doing it but I knew I would have no real desire to talk with my husband about was happening in an illicit relationship I had entered with a stranger. I'd have the affair, keep it in a locked box, and when it came time to tell Tom, if ever, I'd do it in the most euphemistic manner.

I'll never forget the moment in time Roger first put his hand on my back — that cold dark day when I set about to carry out my plan — and led me into his office. My blood froze! I didn't think I could go through with it. It was all new to me having someone touch me and being immediately repulsed and having pins and needles break out all over me. I know I planned it. I had thought about it but thinking about something distasteful and then doing something distasteful are two totally opposite things.

I've a vague recollection of what happened that day. I guess I was able to carry through on my intent although I let him take more liberties with me than I intended to at the first encounter. It's not that we did that much then but being unused to the fine art of seduction, I thought I could confine the first encounter to some sensuous talk and subtle hints. But I couldn't stop his gross hands from touching me and feeling me up but it mostly consisted of him going up and down my backside down from my shoulders to the top of my back thighs and up again over and over while holding me tightly against himself. He tried several times to kiss me but I could not stomach the idea of having my mouth meet his and successfully avoided it for a bit, but he was a smooth professional and I was a clumsy novice and he eventually gained the ascendancy.

When I finally extricated myself from his office I felt I had a neon sign lighting me up and everyone who saw me knew what I had done. What's that saying, a thief feels his hair is on fire? I'm sure I was flushed and red and that my dress was messed up, but I really don't remember too much after coming out of the office other than thinking that I had passed the first test. I had done enough so that it was clear to him that I was very approachable.

I always thought had it ended there and you asked me what exactly he did or how long I was with him, I would have been unable to tell you. It was like a big blur. I never would have been able to recall it but as time passed, he'd often remind me, to my disgust and his delight, of how he felt when he first experienced touching my body. I hated his penetrating questions when we became more intimate later on as to how I felt when he did one thing or another that first time.

I could never level with him – I could never tell him how much he sickened me. I had my plan and I was intent on carrying on. I guess I became like a prostitute since I had no feelings for him — it was business — a business in which I was continually violated but for which I planned to get more and more financial rewards which palliated the violation.

That first day was the longest day of my life. What happened, happened in the morning. He left to go on a trip some time before noon — he went for three days. Thankfully, I had some time to reconsider my decision since I now knew it was not going to be as easy as I thought.

I somehow got home. I was in sort of a daze. I remember the cold going to work that morning vividly, so vividly that I can still feel it, but that night going home is a blank. From the time I escaped from his inner office to arriving home, except for how I felt when I had to leave his office and look at the faces of my fellow workers, that day has been blacked out totally like a black hole. As I said I think even what happened in his office would have been part of this void had I never seen Roger again.

But no one had to remind me of the reception that I got when I got home. Here I was letting this gross monstrosity touch my body so that I could get Tom and me out of the prison we lived in. I remember walking through the front door of our three-decker and shuddering at the thought of what I'd just gone through. But then I thought of Tom waiting upstairs for me and all the dirt and grime which I felt was on my body slid away and fell onto the floor of the hallway where it mixed with the puddles of water which dripped from my boots.

I flew up the stairs, dropped my boots outside the door with the umbrella, reached for the door and found that it was locked. "Tom," I shouted anxiously and happily, "Tom, honey, it's me." I waited expecting him to come running to the door. But he didn't come. I thought that maybe he was exhausted from waiting and went into bed for a nap. I understood that he was under as much pressure as I was so I figured he was sleeping. That was fine — I'd just go in and cuddle in next to him. I fumbled through my bag and found my keys. I opened the door and was welcomed by a chilly, dank, empty apartment. It was like I walked into a freezer. I walked anxiously out to the kitchen – looking in the bedrooms as I passed – and saw that there was no sign of life. I looked for a note, for some explanation as to where Tom was, but there was none. That was still okay, I thought, he must have gone shopping or was out job hunting.

You see, I was always able to find an excuse for Tom. No matter what happened, there was an explanation for it. Tom was given the benefit of every doubt imaginable. So I turned up the heat and put down something for supper. I nervously sat in the kitchen, feeling hurt by his absence, but also concerned by it. It was several hours later when he arrived, several long, anxious hours.

When I heard him at the door, I got up and stood in the kitchen entrance looking down the long hallway. When he came in from outside, I could see he had been shopping all right – shopping in the local barroom. I didn't know what to feel when I saw him staggering down the hallway toward the kitchen. I didn't approach him but slowly backed into the kitchen uncertain and a little confused. I sat at the table waiting for him. As soon as I saw him I knew he'd been drinking but I did not know he was blotto until he stumbled into the kitchen and grabbed a chair opposite me. He blurted out something to the effect that he was sorry but he couldn't stand being home alone while I was doing what I was doing.

As usual, I felt sorry for him. I remember getting up and walking around the kitchen table to comfort him – mindless of my own suffering and the indignities perpetrated on me – I felt sorry for poor Tom sitting there sloshed in the chair. When I reached him to knead his shoulders like I'd always done he cowered into himself and blurted out: "Don't touch me, you whore!"

I withdrew in horror - disbelieving what my ears had just heard.

Did you ever see someone in a state of shocked horror? How they hold their hands on the side of their head, their eyes and mouth held wide open? Edward Munch captured it in his painting "The Scream." I think that's what I must have looked like. I couldn't believe what I had heard. I was appalled. I felt weak. My whole body trembled. I staggered back and collapsed into my chair.

I didn't know what to do. My next reaction was to give him the benefit of the doubt by not believing what I had heard. I didn't have to wait too long for a resolution. He sat for a moment or two and then drunkenly swirled out of the chair, which fell over, leaned toward me with his hands on the table steadying him, and slobbered at me: "Don't ever touch me again, you slut!" He then stumbled off into the bedroom.

I was absolutely astonished. I was aghast at his accusations. The words 'slut' and 'whore' reverberated in my ears and pounded inside my head. I think I sat most of the night in stunned silence at the kitchen table. After a time I managed to bundle myself up and get a few hours sleep on the couch in the cold living room. While I thought of what happened that night I became bitter. I had exactly two choices: stop trying to set up Roger and live forever in penury with my invalid husband, or continue on and pull myself out of this quagmire. After much agonizing, I decided that the best thing to do was to give up my plan and maybe, who knows, maybe I could get another job paying more money and – hell – I remember thinking – "If winter's here can spring be far behind." Spring had to bring us a new life as it did every year to most living things. I figured Tom would be better by then. I'd have a better job. We'd both be able to scrimp and save and get out of this mess.

I felt better after I resolved to quit the job and forget the idea of blackmail. I then began to wonder how I ever convinced myself that such a lunatic plan, that's what I thought of it at that time, could ever have brought betterment to our lives. I would do everything in my power to pacify poor Tom. That's what I thought of him – poor Tom. He was right to call me a whore and a slut. I turned on myself for going along with the idea of allowing Roger to touch me. I felt like trash, like some greasy wretched slime oozing along a filthy sewer line.

Yes, I still I had my redemption in my hand. I just would talk to Tom – poor Tom – wonderful Tom. I should have known he would become so distraught and upset at that thought of my person being touched by another. His talk about the freedom of parties in marriage to loosen the terms of their agreement to allow others into what might only be a part of it, but clearly the most important part, was totally wrong. He didn't mean a word of it. I should have known that.

Despite feeling like some greasy flotsam, I saw there was a light. Yes, Tom was the light. Of course, I thought, "I'm so lucky to have him." I convinced myself that his drunkenness proved how much he loved me. I believed his drunkenness was a sign of the hurt I inflicted on him by my imbecilic plan. By the first light I was deliriously in love with him.

I knew Roger was out of town, so I determined to take that day off. Maybe I'd never go back to Hunt Enterprises again. Maybe I'd use that day to go get another job. I'd get a better job. Having resolved my problems, I felt my gloom lifting from my body like someone lifting one of those lead shields the dentists put on you when taking an x-ray.

I became impervious to the apartment cold. I shook off the tiredness caused by my stint at the kitchen table and the term of tossing on the hard couch and quietly spruced up the kitchen area so as not to awaken Tom. I took a long warm shower. Yes, the hot water held. I scrubbed off the lingering dirt caused by the Roger's touches. I sneaked out of the apartment with some of our emergency savings and went to the local convenient store. I picked up eggs, sausages, muffins, and all that stuff, even a small steak.

I was in the mood for celebrating. It was bitterly cold out – I remember that – but I remember not being cold. People stared at me in my light coat. It wasn't buttoned but fluttered in the wind making me feel as though I were flying through the air. I was warmed by the smile on my face and the warm glow in my heart.

When I returned to the apartment, I turned up the heat. I knew that Tom would soon be getting up. This was going to be a breakfast for him to remember. It was to kick off our new life together.

When I heard him coming out of the room, I cracked the eggs and dropped them into the frying pan. I heard him moving clumsily about the bathroom. I waited anxiously – I had dressed myself in a chic night-gown I had kept from our good days. I was sure he'd forgotten that I had it and would be pleasantly surprised. I was hoping those vile epithets he'd hurled at me the night before were lost in the fog of his drunkenness. If he did remember them and was remorseful, I was ready to pooh-pooh his apology for his inebriated attack on me. I had come up with some cockamamie response I would make to him along the lines that I'd have been insulted had he not gotten drunk when he thought of what I was planning to do. Whose husband wouldn't?

He walked into the kitchen surrounded by a stench of stale beer and fetid smoke. His noisomeness filled the kitchen but failed to dampen my spirits. He hadn't bothered to comb his hair. It was all messed up and filthy looking. He had that gruff day-old beard that looks so sexy on some movie stars but on a person in front of you who's besmirched by a prior day's drunk it's a huge turn off. Even that didn't impinge upon my gaiety.

I remember saying as he slumped into the seat at the kitchen table, "one or two?" referring to the eggs I was frying. "How's it feel?" he said. I had no idea what he was referring to. I looked at him, shrugged, did my best to figure out what he was referring to, and responded, "I'm doing the eggs over easy. You want one or two?"

He repeated himself but added a couple of words: "How's it feel to be a whore?" he said. I was stunned standing there with the egg flipper in my right hand, dressed in my fancy nightgown with a pretty apron protecting it, and again hearing those cruel heart-rending words being shot at me and feeling them tearing into my core. Of course, my knee jerk reaction was to accept the slander, put the blame on myself for the torment I must have put poor Tom through.

I hate myself when I think of my reaction to this barb but I turned, flipped the eggs, and quickly took them out. I was a wreck inside fighting to hold back tears. I put them on the plate next to the sausages, fries, and toast, and

49

walked over to him. "Tom, honey," I said. "Nothing happened. I did nothing." He accepted the plate from me and looked down at it. He picked up his fork and examined the eggs as if in some fancy restaurant to determine if they were cooked to his satisfaction or some dive to see if there was a foreign object in them. He then looked up at me and said: "What difference does it make whether something happened or not — you're still a whore for even thinking of doing something."

What a meek lamb I was with that man! If any other man had uttered such trash to me I'd have tried to gouge his eyes with my nails, or at least responded with a feisty retort. But I accepted that he was right and that it way my fault. To this day I don't understand why I didn't dump the breakfast food on his head. After all it was his idea, not mine that I become a whore. But I tried to placate him.

I pleaded: "Tom, but we agreed on it, remember? We agreed I'd try." He returned saying he never agreed to any such thing. He then astounded me by saying once I had made the proposal in the first place as far as he was concerned I had betrayed my marriage vows. He said I was no better than one of the women who sell their bodies in the back alleys. He was thinking of putting red lights outside the windows.

Without consciously reacting, inexplicably, the red light comment suddenly made me sense something hardening within me. Funny — those words clicked a switch; they were the hammer that fell on the already primed gun, the proverbial last straw that broke the camel's back. My ire was slowly being stoked up to the boiling point as he hit me with gross insult after

50

gross insult as he continued to eat the delicious breakfast I had cooked for him. I focused on him eating the food and I thought, "If he had an ounce of decency he'd not eat a whore's breakfast."

As I just said, I felt myself becoming hardened. As much as it stung, being called a whore over and over again, I was more hurt thinking of myself as a dirty floor mat with Tom wiping his filthy boots on me. I finally found enough of a backbone to tell him, "Stop your bullshit. You were the one who suggested I become a whore." Yes, I said whore, even though I almost shocked myself when I spoke those words in relation to myself. "You agreed with the plan. The whore did nothing but what you wanted her to do. Tell me why did you suggest I become a whore? To throw it back in my face? Do you think I'd forget it was you who suggested I become a whore?" I guess once I broke through the barrier and accepted I was a whore I found a strange fascination in repeating the word.

He stopped eating when I fought back. Maybe the breakfast tasted a little bitter when ketchuped with my words. He looked up at me and said, "All right tell me everything that happened."

I said, "I thought you didn't want to know what happened."

He angrily put down his fork and said, "Well that was then, but now I want to know."

"Sorry to disappoint you," I said, "but nothing happened."

He replied, "You're lying. I know you. You went to work all dressed up and I'm sure you got to see your boss. Didn't you?"

I responded, "Yes. I got to see him as we planned. But nothing happened. He touched my back and ran his hand onto my behind. That's all."

That threw him into a frenzy. He yelled, "First you tell me nothing happened and then you tell me he only touched you on the ass, who knows what you'll be telling me next. Is getting touched on the ass nothing?" This went on ad nauseum but I remember finding surcease to my outrage because he was no longer eating my food. I smiled back at him which sent him spinning out of control

He said stupid things like "If you let him touch you on the ass, then as far as I'm concerned, you slept with him," and other vile things about my involvement with Roger's anatomy. Seeing his words were not affecting me he started to ask me to compare Roger's love-making to his. It was so gross, so sick.

The whole thing was a low, stomach wrenching performance. I didn't see my husband sitting there but some warped and perverted being who I didn't know. "To think," I thought, "I was going to sacrifice my cleanliness to save him from his weaknesses."

I listened to his ranting on for a while trying not to respond either by words or tears. My newly found toughness forbade tears to fall; my enjoyment of the show prevented his evil words from hurting me. Finally, he seemed to run out of breath and stopped talking. I was almost disappointed.

It was then that I told him I was giving up my job. You won't believe his reaction. If I wasn't there I wouldn't have. He almost fell off his chair. Amazingly, he told me not to. He started apologizing for what he had said. Like he went on and on about how sorry he was about hurting me. Tears filled his eyes. He begged me for forgiveness, saying it was just so difficult for him to adjust to me being in such a situation and a lot of other bull-shit.

He went on endlessly seeking my forgiveness so much so that the rest after what I just mentioned is mostly garbled in my memory. I got myself around to enjoying his vile attacks on me and now this. This was torture, listening to him grovel. After a long arduous time, I agreed, just to shut him up, that I would reconsider my decision to leave work. Then, you want to be more disgusted, he begged me to keep involved with Roger. I said I would consider it.

After practically crawling on his hands and knees begging me to go on with the plan, out of the blue he said that because I violated my marriage vows, he'd never sleep with me again. I never saw that coming.

It reminded me of my college roommate Emma. She was in this long-term relationship with this guy, Charlie, who she really liked. I thought he was sort of a pig but what did it matter what I thought. I guess I thought of him like that because she'd keep agonizing over and over about the pressure he was putting on her to sleep with him. She kept bouncing it off us, asking what she should do. We initially said go ahead; it's no big deal, you'll be getting hitched soon. But she refused.

We didn't know why she asked us because after we'd give her our facile advice she'd say there was something in her that was telling her it wasn't right. We could see she was struggling so eventually we told her to do what she thought was best and tried to avoid the subject. She'd cry and tell us she didn't know what was best. She'd really weep whenever she came back from being with him telling us how he badgered her to sleep with him and how he'd get angry and threaten to leave the relationship because she wouldn't. Through tears and torment, she held out.

It was around Christmas of our last year and she was looking forward to a special dinner with Charlie. As expected, he proposed marriage to her. She was delighted and accepted. He put a gorgeous diamond ring on her finger. While she was turning it this way and that, admiring it he said to her, "You know Emma, I never told you this, I made a vow years ago that I would never marry any woman who wasn't a virgin." She softly inquired while still admiring the ring and without looking up, "What would you have done if I, you know, slept with you as you kept begging me to do?" He said, without a second thought, "I'd never have proposed to you." She took one final look at her magnificent ring, took it off her finger, put it on the table in front of her, and without a word got up and left. I loved Emma for that. I admired her strength and character.

Whether it was Emma's example that came to my mind or that the emotionally straining morning had deprived me of all feelings for him, or that he surprised me with his avowal not to sleep with me again, a light suddenly came on in my head. I said to myself an expression we girls used to say in college when someone said something painfully obvious, "thanks, Pete!" As if I'd let him touch me after what he called me and just put me through.

Did you ever see one of those old washing machines with the wringer on top? You know it has two rolling pin-type rollers that turn in opposite directions as you turned them with a large handle. You'd put the clothes between these rollers to squeeze the water out. If you've

54

seen one, then you can understand what happened to me. I'd been joyous, shocked, hardened, pleased, and a hundred other things. My emotions had been put through rollers like those on the old washing machines. I had squeezed out of me every bit of love I had for Tom.

He reluctantly agreed to move out of our bedroom into one of the spare bedrooms with a cot. Truth be known, he wouldn't have thought twice about me moving out had I offered. He suggested that even though our relationship had split that if I did decide to go back to Roger and successfully blackmailed him, we should split the money. I remembered that because I remember thinking that we had gone from a relationship of husband and wife to one of pimp and prostitute in the space of a twelve-hour day.

I can jest a little about it now but at the time I was an emotional wreck going through that tempering fire. Yeah, I thought I came out of it OK, but you don't go through things like that and not have some adverse affects which you'll never understand.

But back to that time, what I've told you is a condensed version of the conversation that ran off and on from nine or so that morning until right up until seven or eight or even later that night. After noon did away with morning and the afternoon came on my feelings toward him continued to harden. You don't have to be too bright to realize when you're in the position I was in that the person sitting at the other side of the table is not the person you thought you married or wanted to be married to.

I thought to my dying day I'd never be able to figure it out. The day started with me blaming myself for his animosity toward me but it ended with me having no sympathy for him. I left the emotional upheaval diamond hard. Why I didn't leave in a straight jacket I don't know. I very well could have. I no longer blamed myself for his obnoxious hostility toward me. His insults, which for a while were painfully stinging, bounced off me like thrown marshmallows.

I hadn't really compromised myself. The little evil I wallowed in was suggested by him and being done for him. It gnarled at me to think he was offended while sitting in a bar, yet I was the one that was being touched by the filthy lecherous fingers. I was being violated, not him. But because he went at me so viciously, I was able to get over my "so in love" state and stand up for myself.

When I think of it, which I often do because it is what made me what I am today; I realize he was very lucky. The way he turned on me like a rabid coyote – the lashing of his tongue – my humiliation and repentance – my agony thinking in my confusion I had wronged him – all come back to me like it was yesterday. He's lucky because if I had known at that time that it was all an act — a beautiful feigned act performed brilliantly — so that he could sleep with other women rather than me, I would have killed him right then and there. No shit. I would have. I'd have taken a butcher knife and planted it in his chest without a second thought.

Think of what he did. I'm busting my butt working and he's lolling around making love with other women. He suggests this sordid plan to me which when I childishly agree to do against my better judgment and embark on it for him and he calls me a dirty whore. I let myself be manhandled for him, and he calls me a dirty whore. Then after humbling me to get the split-up he wants, I'm suppose to live with the idea it was my fault our marriage fell apart. If he wanted to dump me, that's fine, dump me. But no, he wanted to torture me. Then after doing all that, he wants to become my pimp. If ever there were a case of justifiable homicide that is it.

Why do men do that? If they want another bed why don't they just go lie in it? Why do they have to torture the person who has given her all to them? Is that type man so unable to abide the guilt of his betrayal that he wants to crush a woman's character and sear her soul. I suppose it is the men like Tom who kill their wives or girlfriends in order to get it on with some chick. I'm probably lucky Tom's character was too weak to do that.

The day was spent in deep conversation. We went from being married to business partners in an illicit enterprise. I no longer had a poor Tom, my husband; I had Tom the pimp. Maybe it's not poverty that causes love to fly out the window as much as is when a woman wakes up and opens her eyes to see she's involved with some low life that she tosses all her emotional attachment to him out the window setting herself free. Are emotions so fragile that what I believed was deep love could have changed so quickly into such an intense hatred? My feelings changed as quickly as Gregor turned into an insect in Kafka's *Metamorphosis*.

That is one of the reasons my story is so sad. How can I after this experience ever love another person knowing how quickly love can turn to shit? Maybe it would have been better had he killed me since for all intents and purposes he destroyed a fundamental aspect of me. Do you want to hear a story that warns you that your love for someone may last no longer than it takes for a fallen star to disappear over the horizon? I know you don't believe such things can happen but neither did I when I woke up that morning.

I must admit that as they day wore on I was definitely engaging with him for the sole purpose of destroying him. Let me remind you, I still did not know about the other women so you can imagine how much my resolve to do this was reinforced when I learned of them. I told him he could call me slut, whore, whatever he wanted. I said he didn't have to sleep with me anymore as he wished. I stung him when I said I felt as much desire of being touched by him as by Roger Hunt.

Near the end of our discussion I had total control over my feelings even though I felt more tired than any other time in my life. I was drained. I did not feel sorry for myself but was like one of those people prowling the ocean beaches after hearing of a boat wreck off shore looking for something that washed up to salvage for herself. I'd spent a lot of years with Tom and I knew I wanted to get something out of these wasteful years. I bargained better without my emotions clouding my judgment.

I decided that I was going to continue working at Hunt Enterprises to pursue my planned blackmailing of Roger. I told Tom that. I also told him that the blackmail could only be successful if it appeared to the world outside our apartment that we had a close, loving relationship. I told Tom he had to maintain the facade of our relationship until I could spring my trap on Roger. That meant he could not move out until I said he could.

As I said, I thought I'd never have understood how everything so suddenly unraveled. I soon would. Everything fell into place when I later learned that I should have substituted for the word "gym" as to where Tom had been going for weeks on end to "former best girl friend's bedroom" and the words "looking for a job" to "frolicking in bed." For months, he'd been going to Jenny's apartment or some other love nest instead of job hunting. He'd apparently found her to be more sympathetic to his plight than his wife, who was out working her butt off to support him and who he turned into a blackmailing prostitute. I thought when I learned that, "The other woman has time to manicure her nails."

SUNDAY EVENING: TEN-THIRTY

I just took a small break. I intended to call it quits on my writing for the day. I picked up a book and started to read but found nothing was sinking in. My thoughts kept going back to you, Naria. I figure I'll write a little more before I go to bed.

Let's face it, when I went after Roger's money I didn't really know what I was doing but I was desperate. I saw what our vicious circle of poverty was doing to our relationship; at least it seemed to me that our problems were being caused by that. It's difficult to understand how very debilitating it can be unless you've been there. But I'm sure all those living lives of comfort if they'd ever heard a story such as mine will find my actions sordid and think me a low creature. They'd believe they could never fall to my level.

I know that. Having once been where they are I understand why they'd think that. But let me tell you, nothing is out of the question when survival is at issue. F. Scott Fitzgerald in *Tender is the Night* pretty much summed it up when he pointed out, "Women are necessarily capable of almost anything in their struggle for survival and can scarcely be convicted of such man made crimes as 'cruelty.'" I would add adultery to that and point out that all of our crimes were invented by men without consulting women, even the Ten Commandments.

I suppose that's always been the case. History teaches us that those comfortably situated have always looked down upon their less fortunate sisters worrying that somehow or another they'd have to give up a little of their much to those with lots of nothing. Queen Marie Antoinette's supposed response when told the people had no bread of "let them eat cake," exemplifies that attitude of those who have toward those who don't. Of course, for me I don't have to look at history, I only have to look at myself to see selfishness epitomized.

More than men women know that desperate times require desperate measures. There's a story in the Bible in Lamentations that tells how compassionate Jewish mothers facing famine boiled their own children to serve them as food; it is reported by eyewitnesses that in the 1930s during a famine in Ukraine mothers cannibalized their weaker children to benefit their healthier ones. It wasn't the men who did these horrendous things that took other-worldly courage; it was the women.

Today, think of those hundreds of young women in foreign red light districts. They hang in windows like spiders attempting to lure male passersby into their webs so they can get through another day. I've always thought the worst part of that is they have to service any greasy goon who shows and can meet the price. Yes, I know some say they like it or that the money's good, but one can convince oneself of anything, like I did one time. I've never met a woman who would willingly sleep with a dirty sweaty smelly scab encrusted man, yet the red light spiders do it continuously. Love for sale; fascinating young love for sale; all comers welcome!

The nice ladies can think of me how they like, I saw myself as a woman fighting for my life, my survival. At that time I believed my marriage was my life. The degradation I gladly accepted I expected would be discreet, short lived and highly beneficial. I'd save Tom and our marriage.

I recall, as I read what I wrote earlier, I had another reasons for wanting Tom not to move out. I was not ready to let him go. I had a sense that I wanted him near me so I would know best how to get my revenge on him and destroy him. As human's we're emotional beings. If one loses a strong emotion, a vacuum does not develop but the hole that is left has to be filled by another emotion; the stronger the emotion the deeper the hole. That is why it's said love is close to hate. It isn't on the range of emotions because it is at the opposite end of the emotional scale. But it is the same in intensity. So when love is suddenly yanked out a vast space needs filling. It can only be filled by an emotion as intense as love. In most cases that means hate.

There's a saying, Sicilian supposedly, that "revenge is best served cold." That didn't appeal to me at that time. In my mind the revenge I planned was going to be served like a daily dish of pasta with tomato sauce, or better like a feverish nightmare, continuous and never ending. Yes, these were the thought of sweet little Dakota who the day before shook with fright at the thought of being immodestly touched by another person.

I emphasized to Tom that if we did anything that publicly indicated we were estranged our chances of extorting any money from Roger would be lessened. I stressed that if we'd get anything worth while out of my being a prostitute it would be because we'd want to say that Roger Hunt destroyed our marriage. So I told him that he would have to go on for a bit doing what he had been doing which I thought was looking for work. I said as my act with

Roger moved into a more significant stage he could then move out and go his own way. But before doing that he would have to be patient and act the good husband and no one need ever to know what went on behind our closed doors.

I had totally changed my feelings for Tom that day. But that is looking back on it from now. I wouldn't rule out that secretly inside, I was clinging to a hope that the money once gained would bring back the New York days. There was that old feeling, the memories of the nice times we had together, and the fear, the fear of going off into the future all alone.

As you can see, my feelings sat on a roller coaster which I cannot truly recreate at this time. Mercurial thoughts of love, hate, betrayal, pity, weakness, and the like raced through my mind and tore at my emotions. One second I'd be convinced that it was over but the next I decided it's not. I'd say to myself things like, "Yes, Tom's a weakling, but maybe it's just a temporary aberration in his life and the real Tom, my man of strength, will return."

As you might expect much of that day was a day of torment and confusion. Tom paced and paced, all he wanted to do after he told me off and begged me to keep my job was to escape. I thought it was because the sirens were calling him from the local barroom when little did I know it was that tart Jenny from a local bedroom. On more than one occasion I had to insist that he take off his jacket and sit down and review the matter again. I had to pound it into his head so that he'd be like Pavlov's dog and react to any question relative to our breakup that it was caused by Roger's overtures to and seduction of me.

Seeing him squirm in the seat, stand up only to sit down again, rub his temple with great dismay, take water to clear his throat, and things like that showed me he was such a weak man. I never wanted to accept that because I married him. It's a telling commentary on me – a black mark I have to live with that I was so blind to enter into a marriage with such a man.

But I wasn't going to let his weakness screw up my road out of the jungle. I had to implant in his mind a knee jerk response to any question about the dissolution of our relationship. I also had to provide a mechanism for insuring that he was not going to stray from the party line. My desperation to do this made me grow stronger.

We eventually arranged a deal where I would have a good idea where Tom was every day. My initial intent on doing this was just to keep Tom in line. But as time went on I found that I needed this contact with him as an insurance policy. I had no contact with any of my family and my friends were few having burned all my bridges when I went to New York and became a snob. So even though I despised the man I found a strange comfort in the fact that someone, whether it be Tom, Crazy Red, Tiny Tim, or Joe Shit the Ragman, someone other than Roger and his associates have an idea what was going on with my life.

Ironically, a couple of days after this, I called Jenny. She was probably my closest friend ever especially for several years prior to my marrying Tom and leaving the neighborhood. I thought of calling her to see if we still had a close enough relationship that would allow me to stay in touch with her in case something happened to Tom or he would no longer act as my safely valve. We had a long chat just like old times. I did not bring up the subject of our split but was relieved that Jenny was still there for me. It comforted me to have an old close and trustworthy friend to call upon.

Another thing I told Tom that evening was that from all I could see things would never be the same between us again. His vituperative remarks toward me effectively voided our vows as far as I was concerned. I told him that I had not done anything with Roger even though he insisted otherwise. I then told him that what I did with Roger from now on was up to me. I told him I wish I had slept with Roger that prior afternoon then I'd have something to throw in his face – you know, I could have yelled, "All right, you call me a tart, fine, I am a tart, I went to bed with Roger Hunt and he was ten times the man you are."

I said he was entitled to believe what he wanted, but as far as I was concerned I was not married to him anymore and that it was each one for his or her self. He could do whatever he wanted and I would do whatever I wanted as long as we were discreet about it.

Stupidly, he asked me if I was telling him to move out. I had to remind him that I would be delighted if he did but he would have to suck it up for bit and stay because if he moved out now it would foil our plan. I sarcastically said to him "I feel bad that you're going to have to besmirch your character and reputation by living with a whore, but there's nothing we can do about if for a bit." He had to wait until I compromised Roger.

He then said, "Then will I have to move out." I said, "You bet your ass you will." This threw him a little. He didn't mind insulting the shit out of me or seeing our marriage dissolve but he was upset at the idea of not having his meal ticket. Who was going to feed him? How was he going to live without a job? Questions like that came up during the lengthy discussion. I couldn't believe he was so naïve. He thought he could call me a whore, throw me out of the big bed, and then have me support him, feed him, and wash his clothes. He really thought I was a sap. We went back and forth over that.

I told him that once I went to bed with Roger he had to move out. I told him it'd be within weeks, no longer. His moving out would be part of the damages I would claim Roger caused.

He complained that he had no job. He would be unable to get an apartment. He'd end up at the Pine Street Inn, a home for homeless men. He said his mother and father wouldn't let him back in their home.

He was right about that. I never told anyone this and I don't know if I should now – but since you'll keep it to yourself Naria then will because it shows you what Tom is really like which again shows my lack of judgment in falling in love with him.

When we were rolling in dough and sending thousands upon thousands upon silly avant-garde art works that we couldn't get ten cents on the dollar when we had to sell them to survive — funny — the same galleries that pushed them on us extolling their value refused to buy the art back — it was always the same excuse — "you bought that when such and such artist was in vogue — no one's buying her now — so I can't possibly buy it back — but hold on to it and you'll make skillions of dollars." I'd tell them that I was giving them the opportunity to

66

make the skillions of dollars and they'd hustle me gently to the door and mumble about overhead.

Well, back to Tom and his parents. It was during this time we had more money than we could ever waste. We believed we were permanent residents of Easy Street. Tom's father called to speak to Tom.

You have to know Tom's old man – he worked his fingers to the bones for Tom who was his pride and joy. Every extra cent he had he showered on him. His house was heavily mortgaged to pay for Tom's education or his whims.

I particularly remember one time around New Year's that I want to tell you about. We were moored off the Bitter End on the Island of Virgin Gorda in the Caribbean having gin and tonics on our fifty foot plus yacht. Tom was smoking a huge Cuban cigar. The chef was preparing a nice lobster dinner. One of our guests, Peter Amenostos, was talking about trying to avoid paying his graduate school tuition and related expenses. Tom said, "Why should you pay them, let your old man pay them. Mine pays mine." Peter said his father didn't have that type of money. Tom replied, "The only thing that pisses me off is that sometimes my old man will get behind in paying my loans and will ask me to help him. Geezus, does that piss me off."

Peter innocently asked him if he helped his father. Tom laughed and said, "I tell him he's embarrassing me that he can't manage to keep up with his bills and hang up on him." Everyone, thinking Tom was joking, laughed. He wasn't. I knew it. You see I also thought it was a big joke that we stuck his father with Tom's college and graduate business school bills, and we would have done it for mine except I didn't have any.

His father worked for one of the big banks in one of those jobs that has a munificent title with little emolument, you know what I mean, little pay or other benefits. For thirty-seven years he worked there and went to school nights. He started as a mail boy making next to nothing and worked from that nothing job up through the ranks of nothing jobs to the big nothing job with the fancy title which paid him slightly more than next to nothing. Tom's father worked long hours for this pittance but he managed to make ends meet.

But as luck would have it, the bank decided to reorganize. The bosses must have heard one of Roger Hunt's lectures on becoming more efficient. Roger's main idea was that the best way to do this was to fire those who'd been around for a while and who had accumulated a lot of seniority and received a smidgen more pay than others. Then you'd hire people for less pay or ship some of the work overseas. So the bank to which his father was so devoted gave him the boot and he ended up with all these debts and no job. For a half dozen months he looked for a job – but no one wanted ex-bankers in their late-fifties except some supermarkets who'd hire them as bag boys.

So when his savings were exhausted, Tom's old man couldn't meet the mortgage payment on the old homestead. Not only that, he owed it to the bank he had worked for over those years. Tom's dad foolishly thought that the bank would take into account his many years of work and show a little forbearance in their foreclosure procedure. But new folks were now in charge, so his many years of dedication did not count. The bank started to foreclose on his home.

The night I'm writing about, we were having one of our shindigs. We had these every week when things were good. This was a typical one when we invited who we thought of as high and mighty and lavished them with sumptuous hors d'oeuvres, the finest wines, and nothing but the best. I remember hearing this ringing sound. At first I thought it was the door bell and the first guests were arriving and I walked to the door to open it when I realized it was our land line telephone ringing. Funny, thinking back, we both had our cell phones but we still kept a land line.

When I answered it was Tom's father. It was the only number he had. He asked indifferently how I was. He then warmly asked to speak to Tom. I think he blamed me for Tom's attitude toward him but believe me Tom felt that way toward him a long before he met me – one does not change how another feels about his parent.

Tom took the phone into the bedroom and was there about five or six minutes. As I might have told you, we had decorated the apartment so that it was stark white where ever it could be. It was as inhospitable to comfortable living as could be imagined. But that was us at the time, all show.

That evening, we had retained about five or six people to work the party who were going to cost us about two grand just to serve the food and wine, which was costing us well over ten thousand dollars. But we had money and we flaunted it. We had a string quartet, which cost another two to three thousand for a few hours playing time. This was typical for us at the time. It was just another night of entertainment.

I still can picture Tom coming from the bedroom in his black tux – in sharp contrast to the white background. He resolutely walked over to me and grabbed me by the elbow saying, "You'll never believe what that fuckin' blood suckin' old man of mine wanted — you'll never believe it in a hundred fuckin' years — he wanted me to loan him five dimes for a couple of months 'til he gets a job — what a fuckin' bum — I'm humiliated — imagine calling me here at this time when I'm about to have these people over and putting the arm on me." Those weren't his exact words but it was something like that since he'd said similar stuff about his dad at other times.

My reaction was to pamper Tom. I said well I hope you didn't let him get you too upset, the guests will be here soon. Then I added, "You know your father's going through some rough times." He looked at me as if my hair had suddenly turned into serpent curls of bright green — he said, "Not upset — you bet your ass I was upset — the freeloading son-of-a-bitch. I told him that it's a little embarrassing to have a father's who's a beggar and unemployed and said if he'd get a job he wouldn't have to be hitting me up for money — and you know, that I'd just as soon not hear from him again if he thought that just because he was my father he had the right to hit me up for an unsecured loan — and I told him how the little respect I had for him had been destroyed."

You know, something off the wall like that, that was what he thought of his father. Looking back here's something to try to figure out. His father was the only one Tom could stand up to. What does that tell you about Tom? They haven't spoken since as far as I know. His mother kept in contact with him now and again sending money to him – and every time she did and even though we certainly didn't need it – he'd bitch about his parents being so cheap.

Well – back to our split – that's why Tom couldn't think of going home. His father wouldn't have him. However, he finally said when the time came he would move out but didn't know where. If I had to guess he was planning to try to get full time job in Jenny's bed. She was too smart for that. She wasn't about to become his meal ticket.

I think it was about a month before he finally got himself out. He was able to end up with his mother's brother, a guy named Morrissey who had a big house in Quincy. He was an undertaker.

But from that point on our life as husband and wife was over. When I think of how he treated his father I'm amazed at myself that I didn't have a better grasp of his character. But look at me talking. I was just as bad. I think he had me bedazzled but that is hardly an excuse for my own tawdry behavior since – sad to be told – I was just as happy to lock his parents' problems in an out-of-the-way closet in my mind. I have to be honest, his parents could have starved to death for all I would care.

Why is it I'm talking about him being such a decrepit, ill-mannered person as if I wasn't part of who he was? I wasn't blind. Love may conquer all but it can't excuse all. Sure Bonny loved Clyde but that would have made a poor defense had she gone to trial.

Patty Hearst used some type of defense like that when she was charged with an armed robbery she committed after being taken hostage by the Symbionese Liberation Army. It was called the Stockholm Syndrome defense. The hostage becomes so emotionally attached and dependent on her captives that she loses her free will. Hell, I suppose everyone who has ever been deeply in love could use that defense.

Speaking of Patty Hearst, I heard she did quite well after her term in jail so maybe there is something to the idea. But what most amazes me about her is the times she lived in, the early '70s, and that a group calling itself Symbionese. What did the word mean?

A Black Panther who was one of its leaders spelled it out. Wait a minute, I wrote it down on my iPhone. Yes, here it is, let me quote, "The Symbionese Liberation Army is made up of the aged, youth and women and men of all races and people. The name Symbionese is taken from the word symbiosis and we define its meaning as a body of dissimilar bodies and organisms living in deep and loving harmony and partnership in the best interest of all within the body"

That was the '70s in America. You could kill a school superintendent and a few onlookers and claim you were living in deep and loving harmony. But I digress, not that I mind, it gets my mind of myself.

Here's my Stockholm Syndrome defense. I grew up the only child in suburbia isolated in a world surrounded by manicured lawns. My father was wonderful to me as was my mother. My friends came from nice homes and well-educated, mostly professional parents. I associated with people who were exactly like me inside and out. We had the same values. I didn't study or read too much. The social life was too much fun. If I spent one-tenth as much time

reading a book as I did reading and sending my
text messages, I might have learned something
but the addiction to being in continual touch and
being continually inundated with information
from friends makes one live in a small world. I
slipped into a college. How? I could afford to pay
full tuition, some have to do it, and if you can it
seems that adds a lot of points to your SAT
scores. In college I continued similar
associations and actions.

I was cut from the same cloth as Tom,
who I knew in high school, but began dating in
college. After a while I was heads over heels in
love with him to the exclusion of everyone and
everything else, except, of course, my emails and
text messages from friends who might as well
have been living inside my Blackberry or
computer since I saw no one but Tom. We
married and then Tom went to work at an
investment bank and we hit the jackpot. Maybe
if I'd had to do something after college, things
may have been different but I guess our quick
climb to the top of the money tree made me
heady in that rarified air.

Not much of a defense so take it for what
it's worth but that is who I am, not something
you want to hold up as an example of anything
good.

On that dreadful day many years ago I
began to get my revenge against Tom. He
couldn't escape until the whore laid down the
terms of the future relationship. It was strange
– it was really strange the way everything
happened, the day starting with me so much in
love with him and ending with me despising him.
And what really surprised me was how cold I had
become. I felt like ice that penetrated my body
the day before had seized my heart turned it into

cold stone. Funny saying that, but those are two expression for a women out of the old rock and roll days, expressions that made little impact on me until it happened to me, hard hearted Dakota with a heart made of stone.

Tom slept on the cot that night and I slept in the big bedroom. It had been agreed upon but when he left to get the paper, which was a euphemism for a few double shots at the bar or a quickie with Jenny, I went to bed and to cement the agreement locked the bedroom door. The next day I went to work without so much as a goodbye to him.

I'm really tired. I looked at the time. It's after one in the morning. This probably isn't wise putting so much time into this at one sitting. I have to try to limit myself to time so I can let my mind rest at times. If my notebook were a psychiatrist I'm sure there's no way I'd be wanting to be with him as long as I've been with Naria especially on a Sunday night. I'd burn myself out along with her.

Maybe it's all right to do longer sessions in the beginning. I feel really good. It is so much better than blocking things out and not facing them – hiding from myself in booze or drugs or absorbed by TV – maybe that's why I hate myself – I've never taken the time to get to know me like I'm doing with this retrospective. Who was it who said the unexamined life is not worth living? That may be true but it does not explain why. I think I've figure it out. If you don't examine your life you'll never know who you really are and you'll end up living with a stranger. Who wants to spend 24/7 with a stranger on their back?

What I'm concluding is this is helping me. However, I've got to keep in mind I have other things to do. So like in the real world, it'll be best if I set aside specific times to visit with Naria.

MONDAY MORNING: SECOND CUP OF COFFEE

Well, I didn't see Roger again until that Friday. When I saw him, I had a feeling I did not hate him as much as I hated Tom. During the week my hatred for Tom had grown when I thought of how little he had done to save himself from sinking into the quicksand of despair and how he had been dragging me after him. My hatred of Roger was eased by my idea that his was the hand that would lift me from the sucking quicksand, plant me on firm soil, and let me get on with my life, or as I thought at the time what little was left of it.

It tells a lot about human nature when one hovering close to the age of thirty can convince herself that her life is almost over when truly it has hardly begun. I've learned life's a chunk of putty that you mold for yourself; if you don't, you'll let someone else do it for you and you'll not like the outcome. True, I'm not too happy with the result I've brought about but at least what I've created has been my product. When I was letting Tom mold me I had lost control of who I' would be in the name of love, which proved as ephemeral as the morning dew on a sunny day. It seems many women do this with their friend or spouse, or especially their ex-spouse, surrendering her life to him. I wish I could tell each one of them, "Girl, you've only one life, don't let some guy take it from you. Stop chasing after the guy who ditched you. Stop being the friendly bitch who wags her tail every time he comes back looking for something Stop letting him run your life, especially if he's got another pillow. Get on with it, girl. You had a life before him, so have one after, without him."

76

Of course, I didn't realize any of this at the time, because I never reflected on anything more than getting through the next day or so. In the good times I never reflected at all. But the suddenness of my breakup and the treacherous road I was about to undertake made me understand that I was out there all alone. What was going to happen to me was what I made happen. So I bucked up my courage, suppressed my conscience, took a deep breath and made my body into a playground for Roger's hands.

I'll never get over how grotesque his hands always appeared to me. His manicured nails seemed like the talons of a vulture ready to tear into my skin, his words always floated to me on a carpet of fetid air, his eyes were like dull cesspools, the smoky grey iris floating in a sewer of yellow puss, the openings in his nose seemed excessively dilated as if he was a gorilla and he could inhale me in through its gross hairs, the hair on his head felt like the feathers of a cormorant from the Gulf of Mexico after the BP deep water rig mishap that spewed and gushed millions of barrels of oil, and his skin had a slimy slippery feel to it like the skin of an oozing rotten banana.

Sound gross? It was. But so what, I had a plan put together in desperation that I hoped would get me what I wanted. I was like the contestant eating leeches. I was amazed at how I was able to fight off my repulsion of him and get by all the grotesqueries. What empowered me was thinking of the women in the red light districts in Amsterdam and the surrounding areas of Europe who openly display their wares and must put up with a constant stream of similar decrepit males without knowing what rat infested hole they had just slunk out of in order to survive. I only had to deal with one, and it was sporadic.

There was nothing about Roger that I found attractive except that he had a big chunk of cash. All I wanted was a little of it – nothing excessive – just a little for suffering the indignities which I felt whenever he touched my breasts or put his cold blubbery lips against mine or when his foul breath almost suffocated me as he gagged me with his sordid French kisses. I sometimes disappeared into the thought, "I am woman, I am strong," or "If those kids in Amsterdam can do it, so can I," or mostly I'd hum the tune that Elvis used to sing, "Money Honey" to remind me why I was subjecting myself to these indignities.

It was three or four weeks after the first time he touched me that he started hinting that he wanted to up the ante. I had yet to sleep with him, but we had moved considerably beyond the petting and feeling stage. I don't want to go into details because there is nothing in the memory of it that is other than creepy and horrible. Suffice it to say, I'd come a long way, baby, from the early days.

You can use your fertile imagination. It shouldn't be too hard since all of our activity to that time was confined to his office, the floor, the desk or the couch. Well, to give you a hint, we probably were at the stage Bill Clinton was at when he said, "I did not have sex with that woman." There was something in me that kept me from going too far, since I had a choice, unlike those who are directly paid for specific services. I held this belief that once a donkey gets the carrot on the stick, he stops moving forward. It was a good belief when it came to Roger, because he was a real ass. I knew I wanted to keep something out there for Roger to strive after and aim for. Desire quickly wanes when the chase ends especially for the Roger-types who use women. It is one of man's greatest deficiencies not to be satisfied, always craving for something more.

What helped me in keeping control and not going much further was the environment in which we carried on our enterprise; that it was a busy time for Roger, so he was not around too much and had to travel for days at a time; and my wanting to be different from all Roger's other victims who he continually told me about. All his exploitations of them had occurred in his office so I felt if I succumbed there I'd become a blur in his mind with little to distinguish me from the others. There were a couple of times when I worked late that he tried to move the ball forward but I did not want to be taken so I wasn't. I'd escape pretending that I had to get home to cook for my dear Tom.

But as you'd expect with a man like Roger there came a time when he started to really push me. He was telling me how badly he wanted to go to bed with me and of his intense desire to experience me "skin to skin," — that was his expression, "skin to skin." How it repulsed me! I tried to picture myself in bed with him but all I could imagine was being with a humungous boa constrictor – Roger's oily skin was what I thought a snake's skin would feel like, having never touched one. Try to get romantic imagining yourself in bed with a giant snake squirming around you! That's the picture that filled my mind when he proposed that we sleep together "skin to skin." Yuck!

Now that I think of it, it was just about six weeks from the start when he began to demand rather than hint that I let him bed me. He and I were going at it in his office for a good bit every day and now I'd just about had enough of satisfying him and finding myself drained of energy and thought. I was tired and really felt at the end of my string. I remember that because I finally insisted that Tom move over to his uncle's in Quincy. This had to be done before I could get succor from my daily defilement. My plan was to use Tom's moving out as the linchpin upon which to base my extortion.

I was home alone, planning to confront Roger the next day with his having ruined my marriage, my husband moving out, yada yada, you know the routine. I figured I'd base my claim for damages saying that he had been sexually harassing me by telling me if I did not comply with his demands, I'd lose my job. I discovered using the internet that seemed to be the routine other woman used. I'd tell him that Tom suspected I was having an affair, that I'd been talking in my dreams about him and Tom heard me, something like that. It was all jumbled up in my mind since I was strictly flying by the seat of my pants. Looking back, I was worse than a babe in the woods when it came to this. I knew nothing about the art of using sex to gain money or the need to have some corroborative evidence or most importantly how difficult it is to take on someone as powerful as Roger Hunt with all his money, connections, and legion of supplicants who readily do his dirty work.

Ignorant of all this, I planned to spin out the line that Tom suspected I was involved with someone because I stopped having sex with him, the latter part was true. Tom had suspected it was someone at work because he pretty much knew my schedule and when I mentioned the name Roger in my sleep that confirmed it to him. Now Tom had moved out and my marriage was destroyed. I'd tell him that Tom planned to go public with it but perhaps he could pay to keep him quiet. That was my idea – my big plan to extort money from Roger.

It seemed so simple. I actually wrote out the words I planned to say trusting nothing to spontaneity. I thought after I made my speech Roger would start monetary negotiations with me. I was so naïve, I had not even given a thought to the amount of money I'd demand if Roger fell for it but I imagined that at some point we'd agree on a fair amount for my defilement and Tom's departure from our marriage bed. I'd live happily ever after free from the sinewy clutches of Roger, and unfortunately as I then believed the burden of Tom. Yes, unfortunately because as hardened as I had become after my morning talk with him when he said he couldn't sleep with me anymore, it was not easy to wash away all feelings and thoughts of "what may have been" especially during those weak moments that still imprisoned me from time to time back then.

That day and the next day I rehearsed my speech. Now that I think about it, I rehearsed it for three or so days because Roger was on a trip to the West Coast. I had worked it out pretty good so I was well prepared when he got back to his office.

The morning started off like every other. I assumed it would follow the routine we had established. After he'd come in and wish everyone a good morning along with me, he'd go into his office for a spell. He'd then buzz Stella and ask her to send me in for dictation.

I hated that part because Stella was such an ass. She'd put down the telephone and indicate by pointing over her shoulder with a closed fist and open thumb to Roger's office door and say somewhat loudly, "Hey! Lucy! Time for your morning duties!" as a smug, all knowing grin creased her face. Lucy had been a recent invention of Stella's. I think if I asked her to spell it the name would have been written "Loosey" as in, loose woman. She'd then say in an equally loud voice, "Girls, hold Roger's calls. He doesn't want to be interrupted." I'd try to ignore the barb and the giggles and looks as I walked into his office with my secretary's pad. He'd be sitting behind his desk and would indicate I should slip the lock bolt in the door into place. We'd chit chat and even do a little office work for a while before any contact took place. The whole thing was weird but that's what we did and what I expected would happen that morning – you know, a little calm before the storming.

This time, apparently because he'd confined his activity on his trip to business, I didn't get five steps into the room when I noticed he was not sitting at his desk. He had been standing behind the door and as soon as I shut it, he seized me from behind and started running his hands over my breasts. I blocked out what he was doing. He then ran his hand down below and started to feel me there. I tried to resist but he overpowered me. I quietly asked him to stop, knowing prying ears were twenty or so feet away, I quietly pleaded with him to stop but he was like a wild beast.

I wanted to tell him about Tom finding out about us but I couldn't get the words out. I gave up trying but concentrated on trying to go into my cocoon where I could find Elvis and ignore what he was doing to me. I normally could but this time he was too far out of control that my self-defense mechanisms didn't kick in. He was inside my panties with his hands.

He was feeling me hard and it began to hurt. I bit my lip to keep from yelling out. His wildness exceeded my imagination of how harrowing this experience could become. I found myself forced on my back on the floor with him on top of me, trying to take off my skirt. Suddenly, apparently because he had become so excited by his frenzy, he finished prematurely; the fury fled from him, his body sagged, and he became a dead weight on top of me, squashing me into the floor.

After what seemed days, he finally got up and went over to his liquor closet. He poured himself a scotch. I slowly got up. I felt like I had been manhandled by a thug. I knew what it felt to be wantonly attacked. I wanted to scream. This was ten times worst than he had ever done to me before. I had been ravaged. Usually it was smoother and more participatory; you know, at least it was step by step but this sudden onslaught unnerved me. I was physically shaking.

He was now behind his desk where he lit a cigarette. He smiled. He offered an apology for exploding too early, saying he'd now have to head down the back way to the gym to take a shower and change.

I sat there stunned. He had a smug satisfied smile on his face as he took drags from his cigarettes and sipped his scotch. I must have had deer-in-the-head lights expression on mine. "Cheer up," he said. "I told you I'm sorry I got a little too eager. Next time will be better for you.

You'll see. Now straighten yourself up. You're a mess. Go back to your desk. I'm going to clean up."

I found a well of courage rising up in me, probably because his attack had called forth in me the wild beast that allows one to defend herself, so I said to him, "Before you go, I want to talk."

He said he wanted to shower and indicated with an expression of his hands that he didn't want to sit around feeling unclean. He then made it clear what his mimed expression meant by throwing out some vile words describing his condition. One of them was slimy because I remember thinking that he'd never notice the difference on his skin. He concluded by saying if I had to tell him something then, "Do it quick."

I'd totally forgotten my rehearsed speech. I blurted out that I was frightened because my husband Tom knew I was involved with him. This piqued his curiosity. He forgot about being dirty. He didn't at all seem as upset as I expected, but responded in a casual manner, "What happened?"

His interest and apparent lack of concern eased my fears a little yet only tiny and jumbled bits and pieces of the rehearsed nonsensical tale came back to me. I started off stumbling and hesitating sounding something like: "Tom knows, you know, I've, you know, been not, you know, not doing too much with him, and he thinks, you know he says, after last night, I was talking about you, and he figured, you know how it is, that maybe that's why, I'm not doing anything with him because of you. He's moving out. And now I feel like I'm trapped"

I told Roger I admitted to Tom what was going on with us. Then out of the blue and I have no idea where this came from I said: "When I told him about you, I said that I was deeply in love with you." Honest, that was the furthest thing from my mind but it showed I had really spun out of control. I was beginning to sling out pure bullshit like that for lack of any idea what to say. I was probably petrified at what I was doing. Then tears came to my eyes right after telling him I was in love with him. I had no idea why. Now, if I had to guess, I'd say it was because I was in a full panic mode. I realized I'd nothing more to say and felt sorry for myself. I guess from Roger's perspective it was a reaffirmation of my statement of love for him.

"So he's moved out, is that what happened?" Roger finally spoke perhaps motivated by my crocodile tears. "So your husband's fled the roost."

Still teary I responded by nodding my head and saying, "I'm afraid, Roger. I don't know what he's going to do. I don't want to get you involved that's why I'm so worried. You mean too much to me."

Roger smiled through my recital as if I were telling him a joke. His reaction was the total opposite of what I expected. I thought he'd be upset, fearful of having his reputation or that of his businesses tarnished. He didn't bat an eye. I'm not sure why I didn't fall onto the floor when he said, "That's wonderful."

He went to say now that Tom moved out on me then I could spend more time with him in the evenings. He told me he'd talk more about it later and left the office. I went to my desk in a daze. I'm sure I put myself into some type of presentable appearance before doing that but I'm not sure. What the hell difference did it make anyway? Everyone in the office had a pretty good idea what was going on. They knew my best office skills weren't those taught at Katie Gibbs.

Just before quitting time Roger came out of his office and asked me to stay around saying he had some work for me. I shivered thinking that he planned to really attack me. I realized I had lost the routine excuse I usually used that I needed to get home to get dinner for Tom.

When I went into his office he was sitting behind his desk. He gave no indication of the need for further encounters. It seemed the morning blow off satisfied him.

He said he couldn't stay long. He said he'd been thinking that since Tom moved out I did not have to stay in the Dorchester apartment — he called it the "Dorchester dump" — and I could move into one of his condominiums at the Quincy Marina. I remember the conversation after that like it was yesterday. I said: "But what about Tom, what if he comes after you?"

He turned and poured himself another drink. He said: "Dakota, let me tell you something." He walked over to me, took me by the arm and led me over to the coach off to the side of his office. "Sit down a minute and let me explain something to you."

I sat down. I couldn't figure out how he could be so calm. I thought he'd have been extremely upset and would have started to rave. But he was in absolute control. After I sat down, he sat in the red leather chairs next to the couch. He said: "I'm a rich man, Dakota. I didn't get rich by running from things. I got rich by confronting things and getting my way. So let me tell you a couple of stories."

"I hope you're not offended when I suggest this to you. I hope it doesn't interfere with our relationship, but you're a big girl and you seem to be quite sophisticated. And before I go on, I want to tell you that I have deep feelings for you and my relationship with you is very important to me. I like to think it is going to be deep, long-term, and full of meaning. I hope you feel the same about me. But I want to be honest with you, Dakota. I want to be fully candid with you. To my way of thinking, if I lay all my cards on the table then I have the best chance of success."

He leaned back and put his hands behind his head. "Perhaps you know this, I'd like to think you do, but maybe you don't. But let me give it to you straight. You're not the first woman who has worked here that I've had over the past few years. You're certainly the best and the only one I've ever had such a deep feeling for, but you're not the only one I've been involved with. Do you understand?"

I don't know how I did it but I managed to nod my head and keep a straight face when inside me my soul was bursting with laughter thinking that this fiend was giving me this bullshit about being the best of the flock he'd defrocked. I imagined him saying the same thing to each of the women he now wanted to talk about. I said something stupid like I didn't know or I thought I was the only one.

He reached over and held my leg. He assured me that I was head and shoulders above the rest and how none could or would ever compare to me. I remember nodding. I don't know why I was surprised because I began this encounter based on the idea he thought himself a ladies man, but I was. I was somewhat trying to weigh the consequences to me of the whore

87

master telling me that he was a whore master but mostly I was trying to figure the effect of his confession on my expected windfall and how best to bring the subject around to my extortion.

He went on: "I'm glad you understand, Dakota, because I don't want anything to happen to our wonderful relationship. It's something that I treasure and I'll let nothing interfere with it. But the reason I'm telling you about my other affairs is so that you can see that you shouldn't give one thought about Tom being aware that we're involved with each other, you can be sure I'm not going to do so."

This assertion quenched the fire of joy and left me feeling as soggy and confused as a recently rained upon Girl Scout sitting at a drenched campfire. He continued: "The reason I say that is that in my other relations with women I've had similar things happen to me." I looked over to the widow in his office to see if I could see my money flying out of it.

He got up and went back to the bar and poured himself some more scotch. He didn't offer me any. He never did at the office. He thought it wasn't good for the help to drink in the work place. He came back to the seat. He went on: "The first time I was involved with a woman at the office it was with Jayne Hampshire. She was assistant director of our personnel division. Funny, I remember her name even though I don't remember the names of some of the more recent ones. I suppose that's not too remarkable because I've often heard tell that the first time for anything is the most memorable. But anyway, she too, like you, was married."

"She was a pretty girl too - very pretty. She married some short bald-headed guy. I never knew what she saw in him but anyway we started innocently enough. It was at an office party. I was in my office working at my desk and she came in with a drink in her hand for me."

He went on to describe their intercourse in lurid detail – Roger got some sort of excitement out of telling his sexual exploits to other woman – I've heard this is a man thing just like it's a man thing to go around exposing yourself, you know those flashers. As far as I knew, Roger wasn't a flasher and his telling these stories wouldn't be called flashing but it seems to me that the telling in minute detail of one's sexual exploits seems to be another side of the flasher coin.

I had to listen as he detailed how he ended up making out with her on the floor of his office that night and for every night after that for about a month. He'd get into details like, well, I won't describe them, but when he told it to me it was like he was reliving it. Well, anyway, after spreading out in detail his sex life with Hampshire he said: "Then, as woman do, she began to get second thoughts about our affair and began to back off. Just like that – cold turkey." He snapped his fingers. "I'm up to my neck enthralled by her – she was wonderful in bed like no one I'd ever been with up to that time – but just like that she says 'that's it.'

"Great bed," I thought, "the floor of the office."

He continued saying that he was still madly desirous for her but added, "What could I do? You can't thread a moving needle and this one had moved on. Well anyway, I figured so be it. We had our fun. I was getting involved with one of my major projects so I shrugged the affair off and got on with my business. A couple of months later, I got involved with this young

89

woman who'd just come on board. I don't remember her name, but while all my attention's on her this Hampshire woman shows up and asks if she can see me."

He went on after taking a sip from his scotch: "It's funny. When she came back in, even though it was no more than two or three months when we were in the throes of passion, I felt nothing for her. I'd almost forgotten about her. It's amazing how quickly one substitutes one for another when there's only the animal appetite involved. It's like feeding a hunger. One night it is roast beef, the next sword fish, the next veal, and so on. If there's nothing more involved than satisfying the sexual urge then past participants are like last week's meals — some you have a faint recollection of, yet others are totally forgotten."

I remember that he was concerned at my aspect as he said this because he then assured me that I wasn't just another meal to him. I was different. I was someone with whom he'd become deeply involved and all that. I really can't believe that he'd think I'd accept that but he was so sold on his own prowess that he did. Anyway, after assuring me of his undying fidelity to me, he went on with his story about Jayne Hampshire. "So she comes into the office and she accuses me of passing over her for the position of director of personnel because she no longer was making out." – he used the f word – "I had no idea what she was talking about."

"I didn't even know the director of personnel was vacant. But she went on making all sorts of accusations about filing suits against me in court and with some state agencies. So I told her to feel free to do what she had to do but I asked her to hold off for a day, telling her I'd like

90

to see her the next day and perhaps we could straighten it out. I knew she'd go for that, probably thinking she'd get the job of director or get some kind of hush money. She had assumed that she had me over a barrel."

"But I was not as dumb in my relationship with her as she might have thought. You see – I'm sure she believed there were never any witnesses to any of our trysts, but in fact I always arranged that there were plenty of witnesses. My diary indicated that during the times I was with her that I was with someone else. And that someone else's diary indicated he or she was with me at that time. Sometimes, something she never knew, I'd have been having dinner in the executive dining room with others and I'd excuse myself indicating that I had an important call I had to take in my office. I'd come to the office and spend fifteen or so minutes with her, send her home, and then return to the dinner. Although I appeared to be acting with reckless abandon, I was always extremely cautious that everything was done in a controlled environment. My advantage was that I had cover in writing and people who appeared to be, some in fact were, disinterested witnesses. But on most occasions I could expect she would be in romantic heat enraptured by the intercourse between us and she'd have nothing to support her version of the events. Especially in the early stages of these romances the woman is too involved not to be a little careless. I'd always make it look like an encounter was casual when it was highly planned out. I was able to manipulate Hampshire, and all the others, just like I do with my competitors, into making foolish mistakes."

"I remember Jayne because I'll never forget her astonishment the next day when she returned. She sat in front of my desk and said: 'All right Roger, what is it?' I asked her what she meant. She said: 'Do I get the job or what?' I told her that after she spoke to me about the position the day before, I looked into it. It seems that it was given to another person. I expressed my regret. She then started talking about suing me."

"I asked what did I do that she could sue me for? She said, 'I'll sue you for all the time you had sex with me in the office and the promises you made to me at that time.' I expressed astonishment saying 'I never had anything at all to do with you'. She laughed and said 'right'. I then said 'When do you say all this happened?' She said 'Every working night' during a certain period of time. I asked her what proof she had that we did anything like she suggested. She said she had her word and when push came to shove, everyone would believe her over me."

"I said what she said took place was impossible. I took out my diary. I told her to look at it. At no time was she with me. Her laugh vanished. She wasn't dumb. She realized what I had done. It was going to be her word against my diary and all my witnesses."

He gave me a knowing sinister smile as he said: "You wouldn't believe what a fine acting job I'd done. She was in tears after she viewed my diary and list of witnesses. All of them showed that she was not with me. She knew she'd been had and that there was no way any allegation of sexual harassment could prevail as long as I had this backup. Ha, I never saw a person lose her composure like she did. She was like a balloon that all the air is let out of. You

92

should have seen her face, thinking of it made me smile for days afterwards. As much as I loved seeing the tears pouring from her eyes when she realized that her crude blackmail attempt was to get her nothing and that she'd given me a lot of pleasure for gratis, I was really pleased when she got up, said 'you're a bastard', and left the office. I am a bastard if someone tries to take advantage of me."

He went on and on telling me about this one and that one. He told me one filed a complaint with the state agency against him. He told me how his hired gun lawyers had it quickly thrown out. In the one case brought against him in federal court he ended up getting money from the woman he had abused because his lawyers were so good and he had taken such good care to protect himself.

So the gist of all he told me was that he really didn't care what I told Tom even less so what Tom would do. He said he'd simply deny it like with all the others. He said he'd have no trouble arranging to have all the witnesses he needed to show he was with someone else at the time I said I was with him. He said, and I must admit this threw me; he'd make Tom believe I was with someone else but that it was not him. Then he told me how he had done that to another woman and almost got her killed.

I could see that I was check-mated. There was no way I'd get any money out of him in the manner I planned. I pretended I was relieved. I said: "I'm glad to hear that – I was worried. I was worried all the way to the office today until I told you. As soon as I told Tom I wish I never had told him." I then went on to tell him how much I loved being with him. I was fishing about for the right things to say or at least not to say the wrong things. The last thing I wanted him to think was that my original intent was to stick him up. The second last was to have gone through my agony for nothing.

I was really reaching to come up with my next step. I kept thinking I should be careful because he was clever and experienced. He was much too clever for me at that moment. He had been through the routine I was planning to pull on him more times than I could count on my two hands. I needed time to think about how I could get the money out of him. I knew I had no hope with any type of legal action. He already had blocked that route. As my mind whirled trying to come up with an answer, he said: "Dakota, Relax. Everything will be fine."

I told him I would. I repeated how relieved I was that he wasn't upset with me. I went on about how much he meant to me and how sorry I was for having given away our secret. I could sense that he was buying it because he said that when I first brought it up he had a momentary impression that I was trying to get some money out of him. But he said he could now see that I wasn't.

I remonstrated with myself for being so naïve. How could I have thought that this man who'd had a reputation as a womanizer would be such an easy prey? I knew I should have assumed that some of his past playmates would have tried to salve their wounds of rejection with some of his green ointment. So I knew I was in for a real battle. I had lost the first skirmish, he had his Pyrrhic victory. I was bloody but I was far from being defeated. I immediately knew I had to convince him that my involvement with him was a love affair. I told him something at that time, which was a theme I would build on as our relationship continued to develop. The theme I established in my mind was to tell him over and over again that I would feel the most debased of creatures if the beauty of our relationship degenerated into a tussle over money, while knowing to my quick that the total sum of my involvement with him boiled down to one fact, money.

I knew what money could accomplish from my heady New York days; I knew what its absence would bring from my dire Dorchester times. In New York, Icarus-like I had experience the giddiness of the heights but being careless I quickly came crashing down. Splat! Suddenly I was down and out as quickly as Daedalus's son fell into the sea. I remember thinking: "So what! We're broke. But we're still the same people as we were when we had money." Yeah, I thought that but none of my New York friends did. We were chased out of the City and ended up in Dorchester.

Oh, yeah, and there's the matter of Tom – I often wondered if some type of Jenny would have come onto the scene if we held on to all our dough. Probably, but that's neither here nor there now as far as my feelings are concerned. Although there's one thing that I still don't know, had Tom double-crossed me in New York with another woman would I have acted against that woman as I planned to do against Jenny when I learned about her? I'm getting ahead of myself.

I knew to get the money I had to shunt aside any feelings which would interfere with my total deception of Roger. I had to become another Mata Hari. Thinking of her, I flashed back to the morning Tom called me a whore and suddenly realized that from the mouth of babes – Tom was a child – comes the truth.

95

All right, I accepted it. I am a whore. So I resolved as Roger told me of his duplicity to become a whore par excellence. I knew my intent to undertake this role would tax my emotions and destroy my spirituality. I hoped that after my sojourn in the gutter I'd find a way back to redemption. I had no idea what laid ahead or what I would become but having made my decision I did not look back.

So while we talked I moved over to Roger and stroked his hair and made other obvious passes at him. We again started in. I did enough then to satisfy him and send him off feeling that there was much more of that down the road.

That morning coming to work I hadn't planned on the relationship continuing. As I said, before then I'd never gone, as we used to say in college – I'd never gone all the way with him. I'd been close but not quite there. Initially I'd decided not to step over the line, as it's euphemistically called by politicians, believing that drawing that line meant something morally but I could see I was dealing in a great deal of self-deception. I'd done enough that going all the way was really little more than I'd already done from a moral or philosophical point of view.

I wasn't concerned about those aspects of it. There was something else to keeping that final door locked. How do I say it? It was an ace in the hole. The carrot I mentioned earlier. The line I'd drawn was significant because it still did not give Roger all he wanted. By stopping at the edge, as difficult as that had become at times, it still gave me somewhat of an upper hand.

I didn't have much time to go through all this. My plan had turned to shambles. I knew without thinking about it I had two choices then:

96

go on and become totally involved; or go back to a life I abhorred even before I threw Tom out. Now going back I'd be living in that shit hole by myself.

So, much of what I tell may or may not have occurred to me at the time. My mind was pounding out messages to me which gave me little choice so like that general I resolved – and I remember thinking this expression – damn the torpedoes – full speed ahead – or was it an admiral who said that? – whatever.

So when he suggested that I move into the apartment at the Marina to be his personal mistress I didn't bat an eye. My decision had been made. Anyway what else could I do? He had all the cards. I had none, absolutely none. I'd wrecked my prior life, I thought, not knowing it had already been wrecked which is neither here nor there. Tom was out of the house – I didn't regret that although in a sense if I had not come up with the idea of letting Roger move on me – no what am I thinking, you know, I sometimes forget Tom was already with Jenny and think that if I didn't let Roger at me things would have been different but I'd lost Tom by that time no matter what.

I suppose I could have walked away right then and there from everything – gone out West and started all over if all that had happened was that Tom and I had split. I don't know why the idea of going west came to me. Thinking of it, I wonder where the people out west go when they come to these moments.

But – and this might seem queer – I had this overriding feeling that made me resolve to plunge ahead. I wanted to outsmart this bastard. I'd have to use all the resources available to me – my major resource being my

97

body – to do it. I was going to make Roger pay not only for me but for all the other poor bastards he defrocked. But I also – wait – what am I saying. My body was not my major resource – it was the tool my major resource would use – my major resource being my mind coupled with my ability as an actor – I was ten times smarter than Roger, who when you come down to it, was a dumb fuck who got ahead because of gall and ignorance.

I planned to outsmart him and gain my revenge against him. I intended to destroy him. My beautiful body was my weapon, my beautiful body which had all ready been despoiled by this cretin's touch. My weapon had been tarnished and injured. This fiend had crawl over it and abused it. It sorely cried out for retribution. So I couldn't walk away knowing that the only way it would be healed was to use it as a means to plunge a stake into Roger's heart not just for me but for all the other women he abused.

I had this limpid view of my body as being a sword. Like Excaliber or some other exquisite sword, it would be carried into battle and become besmirched, muddied, stained, dirtied, but never broken. It then it could be burnished and would become renewed as if it had never been sullied. So while he went on and on about his conquests I was totally occupied in thinking how good it would feel to destroy him. I knew I needed time. I knew I was facing a vast conglomerate, Hunt Enterprises, which would throw everything it had at me to back him up. I knew I needed to totally engross my mind on these goals. I believed the challenge would be therapeutic.

I looked back on this day in amazement. In the morning, he ran all over my body with his foul hands and drooling mouth. While he was doing this my mind was blank, I was in a panic. Later, when he told me of how I was just one of a number of women but I was more special than others I again gave him access to me so that he would not think I'd been attempting to blackmail him. My mind was off somewhere in a bright coffee shop, planning my future course.

I first decided that I needed time to plan out my vengeance. The only problem with the time I needed was that much of it was going to be spent in bed with a snake but that didn't seem too onerous since my planning to get back at him I thought would mentally remove me from the physical encounters and steel my resolve to make our denouement so much more fatal to him. I'd resolved my revenge wasn't going to be something that was over quickly – it had to be drawn out – something like the Chinese water torture – cool drops of water dripping onto the sweating forehead of the person dying from thirst. It had to be slow and exceeding agony. That was the only way to burnish my sword and free it from stain.

So by the time his animalistic advantages had gained him a release from his passions, I had put the beginning stages of my plan in place. I decided that I liked the idea of becoming his mistress and living in one of the company condominiums – for two reasons: first, it was cheap, and secondly I could have the environment in which I could set traps for Roger and parade our involvement in an open and notorious manner if I needed to make that part of my plan. Yes, as he babbled on, having by these thoughts and goals effectively suppressed my revulsion to him and calmed my repulsion at the thoughts of having him make love to me, I grew more and more pleased at becoming the sword that would slaughter the swordsman.

Roger made several fatal mistakes in analyzing his opponent. His first error was that he looked upon my initial extortionate gambit not for what it was but as a cry for help. Next he foolishly assumed that by laying out his ability to be treacherous I would be cowered rather than emboldened. Then he believed that because he was so in love with himself that I could love the vermin which I believed him to be. Finally, by making these mistakes he showed he could be destroyed.

His mistakes convinced me that given the time I could outwit him. I knew he was conniving and treacherous, but I knew his ego was such that I could destroy him especially since he thought his past triumphs were indicative of future events and he could act against any woman with impunity. I've absolutely no doubt that he felt himself impervious to any harm from me.

Any idea that I could immediately squeeze money from him had cooled. I was resolved to out think, to out manipulate, and to crush this insect after I extracted as much money as I could from him and lured him into my web and slowly suffocated him. I had jettisoned Tom. I had resolved to make my temporary bed with this creep.

When he finished, I told him that I'd love to become more involved with him and that his suggestion that I live in one of the condominiums was a brilliant idea. I told him, feigning sincerity, that I wanted to sleep with him – to go to bed at night, sleep skin to skin, and awaken in his arms – to make love to him over and over again. I suggested we would do that once we had our own place where I would be comfortable and could give him what he deserved. Yuck! I suggested that to do it in any place other than our own place would be to cheapen it.

As I talked, I could see he was lapping it up. One way to a man's heart is to tell him what he wants to hear. I saw a great benefit from this was that the assaults on me at the office could be stopped because I would tell him they take away from the sweetness of being with him in our place. There'd be another sweet part of that. Stella would lose her patsy. Take that, Stella!

I had to forestall the ultimate act of making love to him. It was clear Roger was the kind of guy who wanted something until he got it. When he had it he'd play with it for a while and then discard it. This was blatantly obvious to me. So I'd avoid dirtying the sword until I had my clutches on the condominium and on him and then delay it tarnishing as long as I could.

I'd use Tom, I decided. I'd tell Roger I was so much in love with him that I wanted to separate our total coming together until such time as I had totally obliterated the involvement with Tom from my mind. I wanted, I said, to become fully involved with him but on my terms, on my conditions, and not too soon so that it would be magnificent and last forever. Oh what webs we weave when we first deceive.

It was not long after that day that I was comfortably ensconced in the two-bedroom condominium of Hunt Enterprises in Quincy, overlooking Boston harbor. I suppose if I were a normal person I would have been satisfied with the life I was leading. I had everything. I was wined and dined when ever or whereever I wanted. I had maids cleaning the apartment. My bed was made every day and turned down at

101

night. Roger treated me like a queen as did most other people. My new cache of money, courtesy of Roger's unexpected generosity brought and bought friends. I had new freedom and minimized my working hours.

I was beginning to acquire as much as I wanted. I played the role magnificently. Roger traveled much which gave me the personal freedom I sought and really needed. When he was back, he spent most of the nights with his wife and kids. He spent a few with me but for two months after I'd moved in. I'd still not gone all the way. He was quickly satisfied and did not seek a double header. I suppose his total occupation with his growing business enterprises provided him with an outlet that other men gain through repetition. So, I was in the cat bird seat. The sword was sullied having been impinged upon by Roger's foulness but it was still in good shape. My plan for bringing about his destruction was slowly coming into place.

So while I continued with my idyllic existence at the expense of Roger Hunt and his company's tax deductions, I plotted his destruction. Shortly after moving into the condo, my desire to prove I was smarter than Roger took second seat to my obsession to destroy him and his evil empire. I analyzed things step by step. I considered the extremes of an outright killing of him by poisoning or some lethal injection. But keeping my two ultimate goals in mind helped me narrow the available options. What were these ultimate goals? The slow obliteration of Roger Hunt was one. And, of course, I wanted a good chunk of his money. I hoped for the quick enrichment of Dakota.

So you see, if I poisoned him I'd not have accomplished either of my goals: he'd be destroyed but it would have been done quickly and I would have gained nothing from his death. My first big break in devising my plan was to realize I did not have to kill him to destroy him but that if I could somehow make his life a living hell then that would be just as good. What for Roger would be a living hell? He had fierce ambition for material wealth and powerful friends. Taking away his wealth and smearing his name would utterly destroy him. Doing it in a manner which would allow me to watch him suffer would be delightful. Now if I could do it while at the same time extorting much of his money from him then I'd have accomplished my goals. But what to do and how to do it?

TUESDAY: LATE AFTERNOON

It's been a while, but I'm trying to stay away from you, Naria. Yesterday, I spent too much of the day writing. I didn't get out at all for a walk or any fresh air. That's not good. So as much as I wanted to go on talking last night before going to bed and first thing this morning, I decided that I had to have a life aside from this. I figure I've got to put around 20 or so hours between sessions.

I'm feeling better talking to you Naria, but I don't want to be too dependent on it. I know that at some point I'll finish my story. If I had a real shrink, I could go to her forever whether I needed the security blanket or not. But here I must end at some point. It's important to drag it out a bit especially since each day seems to make me healthier. Hopefully when I'm finished, I'll feel a lot better. Maybe it'll change my attitude toward that person in the mirror.

Where was I? That's the problem with walking away for a bit. Oh, yes, I remember. I was telling about my plan to get revenge.

The beauty of it was that Roger suspected nothing – nada. I just said men are dopes if you tell them what they want to hear. It's so true. They're incapable of separating the wheat from the chaff when you tell them how great they are. I kept hanging the bait out there for him telling him how I wanted the final coming together to be just so right, something that we'd always remember. When he demurred I was able to turn some of the stuff he told me against him so that it worked in my favor. I reminded him how he had forgotten the names of some of the women

104

who had acceded to his demands at the office. I told him I loved him too much so I wanted to be sure no matter what happened to our relationship down the road he would always remember me.

I knew though that I couldn't delay him forever. It was a delicate balancing game and at this point it was going quite well but I wasn't so dumb as not to realize if he got strung along too much he might feel the wait was not worth the game and I could be out on the street on my butt.

A few days after I convinced Roger we should not be frolicking around in the office, he decided that it would not be necessary for me to come to the main office again. He said that Hunt Enterprises had leased a small office on the boardwalk at the Marina Place. This was about a five to ten minute walk from where I was living. The ostensible purpose of the office was to have a place where people who were going out on the company yacht could gather before the trip to freshen up and leave things they did not want to take with them. My job would be to make sure the guests were comfortable and their needs attended to. It was a little unclear what I would be doing during the time the yacht was out of the office for the winter or away for days at a time. When I asked him about it he said he'd come up with something for me to do.

I told him that I'd like to be able to go to the office on occasion during those times so it'd look like I was still working. He said that would be fine. He agreed that the desk I'd been using would be kept for me. You'll probably think less of me when I tell you, Naria, but when this was arranged I could hardly wait to see Stella's face when she learned Lucy had all these special privileges. It was a sight to behold.

Of course, I knew the real job assignment I was being given. I was to be available at all times to Roger, especially if he had a sudden desire for a midday quickie. Oh, well, I thought, "In for a dime in for a dollar."

All of this was transpiring around the time when I finally gave him a date for the big show. What really got him was the way I set up the time we would do it – full out all the way – you know. I had put him off as I said with the story that I wanted it to happen after Tom had been a distant memory and I was absolutely sure I would be his for ever and, you know, all that stuff men suck up. Sensing his impatience, I arbitrarily picked a day a week or so down the road when I knew he would be in town and told him that would be the night. I made it into a big event. I told him what I would be wearing – where we'd go to eat, what we'd have, how he should dress, how we'd come back early for some candlelight and champagne. I told him of the special lingerie I had for "the special moment" and how I'd ordered new silk sheets just for that night and how those sheets would always be saved for our special nights.

You know how it was. I was slowly stoking up the anticipation of the event which, when it happened, absolutely blew his mind, even though I had great difficulty, my feelings switching back and forth from hilarity to nauseousness. I can never figure out how hookers take on all comers – perhaps desperation and practice makes one inured to it or simply jaded. Even though I prepared myself for it and was a highly willing participant, it still left me feeling upset and creepy-crawly. But Roger was walking on water and in my mind that is what I wanted, so I sucked it up and suffered through.

106

One of the worst things about it was that he wanted to talk about it over and over again. I guess that's one of the good things about being a hooker, when the guy finishes he leaves and she can wash him out of her mind and not have to relive what was distasteful from the moment it began.

Thankfully, the next day he flew away to somewhere and I suffered in silence. If I hadn't had a day or two to recover, I don't know if I could have gone on with it. You remember me saying how I thought crossing the line wasn't a big deal. How having come up to the line so many times I didn't figure it'd make much of difference. I wasn't a virgin or anything like that. It's not that I knew many men. In fact, aside from Tom I didn't know any others but I figured having been with Tom for many years and having gone to the line with Roger many times, the little jump over would be a meaningless happening. Well it wasn't. It was like crossing the Rubicon.

Maybe had I been more promiscuous in my youth it wouldn't have mattered so much, but shit – you know there was so little passion involved from my part – I had to fake everything – I probably acted better then than anyone at anytime on the stage – but doing it without any desire or passion is – well it's difficult to really describe – let's say it leaves a real empty feeling, a deep disgust. Aside from the acting it seemed the play went on for an interminable time. One can escape from reality into fantasy only for so long at any one time. It was utter torment pretending to listen to Elvis's lament about the landlord ringing his front door bell over and over again in order to escape from reality while at the same time wanting to escape from Elvis's endless

moaning but being unable to do so since to leave
Elvis meant returning to the salacious snake
crawling all over me.

Let it be I was so nauseous and upset that
if I hadn't been able to escape for a few days from
the condo I might have flung myself from the
balcony. I couldn't stand being there.
Everything I looked at made me think not so nice
things about myself. So I scampered off to my
secret hideaway, New York City.

I'd been going down there on weekends
after our "out-of-the-big-bed" discussion so I
didn't have to be around when Tom was. I didn't
know where else to go but I had to get away. I
guess having had the wildest and bestest time of
my life drew me back there. But tempering my
enthusiasm was the recollection of the cutting
and ostracization by many I thought were
friends. I guess I returned there only because it
was a place I knew. I didn't expect it would give
me back the old days but I wasn't sure I wanted
them anymore. All I knew, as I said, is that I
wanted to get away from the Boston area. I
sought whatever aid it could give me.

I was not expecting too much having left
it with that sour taste in my mouth. But when I
got there I found some of the good old feelings
coming back to me. The hustle and bustle of the
crowds, the familiar places, a chance to be alone,
among many appealed to me. But now, unlike
before, when I savored the rush of the parties,
the mingling with friends, a lust to be part of the
action, what I started to prize most, was privacy.
I wanted to be alone in the maddening crowd.

I guess before the time of Roger's big
night I'd gone there probably a handful of times
walking the streets, mingling with the crowds,
and to my great surprise spending time in the

public library reading. Me, of all people, reading books at the library, buying some at the bookstores, and spending time in my hotel room engrossed in them. I had become a strange new me.

So by the time I found the need to flee after the night of my coming together with Roger, I had pretty much gotten over my hesitancy to go to there. I found it provided me with the needed get-away place, the place to go where I could try to figure out what I was really doing.

By now, I had no money problems – Roger was very generous to me with what I assumed was his company's money. I was beginning to sock away a fair amount of cash. To get to the City, I'd usually get on the T and ride to South Station and buy a ticket to Penn Station with cash – and stay in a hotel using only cash. I'm not sure why I used only cash – there was nothing sinister in what I was doing – it's just I had this feeling that if I used my credit card, someone other than myself would know what I was doing. I didn't want that. I did not want to share the City with anyone.

Thank God for cell phones. Had they not been invented, what I was doing and how I was doing it would have been impossible to do. After the big night, Roger began to consider me his pin pad which he could stick whenever he felt like it. My job description became such that I was to be available to him whenever at his whim.

We had a little row over this once when he came to the condo and I was not around. I'd actually been at the main office dealing with some problems relating to the yacht. He had to cool his heels for several hours before I got back. He was a man who didn't like to do the waiting. Others waited on him, not the other way around.

When I got back he unloaded on me about not being there when he came in earlier in the day. On and on he berated me in a harsh voice for what seemed like an inordinately long time but I have no idea how long it was. I felt it was so unjust especially since I had been at the office. So I finally said, "You expect me to be here whenever you decide to come?" He said, "Damn right I do – that's part of your job." I said, "You know what that makes me, Roger, a prison inmate. I might as well be locked up in Sing Sing if I can't come and go as I want and have to sit around here waiting for you." He's still boiling mad so he said, "That's right, Dakota, get that in your little head; that's what you're going to do. That's what you're being paid for."

Without another word I walked into the bedroom and went to the closet. I took out a suitcase and threw it on the bed. He followed in after me and after watching me for a couple of seconds he said, "What the hell you doing?" I started to throw some things into the suitcase while saying, "I just got an email from the parole board. I'm being paroled. So I'm on my way to regain my freedom." He realized he wasn't going to get any nookie from me that day and he'd been hanging around all afternoon to get some. This made him calm down a bit. I continued to pack. He said, "Now come on, Dakota. None of that. Be reasonable."

I stopped and looked at him squarely in the eyes and said, "You know Roger. I thought we had something nice going on here. I really loved you and thought you loved me. But today I realized you didn't have any respect for me. When you said you wanted me sitting around here because you somehow had bought me, I could only think of how those beautiful young

110

black women felt when they were held in slavery. That's what they were told by the master – 'stay here, don't move, I own you.' If you don't know it Roger, let me tell you something, slavery in America ended a couple of centuries ago. I'm not your slave. I'm not your whore. I'm sorry to bring you this news but you can't own a slave anymore. But here's the good news, whores still can be purchased. Go to the drug store and pick up a Phoenix. It's free. In the back of the paper they list escort services. Call one of them. Buy yourself a whore or two who'll sit around here waiting for you. But that's not my gig."

He didn't know what to say after that. He stood there and stared. I was really pissed off and steaming inside. I didn't know I had it in me to fire back like that but this was still shortly after I gave him full access to me and I was still tearing myself up about it. I was leaving. Roger could have his condo, his job, and his money. I just wanted to get away from it all. I had no thought beyond the moment. I wanted out of there.

To make a long story short, after many a profuse apology from him I calmed down a bit and I agreed to stay on after we made a deal. No more could he just drop in. He had to call and give me sufficient notice to prepare myself for him. This was decidedly to his unliking but he didn't want to lose me right then and there, so he ate some crow and capitulated to my terms.

I think he gave in because I scared him a bit. As he was backing down, I began to realize that wasn't a good move by me since I did not want him to be wary of me. If I was ever going to bring his world down around him I had to catch him off guard. I wanted him to think I was a dolt and easy pushover. So as he was throwing up

111

the surrender flag, I realized I had to retreat a bit myself.

Look, it's simple. Roger didn't need me. There were a dozen dumb blond broads he could have without blinking an eye. Sure, right now I was the apple of his eye and he didn't want me to walk. He was getting what he wanted when he wanted. It'd take him some time to get that again. But he'd quickly start all over it if he saw he couldn't push me around. I realized that if I were going to win the ultimate battle I had to pull in my horns.

"Roger," I began, "I'm sorry for what I said. I don't know what got into me."

This surprised but pleased him. It gave him back his sense of worth and control.

I went on, "I don't want to change anything that we've had. If you feel like dropping in any time like you've always done, you can do that. It's just that, like seeing you so upset because I was not here when you came makes me think I'm disappointing you. I never wanted to do that. You know I didn't mean any of those things I said about how you treat me like a slave or a whore. I don't know why I ever said those things except because I was so mad at myself for having disappointed you. I don't want to change anything if I'm going to you get you upset. Why don't we leave it that you'll call when you can and you can still drop in whenever you want but if you drop in and haven't called you won't be upset anymore? Is that all right, Roger?"

What a phony I was becoming! Later that night, I kept thinking of the speeches I had made during that day, and I truly was amazed. The first one was from the heart, but I couldn't have spontaneously reproduced it or anything like again in a hundred years; the last one was from a conniving mind as I speedily measured each word to determine how it would best sound to my victim, Roger.

Needless to say, when I surrendered I knew as part of that I would have to let him have access to me. The speech, no matter how well done, only became brilliant when combined with the love making. Looking back, I could see I was no longer the ward dependent on Tom. Having been tossed out into the world, I was beginning to make a pretty good show of it.

It was that confrontation with Roger coupled with the cell phones that set me free. Now I could be sitting on a bench in Central Park eating some mustard herring from Russ & Daughters and answer Roger's call. I'd always get a read on where he was. I could say I was any place I wanted to be in relation to where he was. If he were not in the Boston area, I'd act like I was sitting in the condo in Quincy waiting for him. If worse came to worse and he demanded to see me, I could easily put him off for the few hours it would take to get on a train, bus or plane and get back.

Well, as I said after playing the willing mistress and experiencing Roger, you know, it was a while before I could get over that first night but I eventually did, probably because there were many more to follow which caused my feelings to be jaded and my body hardened to his constant demands. I suppose I'm wrong having just said I could never figure out how hookers could take on all comers — they become like I became. After a while, I felt that whenever I opened the door to let Roger into the condo, I was just like those Amsterdam spiders opening their doors.

You know what I did when I began to feel like that? I went out and purchased a red light bulb. I put it in my bedroom. Whenever Roger was coming over for a little action, and he now called most times before coming over, I would go into the room and turn it on. It reminded me what I was after all. I didn't want to try to fool myself; I wanted to know the next time I saw a woman in a red lighted window that I was truly her sister.

But I'm getting ahead of myself. The morning after my all night defrocking by Roger, I zipped down to New York. There was no way I could have stayed in the temple of my doom and slept in the same bed. Walking out of Penn Station it seemed all the filth washed off me. I walked down to East Houston Street to get some herring at Russ and Daughters. During my F. Scott Fitzgerald days in the City we used to shop there all the time. Just walking into that store made me happy.

I then took the subway up to 68th Street and Lexington and walked over to the park carrying my herring. It was a nice day and I walked for a bit before sitting on a bench and opening the herring container. I usually didn't have them cut it up at the store but not having any utensils that day I had them slice them for me. I was sitting there and the cell rang. It was Roger. He told me he was delayed and would be gone for a few more days.

I immediately thought, "Brilliant!" but replied with a smile on my face but a tear in my voice, "Oh, Roger, dear, you promised me you'd be back by Saturday – how can you do this to me – I was so looking forward to seeing you."

"I know, Dakota, I'm sorry, I am too, but I just can't get away now. I'll make it up to you, honey. I will."

I remember I pictured him sitting in a hotel in the Far East with a few nude Asian beauties traipsing around his room and himself smiling as I was, and pretending he was upset. I knew, and that deeply pleased me, that he could not picture me sitting in Central Park. After telling him how great the night had been and forcing a few more promises out of him as to how he would make it up to me, I hung up, openly gave him the finger, and turned to go back to my herring when I realized what I had just done. I sheepishly looked about me to see if anyone saw me. Thankfully, no one did. Relieved, I enjoyed my herring.

But an idea was percolating in my head. You know it was a strange idea. Yes, Roger did not know where I was but he did intrude on me. I guess it went along with what happened to me a week or so earlier when I was sitting in Central Park and one of the persons I knew in the good days, Miranda Diaz, was walking her dog along and came right up to me and began a conversation. It was nice seeing Miranda and all that but – I don't know how to say it – it was like an intrusion into my life. I wanted to be alone and here she was sitting down and prying into all my business. It was friendly and all that and we caught up by lying to each other, but I was bothered by it. I didn't want her to know anything about me but it is difficult carrying on a conversation trying not to disclose anything about your self. I felt that this may happen again and again; in our New York days we had spread ourselves around so much that we had accumulated a stable of hundreds of people who knew us.

But I didn't think much about it until I

finished speaking with Roger. Maybe because having to lie to him and to Miranda coupled with the immediacy of Roger's big event made me think: "Wouldn't it be nice if I had a place to go where no one knew my name or knew me." From that point on that idea started to obsess me.

I couldn't sit there, thinking of it. I was too excited. I had to walk through the neighborhoods off Central Park on the East side. I knew that I could get lost in Manhattan. What I had to do was to come up with a different identification – become a different person – rent an apartment here – disguise myself for a little extra protection – just a little because even though there were too many people in New York City who may know me the acquaintance was casual – then I would be able to have a place to go where I could be away from everyone and to start a new life and not have to lie anymore. My ongoing involvements made me feel dirty and intruded upon my peacefulness.

I want to be clean and new and not have to lie to anyone again but to begin anew. Can you blame me for wanting this? I knew it would be one big lie but I felt I could buy into that better than the constant lying. Wasn't it Hitler or Goebbels or some other Nazi who said "If you're going to tell a lie, tell a big one." It worked for them; for a short while, anyway. It's the little lies that trap people.

I found for the next two days all I did was think of this – the sole idea was not only to get away and not be bothered as I had been doing but to get away and live the life of another person – a new me. I was strangely intrigued by this. I suppose it all went along with becoming extremely dissatisfied with what I had become. I looked back at my life. What was I that was so

116

important to me that becoming someone new wouldn't be better?

I thought of school how each year was a new beginning. You'd finished the prior year and the results were recorded in the book of time as well as the school ledgers. Then a new year started and what had been recorded in the past really had no effect on what was going to be recorded this time. It was what you did lately that counted. You know, if you were an 'A' student, you could easily become a 'D' student and vice-versa. One always had a chance to let the past bury the past.

It also made me think of my Catholic friends in high school and college, the ones that went to church. They had their relationship with God who had certain rules they had to obey. If they didn't follow the rules, then they committed sins. If they sinned they had this burden to carry because they displeased their God. But they also had this thing some called confession and others reconciliation but I think it was all the same. Anyway, they could go see a priest, tell him about their sins, and the sins would be washed away. They could start anew again. Some used to go every week. That was cool. I thought it a swell idea since I guess I was stuck with my sins although I was lucky in a sense because I didn't seem to have nearly as many sins as those Catholic had even though we did the same things.

I yearned for a new start. I wanted to get away from everything after I got my revenge on Roger. I knew I had a chance to do this and each time I was in the City I thought about it. My folks had passed on, I had no siblings, and my cousins and I weren't close so I had no relations I needed to stay in contact it. As I said I had already alienated my friends from high school and college. So from a people to people point of view, once I lost all that really mattered to me in the world, Tom, I was flat out barren of friends. I was at ground zero so why not start all over with a new life taking off my backpack full of lessons and regrets to see what I could accomplish.

To start over, I had to become someone new. I had no idea how I would go about doing it. To get a place in New York City I would have to be someone other than who I am. To be free in New York City I would have to make sure that I encountered no one there who looking at me would know me from previous days.

One part I thought was easy would be to disguise myself, a wig, even a changed hair style, glasses, colored contact lenses, and other stuff. We women can easily conceal our outward looks with a little imagination, of which I had plenty. If I wanted, I could have a little plastic surgery, but initially, that would not be necessary. I'd change my outward appearance like I said with what was available.

I figured I would do it in stages. This was going to be fun. I had people around who knew me. I could test out and perfect my disguises on them. I planned to encounter one or another in my disguise. I knew I would be able to tell the effectiveness of it by his or her response – you know if I asked for directions and they looked at me and without a second thought gave them to me, I knew I had done a good job. But if they did a double take, or hesitated, or looked inquiringly at me as if trying to figure out if they knew me, I knew I needed more work on what I'd done.

Men are easy. They're too involved in themselves or too interested in looking at my boobs to pay much attention to my face, especially if I approached them as a stranger. I remember thinking that woman would have much better communications with men if they talked through their boobs. But talking boobs aside, it was easy to fool men because their attention was always distracted by one bodily trait of mine or another.

But women were another thing. Maybe by nature they are more suspicious or alert to dangers, I don't know. I found them the hardest to deceive. After a while I concentrated in perfecting my disguises and only used women as judges. I became good at it. Oh, the most effective disguise was altering my teeth a bit with the help of a dentist friend who gave me a set of teeth that fit nicely over my present teeth – I told him I needed it for a disguise at a costume party and he willingly obliged, as long as I paid his extortionate fee. Change your teeth and you radically change your appearance. I never knew how much until I did it.

One final great change I made was in my voice. I altered the pitch, and changed the pace. I went to a voice teacher for this. He was very receptive when I explained that as an actress, I'd been unsatisfied with the quality of my voice. I wanted to have a command of differing ways of using it. It was amazing what he taught me and the exercises he provided that helped me gain greater control over the way I talked. He was expensive but a real expert teacher and every dollar was worth it.

So I perfected my outer disguise. With that change, and with the additional confidence that that everyone I once knew in New York believed I had left the City for good, I knew I could walk the streets of New York without being recognized. You'll never understand what a feeling of peace that gave me. It was as if I had been in a jail with four bars on the window and I had successfully hack-sawed through one of the bars and slithered out. Even if someone with extraordinary abilities to remember people met me, I could easily convince the person altering my voice that he or she was making a mistake. How unusual would it be in the City of eight and a half million people plus tourists for two people not to have some similarities? I'm sure I'd have no problem doing this especially since I could turn on a British accent or Irish brogue or Eastern European accent at will.

Doing all this while at the same time studying it on the net and in books, I realized I had one great advantage. No one had my finger prints. Therefore there was no way to trace who I was through that medium.

I recognized that the easy part was changing my physical aspects. What I next had to figure out was how to get a new identity. How do I get different identification papers?

This made me look at myself to figure out what I would do now if I lost all my papers and had to prove I am who I am. I said, "All right Dakota, assuming you don't have anything to identify yourself, how do you prove you are you." Immediately I thought well I'll have people who know me identify me as being me. But I couldn't do that if I changed my ID. I'd have no one who could vouch for me.

"All right, then I'll have to go get a birth certificate, a social security, bank accounts, letters that came to me through the mail, and a driver's license." After thinking that, I wondered if that would be enough. I then thought that it would be but that a credit card and an employment history would be nice additions. I had to figure out how to get these things and not leave a trail back to me.

I figured some would think that's a lot of work to go through to just have a day or two in New York City without fear of recognition. I guess they'd be right about that – now that I think of it. But when I write, this I'm probably condensing into a small period the things I thought about over an extended period of time. There's no question I could go to the City and hide out for a few days with a disguise and cash and not get caught. But deep inside, I wanted more than that.

As time went on I began to develop bigger plans. As these bigger plans grew, so did my need for the additional security of being another person. I'll explain as I go along how all this happened and why it became beneficial to me. I had not thought of that great benefit at the time because when I first started to get fake papers I was more interested in doing it just for the sake of doing it. Plus, the disguise and getting the new identification were a game to me. I had plenty of time on my hands. You know the old adage: "the devil makes work for idle hands." It was later that all I was doing for fun became a necessity.

WEDNESDAY: THREE-THIRTY IN THE AFTERNOON

    I should have mentioned this earlier. Sitting down so long after the fact and trying to recreate what happened in the past causes lapses in memory as to what happened when – not so much what actually happened but you know the chronological part. I'm doing my best to set out the things as they happened in the order in which they occurred and also trying not to repeat myself, which some people say I have a tendency to do. I thought that was something older people did, you know like those people in their fifties so whenever someone says "Yeah, yeah, we've heard that," I feel like I'm really getting old and losing it.

    To digress a little, I said I'd tell you why I choose to call you Naria. I once had a friend, Naria who seemed to live her life vicariously through me, and probably some others. She was a real nice kid and like a real good listener. We'd sit around a lot during and after school. I'd tell her what I'd be doing and thinking and stuff like that, and as with anyone, sometimes something nutty or outrageous would happen to me and I'd tell her about it. But what was nice was Naria was always a patient listener, an ear into which I could pour my tales.

    Although I must admit that Naria had a strange habit. About a month or so after I'd tell her one of these tales I'd hear her telling it back to me and others. It was the same tale I had told her only she had put herself into my place. What I told her I had done she told others she had done it. I had been displaced by her in the telling. What reminded me to tell you why I choose to

122

call you Naria, was that when I wrote about repeating oneself a thought came to me that it's bad enough repeating yourself but even worse when someone else repeats back to you what you told them as if you had nothing to do with it. But aside from this strangeness, Naria was real nice. As for you, my new Naria, I'm confident you won't repeat my stories and change roles with me.

But back to me and the topic at hand. I decided rather than going back and trying to insert everything in its proper place, not that I could, I figured I'd just to keep writing on for the sake of its therapeutic effect. I don't expect anyone to be reading this since I am only talking to you, Naria, and so far, like my friend Naria, you have proved a good and willing listener.

Oh, another thing, at one point I thought it might be a good idea to tear up each page as I wrote it since I was getting my story out of me. But I couldn't do it. Mostly because Naria feels like a person to me so I'd be hurting her but also because I realized it's best to keep what I've written so I can check back to make sure I progress forward and don't go back and repeat myself too much. I have to admit I sometimes feel like I'm a little girl again sitting at my little desk and beginning on a fresh page in my little book with the words: "Dear Diary."

I told you how I was trying to perfect different disguises I had invented. I felt — and by the way, as I said, this was a lot of fun for me doing this, and compensated for the nights of horror with Roger by getting my mind off it and into something else — I had made three excellent disguises. I had tried them out on people I knew at work, others doing my groceries, and some who lived around the condo area. They passed with flying colors, each one. I decided to push the envelope. I initially planned to try it out on Roger. I was thinking maybe I'd put on the disguise and be sitting in the condo when he came over to be satisfied and see his reaction or go to the office and ask for an appointment to see him. I realized this would be too dangerous. If he ever discovered that I was doing this, his suspicions may be aroused. Right now he had no reason to mistrust me. But if I gave him cause for concern he'd have people tracking me all hours of the day and night. It was too much of a chance to take.

I had to find someone else to try the disguise out on, to give what I thought was the ultimate test. Thinking of this I could think of only two people who knew me inside out. Those were Jenny and Tom. I didn't know if I could pull it off on Tom.

Yes, I should mention dear Tom. We stayed in touch almost every day as I hoped we would. There was still a little emotion on my part when we spoke; he seemed to have gone on easily with his life *sans moi* which was good but to be truthful it hurt a little to see how easily he discarded me almost as if I were a one-night stand. I suppose it must be sheer hell if you lose your feelings for some guy but he still has intense feelings for you and you have to be in contact with him and listen over and over again to his whining.

That was one thing that was good about Tom, I guess, he took the break up good and had gone on. As I just said, on one hand that's good I didn't have to listen to any crying after me, on another not so for my ego. Yeah, I think that hurt a little as I look back but I'm not sure I picked up on it at the time.

I mentioned I had a little emotional reaction talking to him. What was the little emotion I had? It wasn't one of love or regret. It wasn't the ego thing I just mentioned but that may have played into it. It was more one of anger that he had lived off me ever since we came back to Massachusetts, that he was such a loser he couldn't seem to get a job, that he set me up in our attempt to extort Roger suggesting I have a sexual liaison with him, and that he turned it all around on me and called me a whore which threw me into a rage and destroyed what I believed was a wonderful marriage. It wasn't that I regretted it happened, as I said, it was this feeling that I was used by him. He caused me to break up the marriage. He wanted me to believe it was my fault.

I eased my anger by thinking that Tom was probably worn out from the continual rejections he got from employers. I probably never should have read that book "Studs Lonigan" in college. It was one of the few books that I did. Reading about the tough time that Studs went through looking for work made me feel real bad for him. When Tom would go out looking, I'd remember how difficult it was for Studs and I pictured Tom suffering as Studs did. So I began to think his suggestion I become a whore and then throwing it in my face was understandable given the pressures he was under. I often thought I should have known that the endless job search was tearing him down and taken that into account before I blew my stack. So I guess when I talked with him along with the anger there was a good deal of guilt. I must have felt that I was too hasty in defending myself from his accusations and did not put myself in his shoes to understand the stress he had undergone.

As I tell you this, Naria, I'm figuring things out, things that were there but until now I've never thought of them. Talking to you has brought them out of my subconscious so that I could examine them. Of course that was it, the more I thought of poor Tom's ordeal and how I didn't give him the help a wife should, the more I turned against myself for my lack of empathy toward him. That was probably what was happening to me without me knowing it; I had taken all the guilt of the breakup onto my shoulders and I was despising my self for my insensitivity and for my rash response which caused our marriage to dissolve.

Discussing it like this, I find I can understand better why I acted like I did. My extreme reaction and the compelling need that drove me to get revenge against Tom I've never understood until now. It seemed at the time when it happened that without reason I flew into a rage and the more I learned about it the higher the bonfire within me flamed igniting throughout my body an uncanny irresistible urge to destroy Tom. That bastard, making me think it was my fault our marriage broke up! I did control my high ire and bided my time only because Roger was my immediate target but I didn't quench the intensity of determination. I could do this because I'd become a big girl through all that. I'd learned that to do it right it had to be well planned. But again I've digressed and jumped ahead of myself.

I was talking about giving my disguise the acid test. I decided the only one I could safely try it out on was Jenny. Jenny was probably the only person alive who knew me from early in grade school and was friends with me all the way

126

through college. Another reason Jenny was the perfect one to go up again was that she was as shrewd as they come. She was always thinking ahead and planning things out but nothing got passed her without her knowing what was going on. If I deceived her, I'd know I had perfected my technique of disguise and I could get by anyone.

I mentioned earlier that I had called Jenny when I felt alone in the world and wanted to find some type of anchor and how I had a nice discussion with her. When I was thinking of using the disguise on her I was also thinking I'd try to renew our friendship. She suggested this when I talked to her on the phone. What a call that was! She told me how she was so glad I called. She said she felt real bad we'd let so many years passed without being in contact and that she'd thought many times that she wished she knew how to reach us. She'd heard we were in New York and were doing real well and she was glad about that. She supposed if she really wanted she could have found us. She asked how I located her and continued to talk like for all she knew Tom and I were still living in New Your City. I didn't indicate otherwise at the time. She asked how Tom was doing. Of course I put on a good front and told her great. She said to give him her best. She said lots of stuff like that and we agreed we'd get together again the next time I was in the Boston area or she was in New York City. I'm sure she and Tom had a big laugh discussing the conversation later. No wonder I was so irate.

My major problem in using Jenny as my test tube was to figure out how to do this, you know, to approach her so she didn't know I was coming. She lived in one of those condo buildings where you had to be cleared by an owner   in order to get into the building, so I could not show up and knock on her door. She told me when we talked that she was a vice president or something big like that for an investment company in one of those buildings downtown where it seems harder to get through security than at the White House. I had no knowledge of her daily activities. I had to puzzle out how I could arrange to run into her and have a conversation. It had to be more than stopping her on the street and asking for directions. I thought if I did that I would not have proven much because I wouldn't really know how much attention she'd be giving me. You know how it is when you're telling someone how to get somewhere. You're spending most of the time figuring out yourself the best way to give the directions and then you look off in the direction where you want the person to go and often indicate while doing that and hardly pay attention to the person because that's not your concern. I decided it had to be something other than that.

It had to be something more intimate but then not too intimate. I had to keep in mind the purpose of my disguise. It was not to make me into someone else. It was so that someone who knew me who saw me would not think I was me and pass on. It was merely to keep people away from me who knew me. But also, in the event someone noticed something about me that reminded them of me, then it was to dissuade them from that belief if they approached and engaged me in conversation. My difficulty was coming up with the scenario in which this would play out with Jenny.

I wasn't just busy on this disguise business during that time. I told you that I wanted to get a place in New York where I could have my hideaway. I wanted to rent a small apartment somewhere in the seventies on the Upper East Side. But to do that, I knew I had to have satisfactory identification and background information to give to the landlord or his agent so my background could be checked. This meant developing a new name and background for myself to insure my privacy. Also while doing these things, I'm engaged in trying to figure out the best way to destroy Roger.

Looking back to that day when I had that all day conversation with Tom that went from eagerly wanting him to hoping anxiously to get away from him, what I call my personal 9/11, or "out-of-the-big-bed" day, I knew nothing of life, especially its harder parts. I've often wondered, had Tom's investment decisions been wiser and the times and the market better, and if Tom didn't fudge the figures like he did and had not been fired and prosecuted and we'd continued our easy ways, whether I could have lived my life out without knowing anything about life. Probably, there are many women who are fortunate enough to find a helpmeet who will keep them in their little safe world, away from the pushings and shovings of hoi polloi. I suppose it's not only women but a lot of guys who also go through life thinking it's all a bed of roses. I don't know if they are not the better for it. There is something to be said for a life of ease. When you go beyond the end you don't get any more credit if you've struggled to get there than if you've glided though.

When I jumped over into life beyond Tom by deciding to venture into the life of a whore planning to get into the blackmail business, it became necessary for me to quickly pick up on

129

what it would take to live like the unwashed masses. To that point, I'd been a Margery Meanwell. I'd never crossed a street unless the pedestrian light said it was OK or done anything that even my Catholic girl friends would consider a big sin and they were constantly finding them everywhere.

My learning to be evil had to come in kindergarten at the school of hard knocks – cushioned by my sugar daddy – with myself as my teacher. I was to find out that having been put out on my own, there was a lot in me that I never knew was there. I think that might be true for most people. Unfortunately most when tossed out of their nest never dig deep within themselves but quickly look for another nest in which to crawl so they can continue their dismal lives going through the same-old, same-old and merely go on slipping and sliding through the remaining days of their life. I had this sense that if I failed in my new life I wanted to fail greatly.

Maybe why I did things the way I did was this thing I have in me. When I see what I perceived to be a great injustice it bothers me to the core. That's why I really never liked movies; I got too drawn in by them and by the end often was an emotional wreck. Something deep down inside me stirs me to right the wrong. But for me, it was more than just making it right again for the victim. I never wanted to just correct the injury; I wanted to destroy the one causing it or if I couldn't do that to teach that person such a lesson he'd never, ever, even think of doing it again.

You know what I mean, Naria? I couldn't just walk away from Roger after hearing how he used his wealth and position to abuse so many unwilling and unwitting women doing nothing more than working in his horrible enterprise struggling to survive. When he told me he couldn't even remember the names of some of his pin cushions that threw me over the edge. How could I just have my day with him, get some money from him and just walk away? I couldn't do it. I had to do what I could on behalf of these women he exploited and savaged to make him pay for it.

Maybe when I condemn others for letting life pass by passively I'm being unfair. They just might not have had the fire in the belly that I had; or, may not perceive the things that people like Roger do as being a great injustice. There's so many people who want to blame the victim, you know the attitude, each woman Roger abused had a choice whether to get involved with him or not so don't cry over her misfortune. It's that attitude that's always sets the masses against the masses and insulates the exploiters from blame or accountability. You know it seems to me the rich can always count on the poor to keep the other poor down.

Before I got involved with Roger, I heard some of the gals in the office talking about another woman who had been fired just before I was hired. Thinking back, I was her replacement. I now don't remember who said it, probably Stella, but it was something along the line she deserved to lose her job because she thought she could rise up by lying down. At the time, I had no idea then what she meant.

When I was thrown out into the cold as suddenly as I had been by my spouse without really any warning, although the signs were certainly flashing all about me, it seemed I had a choice of freezing to death or doing something

131

about it. I don't know if I even considered it, but I could have found a small apartment somewhere, continued at work, backed down from my adventures with Roger, bought a big, flat-screen, Chinese-made HD television set and did some TiVo-like set up so I'd have the day time soap operas for viewing after work to keep me company as I passed into the dreary night, and for weekends climbed onto one of those on-line dating services, looking for some male companionship. I suppose that would fit my definition of freezing to death.

But the sudden shock of the breakup out of the blue — speaking of out of the blue, remember that Tuesday — the terrifying and horrid photographs of the Twin Towers sinking down and disappearing into the enormous clouds of billowing dust and thinking of the many beautiful, mostly young, people who had joyously left for work that bright fall morning whose lives were unfairly obliterated before their coffee breaks and how from that carnage sprang many women who had lost their loved ones who resolved never to forget and who continued with their lives by insisting the truth about the disaster be told and by setting out to help other unfortunate people throughout the world.

Like them when my marriage came tumbling down though not nearly as great a loss as they suffered, it affected me like it affected them. It propelled me forward. Just like the 9/11 widows, I wasn't going to let the bastards win. My life meant something.

It seems to me you either let life run you or you run life. There is in the American woman, at least some of us, a courage that has been passed down through the generations. Almost all of us are the progeny of another intrepid woman who fled penury or persecution and daringly crossed a treacherous ocean, either by herself or with her husband, in most cases penniless and in many ignorant of the language of the new land, who hoped by throwing herself into this great unknown land, knowing full well for her there would be extreme suffering and dire privation, in effect surrendering forever any comfort in her life to give her children a chance of a better future than she would ever know fully aware she was sacrificing her life for her kids. Do any American women today recognize the ultimate sacrifice involved or the courage that it took? Do any think that they have it them to do what that female ancestor did? Aren't those poor women who struggle to come here today possessed of the same spirit that our mothers who came before us had and if we accepted them rather than tormenting them wouldn't we be infusing in America a spirit that is vanishing?

For me, not to take vengeance on the wrongs I had witnessed and experienced would be a betrayal of each of those intrepid women ancestors who gave all for me. I would be denying their spirit. I would be accepting a feckless life. I'd be telling each of those brave souls who undertook all those hardships that it was in vain. She'd have been better off to have stayed in the old world for although she had the courage to cross the ocean and risk starving and drowning, one of her female descendents was afraid to stop a great injustice where the risks were nothing compared to what she had faced.

I was fortunate. I knew I had that woman's blood coursing through my arteries because of my reaction when I perceived an injustice. I had no idea which one of my great grand mothers or grand mothers had it or how many had it. All I knew was at least one had it and it had been passed on to me because of the steely resolve it gave me to act to right wrongs after I finally opened my eyes to them.

There was also another side of this. I just spoke of how I wanted to avenge the injuries given by Roger. It was not that alone that inspired me to go forward. Not that that wasn't enough but sometimes if you have a little extra it sees you on through to the end when things seem the bleakest.

It seems to me I was made of sterner stuff. I have to accept that there was that David-Goliath aspect which held an enormous attraction for me. Examining my position, as I did when I resolved to go forward, I was intrigued by the position I was in. I was not going to be like Jeanne d'Arc that young woman from the village of Domremy, France who went forth at the head of a large army although I may well have end up like her; I was going to be like David taking on this behemoth one-on-one, with no allies or assistants I could call upon to render assistance. I only had myself. It was to me against a vast international conglomerate, Hunt Enterprises.

What do you think of that, Naria? Pretty gutsy for a girl don't you think, especially for one slandered with the name whore? One who never had fought for anything hard in her life?

And here's where what I mentioned earlier comes into play. While I'm doing the disguise thing I'm also working on the coming up with a new identity and planning to get Roger, so when I was doing some things contemporaneously, they're set out here as though they happened at different times but I think you'll understand this was all part of an ongoing adventure.

I'm going to call it quits now. I've got a dinner engagement and have to get ready.

THURSDAY MORNING: WITH COFFEE AFTER BREAKFAST

Good morning, Naria. I got to bed early last night. I had a very peaceful night's sleep which I haven't had in a long time. Talking to you is helping me. I know I'm back sooner than I should be. You know with my good sleep and feeling so restful I hope I can make an exception to my rule of having almost a full day between talking with you, if you don't mind. Speak up if you do! Not hearing you say you mind, then I'll continue talking to you.

I loved my idea of being able to get away to New York. It was a bastion of safety and sanity for me. The more I realized how important it was for me, the more I feared I would lose it. Thinking this through I believed that if anyone knew I was there, anyone at all, it would get back to Roger. He and his willing henchmen would find a way to take it away from me. That made me realize again I could never live in New York City under my name. It became imperative for me to establish a new identity.

On the train ride back and forth, I had the time to think about how I would accomplish this. More and more I convinced myself that without a new identity I'd never be free. As part of this, in the plan I was developing to destroy Roger it became crystal clear to me that during that process I would want a place where I could go and get away from all the turmoil I'd be causing. I never had the sense that if I didn't have New York City I couldn't have carried out my plan. However as I realistically examined my plan and how it would play out, it almost seemed to me that fortuitously my wish for a New York

136

sanctuary which I was determined to fulfill was coincidentally going to make my life a lot easier as I exacted my revenge. Especially at that time since I had become used to going there to cheer myself up.

Being Roger's whore, I was able to learn much about him. I recognized how a powerful rich man acts just by listening to him talk on his cell with others. What Roger wanted he got. He could pick up the phone and call any politician in DC or in the state or any person in law enforcement from the attorney general to the district attorney to the police chief or any of several FBI agents. He did this on occasion, just to say hello. He never had to ask any of them for anything but always offered things for them, especially money for the campaign chests of those who were in politics, or free box seats to law enforcement officials at the Red Sox or Patriots games, or whatever type game or entertainment they were interested in attending. He was always having fine cases of wine delivered to their houses, anonymously, of course. A week or so later he'd mention in an off-hand manner having had a bottle of that wine and how good it was, so the recipient clearly would know who sent it, if he didn't know already.

Roger never asked for anything as I mentioned, but his lawyers did on his behalf. I was always amazed how willing his lawyers were to do the tricks Roger wanted done. Roger always dealt through his lawyers who jumped to his every whim. I remember him talking to one, I'll call him Bob, who was telling him about a court case that had Roger all excited. Bob was saying that the case said now corporations like Roger's Hunt Enterprises could spend as much money as they wanted to support or crush politicians. I guess they couldn't do it before. Roger says, "Bob that's unbelievable. You know what that means! We're going to start deciding who sits in Washington and what's done there." Bob agreed with him and started making some suggestions. Roger said, "Draw up a list. I want to talk to each one. We'll decide then."

Roger went on to say that the politicians will really be crawling all over themselves to please him. He and Bob talked about a couple of Congressmen who loved to travel the world first class and stay in the finest hotels and eat in the finest five star restaurants and not spend a penny of their own. They always took it out of their campaign funds so if Roger kept replenishing them they'd be eternally grateful to him. It was an eye opener to me to see how things really worked from the inside.

I don't want to single Bob out. He wasn't different from any of the other lawyers who talked to Roger when I was there. They all talked about doing things that would make a criminal gangster blush but apparently it was all legal since they had licenses which protected them. One time I remember Roger's company had taken over a large amusement park that had three large roller coasters. The people who constructed them took mortgages back on them. This lawyer, Judy, suggested Roger's company stop paying them. Roger said if they did they'd come and take the roller coasters back. She said, "I figured it would cost them more to take them out than you owe so they'd never do it." Roger said, "Great idea. Screw them." He told her to go through every other item in the park and figure out which other things were too expensive to take back and to have his people stop paying on them. There was nothing but sleaze in the place.

I overheard all this because whenever the lawyers or other business people came to my condo to discuss things with Roger, I'd sit on the couch reading the Soap Opera Digest or studying my hair for split ends. I always wanted to appear like the prototypical dumb broad in front of Roger and the people he had around. It worked well because they never thought anything more of me than a side table and talked openly.

I tell you all this, Naria, so you'll see why I knew how hard it was going to be for me to have a private place in New York so Roger would not find me. I knew how powerful he was and how he and his lawyers ran people. If I left any type trail, they would be onto me. I guess knowing this made it easier when I got my revenge, especially against Tom, but I'll tell you about that later.

When I started, all I wanted to do was to protect myself from Roger's snooping eyes. It became a habit with me that after every time I let him use me as a play thing and he went out of town I escaped to the cleansing streets of New York City. I think every whore needs an escape some how to reclaim herself. Maybe I'm wrong. All I know is that I did.

When I started to decide how I was going to change my identity, I first thought I had to figure out what new name I was going to give myself. I played around with hundreds of different names until I caught myself. You see at this time I still wasn't that disciplined and when I could get off in fantasies like day dreaming of things I'd do it. I'd soon learn that to survive I had to live a highly disciplined life with no time

139

off from the strictures of following a predetermined routine. Discipline, which had been alien to me up to that time, now became my byword.

Right off the bat, I resolved that I'd ensure that every step I took there were to be no leads back to me. I wanted a new name with new identification to support the name. That was my goal. I knew that would take a while. I had time. I needed time. I needed it to squeeze as much money out of him as I could before I took him down.

You know, I got to tell you this. It's one of the things that kept me going. I used to tell Roger when I embraced him: "Honey, you don't know how good it feels when I squeeze you." The dope would smile his idiotic grin at me. I'd smile back, thinking he wouldn't be smiling if he knew what I meant.

I decided to proceed systematically, step by step, inch by inch. To start I felt I had to split myself into two. One part, the whore, Dakota; the other the New York recluse I called Jilienette.

Dakota was the happy whore living in the harem of a rich man, servicing his every need and being his companion about town when he wanted to show off his taste in women. Ha, I remember how much money I got off him for clothes and jewelry. I suggested to him that a man of his stature wouldn't want to be seen with a woman who was not dressed to the nines. I said all the other women who saw me so well clad and bedecked with jewels would covet him and envy us. I'd show him the costs of some of the clothing that was in the high scale fashion magazines and tell him I had to have oodles of money to buy them. When I'd buy a dress I'd tell him I needed special jewelry to go with it or it would look shabby. He didn't care how much I spent — you got to understand Roger had so much money that no matter how much of it was spent in any one day it would never be half as much as came in to him that day. Roger was filthy rich — and the rich are truly different — they have no limit on the amount of money that they will spend on themselves or for their personal pleasure — that's why some can spend hundreds of millions running for a public office — but if it isn't spent on themselves, they are cheap bastards. I was one of Roger's pleasures. I guess our deal was he keeps me happy and I keep him happy. Isn't that so American?

But outside of spending on himself and pleasure, the joy Roger got out of all his money was screwing other people. It was a special pleasure. He loved nickel-and-diming his lawyers over their bills and when they backed down significantly Roger would talk about it on and on, almost as much as his love-making. His attitude toward lawyers was they were a dime a dozen and that there was a long line of them he could use to do his bidding. He loved to cheat the working people, the ones who sweated away doing hard work with their hands. He'd agree on an amount to pay them for their work and then make them settle for much less than they agreed. He would always laugh after leaving an expensive restaurant when he left a waiter a tip of about 2%.

But with me, as long as he thought I was spending it on the right stuff, you know stuff that made me look good so he could look good; there was no limit to what I could do. Roger traipsed around town with me on his arm thinking he was enhancing his status by showing off his magnificent generosity to this woman who was setting the fashion trend with clothing that cost in the tens of thousands of dollars and jewelry costing even more. I'd buy these expensive things, show Roger the receipts, he'd reimburse me, and I'd return the items. I banked all that money for my future. I wore clothes from the markdown section of TJ Maxx and costume jewelry. I'm sure most other women knew where the clothing I was wearing originated and that my jewels were fake. I'm sure they figured Roger was too cheap to dress his woman in some decent clothing. I loved doing this because it was a little sample of the revenge I was saving for Roger down the line. In truth, Roger was a dick head when it came to style and fashion, as are most men, especially straights.

Jilienette was a serene New Yorker who lived an intellectually comfortable life surrounded by quietude, ethnic foods, traditional 19th Century-type entertainment, and far from the man-world of sports and violence and American commercialism. Her new friendships were to be found in her books and with people who loved books.

The division made it easier to get into the proper mode of doing things. Dakota was not required to think and was suppose to act like a complete knucklehead; Jilienette had to be continually wary and aware of the consequences of each step that she made. Dakota could be the Boston floozy; Jilienette the New York sophisticate.

Obviously, much of what I did I could not have done without Roger's money to work with. Maybe I could have carried it off without it, but it certainly made things a little easier especially since I was hoping that Jilienette would not have to work too hard once she ensconced herself in the City.

Let me say something about Jilienette. I picked that name because I wanted a woman's name that no one else ever had as far as I could tell. My big decision in picking that name was trying to decide if it should have one or two n's. I settled on one. I knew, or assumed, my new name in New York would not be Jilienette because the name I would have there would be that of a person who lived at some time or other. I knew I would have to have a real person's identification to come up with a social security number. I had no way of knowing what that new name would be so I had to come up with some name during the metamorphosis to help me think like two persons. Jilienette would always exist only during the transition period. It was her responsibility to take the steps to secure my new identification which I needed to get a place in New York. Once I had that, I would kill her off.

I assumed I would have to give her a last name for certain things. Jilienette became Jilienette Nevada.

I started off by wondering what Jilienette would need to establish a new identity. It immediately occurred to me that she would need some type of cell phone where people could reach her. I was stymied. I knew to get a phone one needs some identification. All I had was Dakota's IDs. I couldn't use those because they would provide a lead. I had to cross out the idea of getting a cell phone for the present.

I don't know if you remember the story of the Craigslist killer. It was a tragic story that happened in Boston. I followed it in the newspapers. A young woman from New York

143

offering services was killed in a Boston hotel room. Her killer fled after shooting her. The only clue at the time was a couple of photographs taken by a hotel security camera of a light-haired young man in his twenties leaving the hotel around the time of the shooting.

The Boston police through checking the woman's background learned that she was involved in that ancient profession that enabled women to come up with some extra money. She had advertised her services on Craigslist. The cops reasoned that if she did that, then the person she had the appointment with for that evening set up the deal over the internet using a computer. This is the normal manner in which those transactions are carried out. A lot of women used Craigslist to sell their wares since they could go into business on their own and did not need to share their earnings with anyone else, such as a pimp.

The Boston police were able to track back and identity the computer that was used to make the date with her. Learning this, somehow they tracked it back to an apartment in Quincy. I have no idea how it's done, but they did it. There they discovered a man that looked like the man who was seen leaving the hotel and when they executed a search warrant came up with other evidence tying him to the crime.

He turned out to be a very unconventional suspect; a medical student. The whole case was a tragedy for all involved. The man ended up taking his own life. Two lives were lost over an ephemeral sexual encounter, although some said the man did not want sex, but just wanted to rob defenseless women. Whatever the reason, I've never understood how two young people died over a solicitation for sex.

What happened months after this was a concerted attack was launched against Craigslist by the attorney generals from several states seeking to shut down the section where women advertised services. Craigslist succumbed to the pressure and closed that section. This was another tragedy. The women were no longer able to operate on their own, but were thrust back into other groups and pimps who acquisitioned much of their money. The attorney generals felt good in the same way the prohibitionists felt good when they outlawed alcohol. Closing down Craigslist is not going to stop prostitution anymore than barring the sale of alcohol stopped drinking.

I'm sorry; I went off on a tangent. The reason I talked about Craigslist in the first place was because this made me aware how easily it is to trace anything done over a computer. This was not the only case. We've all I'd heard of cases where clever, highly-skilled hackers invade other computers and even though they set up intricate defense systems to hide their intrusion and identification, the FBI or some other agency could always find them. I figured if the FBI could track back to a computer certainly Hunt Enterprises had a similar ability, if it didn't, one of Roger's lawyers would get the FBI to do it for them.

As Jilienette, I decided that if I were going to use a computer, it had to be done in such a manner that it could not be traced. This was my first challenge. How to make sure that under no circumstance could the computer Jilienette used be traced back to me. That meant that any computer which I would use to set up my future identity had to be a virgin computer, one that had never been used by anyone before.

145

I should mention that one of my disguises was specifically for Jilienette. This helped me keep in the proper frame of mind. I kept in mind that at some time the computer and Jilienette's disguise would also have to go out of existence. I planned to buy a new computer with wireless capacity so I could use it at different hot spots that were available for the public such as libraries or the public areas in many of the coffee shops and restaurants. If Jilienette only communicated over those type lines on a computer that was eventually going to be demolished along with her they'd never be any connection back to me. Buying the lap top computer was easy because they are ubiquitous. All I needed was one with Wi-Fi capacity which most of them seemed to have. I decided that the best way to do this was to do it out of state to Nashua, New Hampshire. It's only about thirty-five to forty miles from Boston and I could go there against the traffic. So I got into my Jilienette mode and drove off too Nashua to buy two Dell laptops. I planned to go to different vendors using a different disguise at each mall being aware these companies have security cameras that were recording my every move. I never had much of a connection with that state other than going up there to ski on occasion in high school so if the investigation started in that area I felt confident it'd never focus back on me. I planned to only use one of the computers but in case it crashed I wanted a back up machine. If I didn't use the spare during the Jilienette phase, I could do so when I got my New York identification.

I planned to do most internet work in New Hampshire. In case of real need, on weekends I'd use Boston area hotspots figuring any investigator, in the oft chance that Jilienette became investigated, would think she lived and worked in New Hampshire and on occasion went to Boston for weekend shopping.

Driving up there to buy the lap-top computers, I realized I had a problem. My car with MA plates was traceable back to me. Security cameras in the parking lots would pick up my plates. That set me back a bit. I thought it best not to park in any of those lots. I ended up parking down town in a large condo complex and taking a cab to the shopping malls. Driving back to Boston I felt good that I had accomplished what I set out to do having used the disguise to secure the computers and purchasing them by paying cash. There was no tracing me to the computers unless I made a mistake in the future.

I had to keep in mind the main reason I was doing this was to set up my place in New York so no one would bother me. I expected I could still go on with my life in Boston in the usual manner. A few days later I went back to Nashua and sat at a Panera Bread with my new computer and went on line. I read what documents I would need to rent and apartment in New York City and to get a driver's license in New Hampshire. I also tried to find out what I could about social security numbers. I realized one could not just make one up since there is a way to check through the Social Security Administration to make sure the name matches the number. These were all good things to know.

I was stuck with trying to figure out how to get a social security card and a license. It seemed to me a common scheme, at least from what I could tell from the net, was to try to locate a young person who died and use that number.

That seemed so common to me that I figured if I did something like that another fifty persons would be using the same number and we'd all get exposed. I had to come up with something else. I needed a woman about my age whose license I could use to get a license in New Hampshire and whose social security I could also use.

Next, I figured to get a New Hampshire license, it would be better if I had a NH address. The next time I was in Nashua using the internet, I was able to start the process for renting through Craigslist a furnished one bedroom in a condo complex for three months for $1250 a month. It had been advertised for $1,000 a month for a year, but I told them I was being reassigned temporarily to Nashua and only needed it for a short period of time. When I went to look at it, I waved a $3,750 cashier's check that I purchased with cash from local bank in front of the owners, Mary and Sabby Greenwood, who lived over in Bristol. After a short discussion, without asking too many questions lest the check be taken away, they gladly let me have it. Jilienette had her home.

I called the local utilities and asked them to send me the bills in my name since I had agreed to pay for them. The condo had a landline, so I didn't need another phone. I quickly went back out to a wireless site at a Starbucks, jumped on the computer and got a Google email address, Jilienettenevada@gmail.com. I tried to get a Google voice number but I had no way to verify my number without leaving a trace. I didn't want to leave my NH condo telephone number because it might be a lead.

A couple of days later, I was able to lift a cell phone from one of the people going out on Hunt Enterprises yacht for a day trip. After she

148

left, I took off and went over to Dedham where I went to a Panera's to get back on the net. I then was able to set up my voice account using the borrowed cell phone as the verification number. When the yacht got back, I asked whether anyone had dropped a cell phone in the office as they sat around waiting for the trip. The woman's whose phone I used was very pleased that I had found it. Jilienette now had a Google voice account to use.

I next had to find a woman my age who looked something like one of my disguises and borrow her wallet so I could get her license which I would use for my New Hampshire license. There were a couple of girls who worked at our headquarters who fit the bill. I'd go back there now and then. Everyone knew I was the boss's whore and although they didn't like me, they respected me knowing I had his ear and he was a really mean prick if he wanted to be. When I was there, we'd talked. They were all friendly enough to insure I wouldn't run back to Roger and complain about one or the other.

One who looked a lot like me had a really nice name, Patricia Cofer. She was called Patty by some and Cora by others. Initially, I thought people were calling her by her last name, Cofer, which would be strange but I'd learn later that it was Cora, not Cofer. She got the name Cora in high school because she was a big fan of Edna St. Vincent Millay, whose mother's name was Cora. That's all I know. I can't figure it out but pass it off as high school stuff.

She became my target. I watched her closely to see if she was careless with her bag but she wasn't. So getting access to that seemed impossible. I came up with another idea to try out and if it backfired it wouldn't tell against me.

149

I got there early one morning and pretended I had some work to do at my desk. I chatted friendly enough with everyone. After being there a while I walked over to Cora holding my license and a stack of photographs. I said, "Cora, does your license look like mine?"

She looked at mine and said, "I think so."

I asked, "Are you sure, I've heard they've come out with a new one."

She opened her bag and fished around in there a bit. It looked like she just kept it in there without being too finicky about it. She finally found it and handing it to me said, "I think so; here look."

I took it and compared it to mine saying, "Yeah, it looks like mine." Then to distract her while handing her back my license instead of hers, "Did you see these photographs of Circue du Soleil, Cora? They're great." She took the license threw it back into her bag without looking at it because she was attracted to the photographs I was holding. I knew she absolutely loved that circus and talked it about all the time. "I thought you'd like them."

She was profuse in her thanks. I quickly left and within a half hour I was in the Merrimac, NH office filling out the forms for my license and having my picture taken. I used her license for my identification and gave my New Hampshire address. On the application, I spelled the last name so that it looked like Cofen, a slight change in the spelling. I hoped it would not be noticed. It was. When my license came, the name was correctly spelled as Cofer. After filling out the paperwork, I was quickly in my car and back to the office. I was gone a little over three hours and Cora had not noticed the switch. I went up to her at her desk.

"Cora, you'll never guess what happened. I was at the bank and they wanted my ID and look what I gave them." I showed her her license.

"How'd you get that?" she asked without thinking.

"When I looked at yours this morning, I must've given you back mine by mistake, could you check?"

She looked in her wallet and took out mine and we exchanged. I tried to let it pass without much ado. I hoped she would never remember it. It was a chance I had to take and it did leave a trail back to me, but it was a risk I thought was acceptable. I made sure I avoided her after that so that we wouldn't discuss it again. I notified the postman that Patricia Cofer would also be receiving mail at the address. I started to send letters to her at that condo so that it would show she received mail there. I also added her name to the utilities.

I finally knew who I was going to be. As to the social security number, I had access to the employee records at Hunt Enterprises through Roger's computer so I got Cora's from there. I had to be careful about using Cora's social security number. I had to insure I undertook no financial transactions that would involve reports to the IRS.

After the license came — which had a picture of me in disguise — I went to a local bank in Nashua and set up an account that did not pay any interest. Having a Nashua address made it a lot easier. I funded the account with cash deposits through the ATM machines slowly building the accounts up. I then opened a brokerage account with the same information and connected that to the bank account. I sometimes funded that directly with cashier checks. I was able to build up a nice balance in both accounts.

There are two major aspects of identification, the personal and the work. Personal required a social security number, a license, and a credit card. I was afraid of applying for a credit card but I was able to get a debit card from the bank where I set up my account. The work consisted of a job with payroll verification and pay stubs, and an employment history.

Work was much easier than personal. I rented a small office in a back room of building on Dorchester Avenue on a month to month basis near where I used to live in order to have a MA address. I set up a MA corporation, the Rock Hill Corporation, using one of those on-line lawyer services. The stationary I made identified it as a Division of Hunt Enterprises. The telephone was that of Jilienette's Google voice. The email was like Jilienette's, set up with a Google assist. I needed to make it a division of Hunt Enterprises so that when I went to New York I'd be able to produce pay stubs for Patricia Cofer from that company. When I was doing that I was thankful NH had issued me the license under the name Cofer that way it corresponded with the work records. I was angry at myself for having tried to change the name because it would have raised suspicion with the New York rental agency.

After six months, my credential had checked out and I had signed a lease in New York City for a comfortable small-one bedroom apartment for a year under the name Patricia Cofer and I had a New York driver's license under the same name. I opened NY bank accounts and transferred my money there. I vacated New Hampshire, destroyed the computer, eliminated the Jilienette disguise and buried Jilienette. I hoped I had a safe hideaway in the City.

While doing all that identification stuff, I was also busy setting up the basis for my plan to destroy Roger. Oh, and then there was the matter of Jenny. She was going to be the one on whom I did the big acid test seeing if I could get by her with my disguise. It was because of that venture that I realized it was going to be necessary for me to go even further underground.

FRIDAY MORNING: A LITTLE AFTER BREAKFAST

I was tired after writing yesterday, so I got away from this until today. I don't know why I insisted on laying out most of the steps I went through in my changing my identity. It's not that germane to what happened, I should have said: "Suffice it to say, I was able to establish another identity to allow me to rent an apartment in New York City." I suppose the reason I did it was I like to look back on what I accomplished and how I can see in doing the things I did I was growing day by day. It took some while to adjust to the name Patricia Cofer. I called myself CC. When anyone asked, I'd tell them the Cora story and how I became Cora Cofer or CC to my friends. I really never got comfortable in my skin with that name or the way I went about getting it. I didn't know whether it was because I had taken advantage of Cora who was a good kid, or whether I felt I had left too much of a trail. I was just not that comfortable. I planned to come up with another name but I never did.

I don't know why I didn't; probably because like with other things in life I got used to it. I didn't have it in me to start all over again. I felt no need and adjusted to it.

Let me tell you about trying my disguise out on Jenny and then I'll tell you about meeting with the fanatic lawyer who was to help me destroy Roger, or at least she did until Roger offered her a job, but that's still to come. Think of some lawyer jokes and you'll understand what she did. But let me go over to talking about Jenny.

I mentioned how I wanted to set up my encounter with her. I was going to engage her in some type of conversation during which she'd have to have her attention focused on me. I'd watch her eyes. I knew them well enough to see what was going on in her mind. I'd no doubt if she saw through my disguise I'd be able to read it in them. But how was I going to do it? I had trouble seeing how it could be arranged without me giving myself away.

I called Putnam Investments, where she worked, and tried to learn something about her like asking when she wasn't in if she was at the gym or did she go to lunch at the cafeteria, but the persons were well trained, or really didn't know anything about her, since the uniform reply was: "Would you like to leave a message in her mail box?"

Finally I figured I'd give Facebook a try. I had never had my own Facebook page – as I said, with Tom I was in need of no other friends, even during the bad times – aside from that, I have always had a different take on social interactions than most of my friends. I love to socialize in person to feel the closeness of people and see the expressions on their faces such as bright smiles or puzzling frowns which you miss otherwise. I never liked to socialize through electronic means because of the impersonal nature of them.

The only type of communication I've ever enjoyed when a person was not present was a long while ago when I loved to write long letters in long hand to friends who were a long way off. Just to sit there and compose your thoughts while thinking of the person always seemed to me like I was spending the time with the person and bringing him or her closer to me and closing the gap between us. When Tom came along in college I let that habit of writing lapse. I suppose I will never do it again given my present circumstances.

I never like to talk for any length of time on the telephone. I used it for quick messages but not much else. When I learned about Twitter, Facebook, messaging, and all those other social sites or mechanisms for interacting impersonally with people, I found them grotesque. It wasn't that I was a Luddite or anything like that who was opposed to all that stuff, as far as I was concerned anyone who wanted to get involved with them should feel free. It was just, for me, that's not the way I like to do things. That's why I'm talking to you, Naria, like I am, writing all this down in longhand. I could use word processing on a computer but I'd never have felt as close to a computer as I do to you.

I should mention I think one of the most hideous of the new stuff is the idea of reading books in electronic format. I'd never cared too much for books prior to my breakup with Tom, but since then I've come to treasure them. I love the feel of the paper, just having them around and looking at the titles can bring back memories of their contents. There is a sense of permanence to them which is lacking in computers. I'm warmed by bookcases, turned off by computer screens.

I guess deep down I feel I should have been born a hundred years ago in a small town where I had a small house with a white picket fence, knew my neighbors, and led a quiet life. Sort of the life I feel when I read the novels of Willa Cather, or even Edith Wharton, although she writes of a different class of people. But in those novels you talked face to face and did comfortable routine things and were not rushed. The time in America where it seemed peace was valued, standing armies frowned upon, and politics was not controlled totally by the big money people like Roger. I know for many those days weren't so good, especially if you weren't white, but in attempting to bring about equality for all colors we didn't have to destroy the life style all could have luxuriated in.

I guess you'd say I seek now to ride along in a car on the slow track. I treasure most my time alone or in quiet conversations, although my hurly-burly days in New York would seem to tell otherwise. Maybe Tom was just not right for me, although I felt he was all I wanted. I've often wondered if the person whom I now think I am existed back in those earlier days. All I know is that now I feel all these electronic devises seem to intrude into my life and drive out the opportunity for thought and reflection. It's like walking down the road and having marching bands on both sides of you blaring away; it's like being in New York and partying night after night. How did I ever do it?

With Jenny, I was at the end of my wits in attempting to intuit a way to bring about the encounter with her. I had tried sitting across the street from her condo building early one morning hoping to see her come out the front door and walk down the street. After sitting there an hour or so and seeing less than a handful of people exit, I realized that most of the people must be going out other doors. They were. There was an adjacent garage and also a garage under the building that the owners used to reach their cars to go to work. There were too many ways she could escape my notice.

Frustrated, I turned to Facebook as I said which I joined under my real name. It was quite easy. I supposed they make it like that so that people like me will join. Once I joined I searched for Jenny. Because of her unusual last name, she was easy to find. I sent her a message something along the line, "Hey, old friend, how about again becoming friends again?" I'm not sure that's how you write on those sites, you know, it seem everyone uses a code like "How R U" or "LOL," which I learned meant laughing out loud rather than lots of luck as I used to believe. Then I see LOTE; I have no idea what it means.

I didn't hear back from Jenny until the next day. She said she'd make me her friend or whatever you say when you do. This allowed me to look at her page where she kept everything she was doing. I was hoping I would find out something more about her by reading what she had posted. Maybe she talked about like going to the gym or a specific restaurant or museum; well you know what I mean.

The best I could come up with was that she had a routine of going out on Friday's after work to a lounge in the financial district in Boston for a drink with her fellow workers. I did not find the name of the place but figured if I dug deeper at some other time she might have mentioned it. She did say that she usually enjoyed a Sunday brunch at the Seaport Hotel in South Boston's waterfront when she was not out of town. I thought that might be a good place to encounter her when we were standing at one of the tables laden with food and trying to decide what to select.

While on her page, I decided to take a peek at her list of friends to see if any of our old high school friends were in touch with her. To my surprise, Tom was listed as one of her friends. I didn't know he even knew about Facebook, and felt a twinge of loss for some strange reason. I don't know exactly how to say it but seeing him listed as a friend of Jenny's, even though she seemed to have hundreds of others, made me feel strange. I didn't know whether it was because he knew how to become someone's friend on the computer or whether he was no longer my friend or whether he was a friend of who used to be my best friend. I wanted to shout, "How can he be your friend?" It was just a funny feeling seeing his name there.

When I saw she had a picture album, I figured if I looked at it there might be some Friday night photographs that might disclose the identity of the place she went, or some other photographs that would show where she often went. When I first saw her I was surprised: she looked really good, as good as she ever did, if not better. Her photographs showed that she'd done a lot of traveling to various spots around the world. These were in folders labeled with the country or foreign city where they were taken.

Then she had a large group of photographs that were in a folder labeled "Party Times." These were photographs taken at parties she had at what was probably her place. I didn't know what her place looked like but it wasn't hard to tell it was hers because I didn't think she'd be partying at someone else's place so many times. Going through them quickly, I was surprised to see Tom had been at one of them. There was no way to tell when it was, but he was standing with that liquor-induced grin on his face with his arm around Jenny's shoulders and his head bent slightly toward her in that stupid way he'd pose when taking photographs.

I stared at it trying to accept that I had no control over what Tom did after he left me so I said to myself "So what, Tom was at a party with Jenny. We're not together anymore. He can do anything he wants to do. After all, look at me, the high priced call girl whoring for Roger."

That thought motivated me to move on from staring at the picture but I hadn't gone on but to two or three others when I found myself scurrying back to it. There was something. Yes, that was it. I enlarged my computer screen and looked more closely at the way Tom was dressed. The shirt he had on, that is what I stared at. That was the shirt with the little rip in the pocket, the frayed collar and the faded yellowish look. He used to wear all the time no matter how many other shirts were around. It was his favorite shirt.

A few months before we split, we had a little spat over it. I told him to stop wearing it because it was becoming ratty looking. I said it was enough we were down and out and just scraping by but that didn't mean we had to dress the part by wearing a shirt that looked like it was taken from some Salvation Army reject pile. He shrugged and didn't respond.

That night when he took it off, I hid it, thinking he'd never get a job wearing it. He complained a bit about it being missing but started to wear the better shirts, not that they were anything to write home about. After a week or so the shirt issue faded. I threw it out in the trash. I hadn't seen it since that time. But there it was. I stared at it.

"Calm down," I said to myself. "It means nothing." I got up and walked around the room.

160

I said to myself but out loud, "Let me see – I threw that shirt out – when was it – it had to have been late spring – probably, that'd be six or eight months before we went our separate ways – that was not too long after coming back here from New York – what the hell's he doing with Jenny?" I had to go back to the computer screen again to see if it was Tom leaning on Jenny's shoulder. It was.

"Relax," I said out loud, "relax, it's no big deal – so what he must have bumped into her – but he never told me – why? Why – what's he doing at a party with Jenny and he never tells me about it?"

I went on through other photographs trying to see if he appeared again, but he didn't. I went back to the offending picture and examined it again. I studied Jenny's dress and then looked for it in the other photographs but it never appeared again. As far as the photographs were concerned, this was the only event she wore it at and there was only one picture taken of her at that event. There had to be more. You usually don't have just one picture from a party. I went back through all her photographs again. There were no others.

Trying to track down other photographs calmed me down. I was flabbergasted by the picture. I didn't know what to make of it. How could Tom be at a party with Jenny at night and not mention it to me when we were living together, "Not living together, you fool." I said to myself, "Married!"

I didn't know the picture was taken at night, I thought. Then again I said to myself, "Of course it was, all parties are at night."

Then I thought it couldn't have happened. Tom was with me at night all the time – when was he not with me? Then it occurred to me that many times after we ate dinner he would tell me how cooped up he felt being out all day pounding the pavement trying to get a job without landing one and how it seemed the walls of the apartment were closing in on him. He'd ask if I minded if he went for a long walk to get some air. Why would I? I understood the stress of endless unsuccessful job hunting. Of course he'd want to go out and get some air. Then there was the time, it was one of those hot summer nights when the apartment seemed to have been moved inside a sauna, I suggested I'd go with him. He said no. He needed to be alone. Other times when I said it'd do us both good to get out, he'd insist he had to be alone.

Then he'd go out. I'd often try to wait but he never seemed to come back until long after I tired and went off to bed, after all I had to get up for work. It seemed he'd get back very late. He'd apologize the next day telling me he went for a long walk and ended up stopping in the bar with some of the locals and had a beer of two but then he'd do it a day or two later. The same thing! The same apology!

This happened more than a few times but it never crossed my mind not for a second that what he was telling me was nothing but the truth. After all, I remember once thinking when a speck of doubt jumped up from my subconscious that "Tom would never lie to me and anyway he couldn't have been going anywhere wearing that ratty shirt" – that ratty shirt that he was at the party with!

I didn't like what I was thinking. I figured I wasn't putting this together right. There had to be an explanation for all of it, an innocent explanation. There just had to be, I hoped. Because if there wasn't, I didn't want to finish that thought so I didn't. I was like Scarlett O'Hara – I said to myself, " Fiddle–dee-dee. I'll think about that tomorrow."

Tomorrow came and I felt much better. I couldn't imagine in my longest days Tom having anything to do with Jenny. I went back to the Facepage, I mean Facebook, sure that I must have been tired the night before and that by examining the picture I'd find some other meaning to it. Did you ever notice how all photographs stay the same? Well this one was no different than any other. There was Tom still standing there with his arm on Jenny's shoulders wearing his ratty shirt. I was now standing in yesterday's tomorrow when I said I would think about it. I was thinking about it and I didn't like what I was thinking. I was sure there was an explanation for it. There just had to be.

Fortunately, I did have other things to occupy my mind. I'd made the appointment with the lawyer I had mentioned and I had to plan out how I was going to play that. I was also involved in changing my identity so my mind was occupied by that. I let the Facebook photograph problem drift off into the background since I had to have time to figure out what to do about it.

It still bothers me to remember this. I'm going to take a little break and go for a walk over to Central Park. I'll continue on this afternoon. But it is a nice day and I've got to get away from living that moment again.

FRIDAY AFTERNOON: AFTER NAP

I needed that break. Writing about going on Jenny's Facebook and making that discovery brought back that old feeling of years ago. It was like – did you ever experience the feeling that occurs when inhaling a certain scent from the air and being transported back to another place and time? That was what it was like to me earlier today writing about that. I felt like the computer screen was in front of me and I was staring again at that picture and the same emotions flowed into my body almost a vividly as the first time when I was analyzing it closely.

No matter how I sliced it, there seemed to me something sinister about that photograph. If it could not be explained, something had been going on between Tom and Jenny that I did not know about. But I did not want to believe it. Hadn't I just had the recent conversation with her where she said she thought we were still in New York and she asked to be remembered to Tom? Hadn't she just included me among her many friends on her page? I was just not thinking straight I decided and I'd be able to get to the bottom of it at some point so I tried not to think the worst. I was always trying not to think the worst refusing to look at what was staring me in the face.

There was something that happened while I was trying to come up with a logical explanation that seemed humorous looking back. One scenario I manufactured in my mind was that when I threw Tom's shirt out he retrieved it from the barrel. I figured he hid it from me over at Jenny's house. I was content with that explanation for a bit until I realized that was as

164

bad as any other explanation I had thought of, if not worse. That would have meant he was keeping his clothes at Jenny's and what justification would he have for doing that? It certainly wouldn't have been something that made me feel any easier. I fought against all the sordid explanations and refused to credit any thing other than that there existed a very simple and innocent explanation for the picture and that I was incapable finding it.

Although that was a set back, I did gain something from my trip into the Facebook world, I learned where Jenny would be on some future Sunday. On Saturday, hiding behind what I thought was my best disguise; I drove over to the Seaport Hotel. I spoke with the restaurant maitre d' about the brunch. He gave me the details. Reservations were not necessary. I could walk in anytime between 9:30 and 1:30 pm even though the published hours for the brunch were 10:00 to 2:00.

I was at the restaurant duly disguised the next day, Sunday morning, at a little before 10:30. A woman, not yesterday's maître d', was at the desk. I told her I was expecting to meet someone for brunch. She let me peruse the patrons to see if my friend had arrived. Jenny was not there. I walked back into the lobby area. I took a seat where I could watch everyone entering the restaurant.

I eyed each person who came in from the elevators. Each person caught my eye and returned the look for a moment or two. The movement of people into the restaurant was quite steady up until about 11:45 when it seemed to start to slow. It dwindled to a trickle after noon. I was tired of watching the people and getting hungry myself. I took out my cell phone, turned it on to check if I had messages. I had two. As I dialed to listen to them I left my position and walked to the restaurant. I was hungry so I planned to have something for myself.

I approached the desk holding the phone to my ear. Yesterday's maître d' was there. "I'd like to have the brunch, please."

He smiled, "I see your friend did not appear."

This surprised me. I was at a loss for words and my face must have shown my confusion. "How did he know what I was doing?

He quickly surmised my bedazzlement and added, "You've been sitting out there quite a while – I assume you were waiting to meet someone here."

I recovered, "Yes, yes, a friend. A friend was supposed to meet me. She just left a message saying she got tied up."

"So you'll be eating alone?"

"Yes, I will."

He went through the process of taking my cash and returning a receipt to me. In my disguise I always operated with cash. I entered the dining room and smelled the food which reminded me how hungry I was. I took a small table near the wall and away from most people. A waiter came and poured me coffee. I walked up to the various food displays, and picked up a croissant to nibble on while I planned out my attack on the food. I no sooner sat down than Jenny walked through the door on Tom's arm. The maître d' chatted with them as if they were old friends. He walked them to a table on the far side of the room from me. They made quite a pair, I thought, but the hurt inside me was tearing away at me as any innocent explanation

166

for the computer picture flew quickly from my mind.

When they were seated, their sides faced me so I could only look upon their profiles. I could not take my eyes off them. They talked easily and answered each other with touches and smiles. At times they held hands across the top of the table. She got up at one point to leave, probably to use the lady's room, and as she walked by Tom she leaned down and kissed him. They were very much involved in themselves and never once glanced in my direction.

I had not expected this: Jenny with some friends, yes; Jenny with another man; perhaps, but not Jenny with Tom. While watching them, as you'd expect, the Facebook photograph kept popping its ugly visage into my mind. I don't know how long I stared. I only stopped when a waiter approached the table and asked me if I wanted a warm up on my coffee. I looked at my cup. I had not had any so I asked him for another. This time I sipped the coffee deciding upon my next move and wondering whether I had the strength to make a move. I don't know why but my knees seemed shaky. I felt enervated. I didn't know if I'd be able to move from the table.

I paid little attention to my coffee and food while still watching their every move. It wasn't fun. They looked like they were very much in love. I hadn't even begun to consider the implications of what all of this meant. The wound was all too fresh and raw for anything more than reaction, a desire to somehow quickly bind it up. I thought the only way to do this was to run out of the restaurant out into the air. I think what kept me there was the idea I had paid dearly for the brunch and that meant I should have a lot more than just a coffee and half a croissant.

I moved the coffee aside and indicated to the waiter that I'd like some red wine that was part of the deal. He poured me a glass. I had a few sips with a shaky hand and felt myself slowly coming back under control. "Keep in mind, why you're here," I told myself. "Keep in mind your goal. You're here to test your disguise. Only that at this time."

I had sufficiently gained my composure that I sensed myself not thinking of Tom being there with Jenny as a complication which helped me move my mind from the hurt. I remember thinking I did not want to test my disguise on him. "Why was it?" I wondered. I couldn't recall. Funny how sometimes something you know quite well can be swept away with a new tide like sand castles when your mind is consumed with other thoughts.

I finally convinced myself that my choice was to let the opportunity pass or make the most of it. I went for the latter. After a few more sips of wine, I decided to go up to the buffet tables at the same time they did. When they rose from their table and moved toward the brunch I did the same thing. We approached it from opposite directions. The dishes were closer to me. I looked right at the both of them as I walked toward me. They were chatting but each one did look over at me one or two times without showing recognition. That gave me more courage.

They walked behind me and picked up a dish right after I did. I was standing three feet away from them as I walked away toward the first table where a cook was taking egg orders. They followed behind me and stood next to me. Jenny was closest. "Here it goes," I thought.

168

I turned to her and said, "I never know whether to say over easy hard or hard over easy."

She looked right at me and smiled. She returned, "I think it's the same thing."

I said, "I always thought that, but someone told me there is a difference and I absolutely forget what it is." While I talked I stared right into her eyes. She looked back at me without the slightest indication she recognized me. "Maybe she's too enthralled with Tom to notice me?" I thought.

I looked up at Tom. He smiled back at me without any showing of recognition. There was no sign of uneasiness or compunction. He plastered his face with a pleasant expression of interest he'd have given to any good-looking chick standing near him.

"I really don't think so," Jenny said. She turned back to Tom and said, "Don't you agree honey?"

"Anything you say," he responded and she kissed him and smiled.

I wasn't going to push my luck too much, so I turned to the cook and said, "Are there any boiled eggs?"

He lifted a metal lid off the container and asked me how many I wanted. I said one, took it and moved on to the next table. While I filled my plate and they filled theirs, we looked at each other as you will with strangers but nothing more. I was elated that my best disguise could protect me. I went back to my table pleased with myself.

They returned to their table. I waited to see if they talked about me depending on the human instinct of looking over at a person you are talking about to indicate that fact. They never bothered to look my way again. I was surprised at how hungry I was and how huge and appetite I had developed. I ate more than I normally would. Maybe I was ingesting all that food because my mind was going at Mach 5 speed. I should have been surprised that the room wasn't rocked by its sonic boom. I was processing the implications of the Facebook and brunch events.

My first decision was to come to the brunch next week without a disguise. I knew my disguises were effective. I'd now save them for New York or when I was taking steps towards building my identity.

You would not believe how much I wanted the week to fly so I could accidentally bump into them at brunch. I was so anxious for it to happen. It always happens that when you want something to pass quickly it doubles down and slows up. I remember that was the case in school when some classes seemed to go on interminably and I'd stare at the wall clock's second hand that seemed to take a minute to tick away a second. I might still be waiting for that week to pass had I not had the other things to do to keep me occupied.

I mentioned the lawyer. She plays a part in this whole saga, but before I begin to tell about her, I've got to tell a lawyer joke. There was this woman attractive in her early twenties on a plane trying to get some sleep. The guy next to her, a lawyer in his late forties, kept pestering her about playing a game. He said it'd help the time pass by quickly. He'd ask her a question. If she couldn't answer it she'd give him five bucks. Then she could ask him a question and if he couldn't answer he'd give her five bucks. She said she wasn't interested and shut her eyes.

The lawyer frustrated said, "Listen, if you can't answer, you give me five bucks. If I can't answer, I'll give you five hundred bucks." The woman figuring the lawyer would never shut up said, "All right."

The lawyer said, "What's the distance between earth and the sun?" The women reached into her purse and handed him $5.00 and shut her eyes. The lawyer poked her and said, "Wake up, wake up, you got to ask me one."

The woman said, "What has four wings, flies forward through the air at night but during the day it can only fly backwards with three wings?" The lawyer looked puzzled. He took out his laptop and powered it up. He opened his cell phone and begins to dial. She turned around and fell asleep. Two hours later he woke her up. He said, "I give up." She stuck out her hand and he gave her five hundred dollars. She thanked him and turned back to resume her sleep.

The lawyer nudged her, "Hey, hey, wait a minute. You can't go to sleep. What's the answer? What's the answer?" The woman reached into her purse, took out five dollars and gave it to the lawyer. She turned and went back to sleep.

It's a benign enough joke but it sort of shows what I think of lawyers, Naria. Lawyers think they're smart but are easily outwitted. Maybe they know something of the law but most are dopey when it comes to life. It's easy to make them into unwitting dupes. Their egos make them miss the obvious.

For my plan to destroy Roger to become effective, I knew I would need someone with some power working on my side. I knew how Roger could manipulate things so I didn't want my plan immediately squelched once I executed it as Roger had the power to do. You may not want to believe it but our justice system absolutely favors the rich and mighty.

As I mentioned, Roger was extremely wealthy and highly connected and surrounded himself with shady lawyers and willing dupes. The Mafia's belief that everyone has his or her price is true. It's amazing for how little money some people will sell out. I knew full well that without someone with some clout behind me my project could not succeed especially from what I figured that after I did my thing I would have to depend on the district attorney, who was a friend of Roger.

I found that lawyer I was to retain one night when I was tired of reading but not quite ready to go to bed. I turned on Fox News. There was this woman lawyer talking with Bill O'Reilly who was going on and on about how bad the judicial system was and how men were getting away with raping women and sexually assaulting children. She constantly referred to criminals as male and victims as female. I listened to her rant, half paying attention to what she said until she indicated she worked in Boston. This caused my attention to snap back to her, and as we used to say in high school, "Dawn rose over Marblehead." I realized she was what I needed to insure my plan worked: an outspoken woman who hates men and can shine a national spotlight on her causes because of her connection with Fox News.

I looked her up and found her office. The next day I had made an appointment to see her. She shared a suite of offices with some other lawyers. Each had his or her name on the door. Her name did not stand out anymore than any of the others. A burly male receptionist at a desk who looked like a night club bouncer protected the lawyers from the uninvited visitors, or more likely their disgruntled clients.

"Can I help you?" he asked.

I smiled. "Yes. I have an appointment with Attorney Alison Huntingmen."

"What is your name?" I told him. He asked me to take a seat which I did. Magazines sat on the table in front of me. I ignored them probably because I did not want to spend any time away from my thoughts which were not on the lawyer but mainly on how I would go about interacting with Jenny and Tom on the upcoming Sunday.

I was there probably fifteen or twenty minutes before I was told Alison would see me. I've never liked to be kept waiting after the scheduled time of appointment, especially when I've made an arrangement to see a person days prior and the delay is not caused by people waiting in front of you. It's rude. It says to me, "You're time is not as important as mine so you'll just have to wait until I'm good and ready to see you." But it didn't make a difference then. I wasn't there to make friends with Alison. I was there to use her so I had to accept with whatever grace I could what she tossed at me.

I was escorted to her office. Her desk was cluttered. Her walls were cluttered. Photographs of herself with people who she apparently considered important such as Cable News personalities and some politicians were hung on the walls in no particular order. Apparently she thought they were silent testimonials to her greatness. She was on the telephone talking to someone when I entered. She pointed to a seat indicating I should sit there. I had to listen to her pompously giving orders about how she expected things to be done. As she was doing it since I was a little pissed at her I silently derided her clothes and make-up.

I assumed no one was on the other end of the telephone. It was just for show. It is an old lawyer's trick to have their secretaries keep ringing them whenever there is a client in their office. They know it makes a good impression if they look very busy and in great demand.

After finishing her act, she slammed down the phone. Then she picked it up again and said: "Charlie, hold all my calls. I don't want to be interrupted." Satisfied she had fooled me with all her hoopla, she smiled at me and said, "Now, what can I do for you?"

I immediately dangled the prospect of untold riches in front of her so I could capture her attention. "I'm not sure whether you can represent me. I first have to ask you a couple of questions, if you don't mind."

"Shoot," she said leaning back as if ready to duck as they came at her.

"Have you ever heard of Hunt Enterprises or Roger Hunt?"

She brightened. "Who hasn't?"

"Have you ever done any work for them?"

"No, I've never had them as clients, if that's what you're asking."

"I'm not sure if that's it exactly. What I'm trying to find out is whether there is anything that would stop you from representing me, like to protect me against them. In other words, do you have any connection with them where what I tell you would stop you from being my lawyer."

"No, nothing. But let me suggest you tell me why you're here and then I'll have a better feel for what to tell you. For instance, if you have some type of contract claim against Hunt

174

Enterprises, I may not be the best lawyer to handle that. You understand. I'm not the type of lawyer who does contracts. Understand?"

I could see the fish was nibbling at the bait. I replied, deliberately talking in a way that I figured would appeal to her: "No, no, it's nothing like that. I know you're a fighter for women who knows how to protect your client. You see I'm involved with Roger Hunt. I'll level with you since from what I've heard you say on TV you've seen and dealt with just about everything. I've been put up in one of his company's condos as his whore. I don't want him to know I've sought legal advice. He wouldn't be too happy if he did. I have to be sure what I tell you won't get back to him."

She leaned forward to me, a womanly tendency when one is about to impart a bit of gossip. She told me about the lawyer-client privilege and how what I told her would be as sacred as if it were told to a priest in a confessional and how the rules that govern her conduct would prevent her from telling anyone what I told her without my permission and if they hung her from a cliff by her fingernails she'd not breach my confidence. I listened patiently not believing a word she said, thinking "Sure, like lawyers aren't human."

She ended by saying, "Does that make you feel better."

I assured her it did. I quickly jerked the line hooking the fish. "I want to assure you I have money in my own right to pay you for your services and advice but I have to know I can totally trust you."

I again had to hear how she'd keep my confidences even if she was faced with being drawn and quartered.

175

I thanked her and told her I was putting my total trust in her. I then looked around as if I was checking to see if anyone else was in the office. My uncle Joe used to do that and I always though it a nice touch since it made one feel like a really important piece of news was about to be disclosed.

I began, "I'm not proud of what I've become. I was happily married working as one of Roger Hunt's secretary. I don't like thinking of it but to make a long story short he seduced me with his talk and money. Eventually, my husband moved out on me. Roger moved me into a condo owned by his office. My job was to be available to for him whenever he wanted. I don't blame Roger for this. I blame myself. I enjoyed the excitement of it, you know how sometimes we forget who we are and put aside our values and make huge mistakes without realizing it. Well, that's what happened to me."

She asked for more details as to where I worked, when Tom left, how long Roger and I had been together. It interrupted my fable for a bit but I was quickly back to it.

"It was not too long ago that I sort of came to my senses. I guess what happened was I was at our condo and I couldn't find my lap top computer so I went into Roger's private room to use his. He was on a trip so even though I wasn't suppose to go in there, I took the liberty thinking he'd never find out about it. It wasn't to snoop or anything it was just easy, you know, rather than going to my car where I'd probably left it, it was easier to use his to look up something quick."

Here was where I would be reeling her in. When I first saw her on TV that night, and a night or two later, she had been railing about child pornography and the men involved in

176

viewing it because if they didn't view it there would be no market for it. Her movements when discussing the subject spoke of an extreme aggressiveness that no one would not dare do otherwise than agree with her or else subject oneself to being physically pummeled. She said those who view the child pornography were worse than the people who made the children engage in it.

I continued my tale, "I turned on his computer and went on the internet. I started to type in the address line; you know how you do it and how as soon as you enter the first letter a suggested site pops up. I was looking for some information on stock portfolios so I typed the letters 'p' 'o' 'r' and the address line filled itself out. Without paying much attention, I hit the enter button, and I was at a site filled with photographs of very young children; boys and girls, engaged in outrageous sexual actions. It was the most disgusting thing I ever saw and I quickly got out of it. I guessed Roger must have been to that site at one time or another and that bothered me enough I wanted to be sure it was not just one of those strange things that happen when you're on a computer where all of a sudden you find yourself at some strange site without even knowing how you got there. You know what I mean?"

She nodded. She was totally involved in listening to me. I could see she was getting ready to mount up on her horse to begin a crusade against Roger if the right words were spoken. Her eyes were narrow and her lips drawn tightly together.

"So I figured if Roger was involved in child pornography, he's probably downloaded those type photographs on his computer and not

177

just go to the internet to see them. I wasn't sure I was right about that but that's what I thought anyway."

She piped in, "In my experience you're right. If a man is viewing child porn photographs he will invariably have downloaded some of them onto his computer."

"I thought I had heard that," I said to her knowing she had said it a few days before on Fox TV. "Anyway, you're right about that. I went to his picture program and I'll tell you I never saw so many disgusting photographs in my life, photographs of little kids totally nude, three, four or five years old, doing such awful things – many seemed to be Asian but a lot of other types, too. I went through a few of them to be sure there was more than one and finally I got so repulsed I had to shut the computer off. I left the room – it was so bad I forgot to look up the information I went in there to look for."

I took a deep breath and shook my head as if recalling the images. "That's when I began to want to get away from Roger because I was sick after seeing that. He was a sex maniac, I decided. But, I should have known that because he was always telling me stories about how he used this woman or that woman. I was beginning to understand he looked upon women and little children as things that existed solely for his sexual pleasure. I can't believe I'm telling you this. I feel so trapped and I know there is nothing you can do."

I stopped and lowered my head trying to make my eyes water but I couldn't because my feelings were so far from what I was saying that it was impossible. So I kept my head bent and held my hands over my face as if I were in agony.

"Are you all right?" she asked.

I shook my head. I let the silence take over for a while to let her get really mad. I then looked up and said, "Can you tell me something. I know I'm not a good person. I've been called a whore by some which hurts but it probably is what I am even though I don't like to think that I am. Can you tell me because of what I am does that mean whether I am willing to have sex with Roger or not I have to do it?"

At the time I asked this question Alison was already popping up and down and this set her off, "Absolutely not. You have a right to your own body to do what you want with it. If you don't want sex with Roger or any other man, that is your right."

Pretending naïveté, I said, "But what if he forces himself on me, like when I tell him no he forces me to do it: can he do that?"

"That's rape," she shouted. "He's raping you. That's a serious crime. Every woman has a right to her own body and she can't be forced to do what she doesn't want to do and if she's penetrated against her will then that is rape."

"Is it only when he uses his thing that it is rape?"

"What do you mean?"

"I hate this and tell him not to do it but he likes to put other objects into me, not just his thing. Is that all right?"

She's now leaning forward and is very angry, "No, no, that's the same thing. You've got a right to your body! Whether he puts his penis or anything else into you against your consent, it is rape."

"Oh, I'm so frightened; he does it all the time. What can I do? I'm been being raped for months and what can I do. Can you do anything to help me?"

179

"Of course I can. I'll get a restraining order to prevent him from coming near you and that'll protect you."

"You don't understand. Roger is very powerful. He's surrounded himself with evil people who will come after me."

"The state is more powerful than Roger! Don't you worry; you can get a restraining order to protect yourself."

"How do I get one – can you just get it for me."

"No, you have to go to court and talk to a judge>"

"What about Roger? Will he have to go to court?"

"Yes, after he is notified of it."

"Can he talk to the judge, too?"

"Yes, he has a right to be heard."

"Oh, that's what I thought – no one will believe me over him. He owns everyone including the judges. There is no hope, is there."

"Don't think like that. There is hope. That's what the system is for to protect women like you. I will be with you all the way and I'll make sure you are protected."

"Can I do anything about all the rapes he did to me?"

"Yes, you can file for a complaint or talk to the DA."

"The DA is Roger's friend. He won't believe me. You know, Attorney Huntingmen, he won't believe me."

"Call me Alison, if you don't mind."

"Alison, that's such a nice name. You know he won't believe me. No one will believe me. It's only my word against his and he'll say that I'm a whore and just looking for money. I

180

know how these things work. I never should have come here."

I again put my head in my hands and rubbed my eyes so at least it would look a little like I was affected by all this.

"You're wrong, Dakota. I will be by your side. You can be sure you'll be heard."

"Can you guarantee me that Roger will be charged with rape?"

She hesitated a bit. "I can't guarantee anything. That's not my job. I can only assure you I'll stand by your side."

"But what good is that if no one believes me except you – if you could guarantee me Roger would be charged and he couldn't get out of this I'd do it – but you won't do it. I should have not come. I'm not blaming you, Alison. I appreciate you telling me the truth about what I can expect. It's just I know there's no help anywhere. People like Roger with all his money and friends can do anything they want. People like me, the little people, have to do what they want. I appreciate your time. I need time to think over what I'll do but in the meantime I guess I'll just have to be raped by Roger – it's dreadful to think of it but without any guarantees, I don't want to go on with this. Oh, Alison, I feel like my life's over."

I put my head down in my hands again. She was at my side holding my shoulders. Nothing was said for a few minutes. She then said, "I'll be there for you. I'll stand by you."

Without looking up I said in a frail voice, "Oh, Alison, you're so kind. I don't know what I've have done without you."

After that the conversation involved her trying to convince me to change my mind about bringing charged. I adamantly refused. She said if I changed my mind she'd be ready to rush off to court at a moment's notice.

She was so caught up in feeling sorry for me and despising Roger that she almost allowed me to leave without doing what was most important to her, make arrangements for her fee. I brought it up and insisted I wanted to pay her for her time. I was there about forty-five minutes. She extorted five hundred dollars out of me. I was glad to pay. I needed a greedy zealot on my side. I asked her if I could have another appointment a couple of weeks away and I'd use the time to think over what I wanted to do.

I had accomplished what I set out to do. She was totally appalled at what Roger was doing and was urging me on to war against him. She was fully on board. I just had to keep her fires stoked up.

I'd meet with her every couple of weeks after that. The sessions would be short with me inventing horrible things about Roger and telling her how glad I was that she was there and was willing to take my case if I decided to go forward. As I got closer to the time I knew I would have to come up with a show and tell demonstration. I had figured out how I would do it.

She kept urging me to do something and threatened at times, she was so irate at Roger's ongoing involvement in child pornography and his rapes of me, to go forward without my consent. I had to remind her of what she told me in the beginning that what I told her was confidential although I was sure by that time she had plenty of other people giving her advice on how she should have me come forward. I'm not sure whether she gave away Roger's or my

182

identity but I was sure the story was out there in some manner or another.

I'd asked her, "Is it your experience that men become more violent after time?"

"Why do you ask me," she said. "Is Roger showing propensities toward that?"

"He's saying things like the best sex is when you have the pain and the suffering together, stuff like that. I don't know what he means."

She replied, "Yes, there are people who believe that. It is not that uncommon."

"I'd never do that and I'll tell you this if he forces me to do it, I'll definitely come forward."

"You should," she pleaded, "you should."

"And do you find men become more weird-like after a bit?"

"What do you mean?" she said.

"The last time he threatened me if I didn't let him bring in other men and let him watch me and them, I'd be sorry."

"Dakota, you can't let him do that," she urged, "you have to go to the police.

"I will," I said. "And I should mention the other day when I said I was sick, I really was with this huge headache, and told him I didn't want to do it, he picked up this club-like thing and said 'It'll be easier if you forget being sick and do it with me rather than having me have to persuade you with my friend Billy here.' That was the first time I really was scared that he'll start hitting me. If he does, what should I do? Oh, what can I do? I don't want to be beaten. I'll do anything," I wailed, "Anything he wants as long as he doesn't beat me. What can I do?"

She gave me some numbers I could call. She gave me her cell number if I promised never to call her except in emergencies.

But I'm way ahead of myself, let me get back to where I was at the time.

SATURDAY MORNING: BACK FROM A RUN

How can one not think of Mr. Rogers on a day like today? It's a beautiful day in the neighborhood and everyone seems to be out and about. Central Park was heavy with runners, people strolling, and some pushing strollers and baby carriages. Whenever I think of baby carriages I think of Copenhagen just like seeing bicycles reminds me of Amsterdam.

My run was leisurely and I didn't go too far, just enough to build up a little sweat and feel I was working out. I'm feeling more energetic since I've begun writing and the big change is my sleeping habits. No pills and still a good night's sleep. Naria you're going to make me think there is something to psychiatry, especially if the practitioner is someone like you who knows how to listen.

I told you how slowly the week was passing as I anxiously await my time to confront Jenny and Tom at the brunch. To make matters even worse, Roger had plans for us to go away with some of his friends for that weekend. The dénouement had to be delayed for another week but that latter week moved more quickly. I found myself that Sunday standing with my credit card at the desk at the Seaport Hotel buying a brunch ticket. I was not, as I indicated, in any disguise. I took a table at the other side from where I had taken it before, the side where Tom and Jenny sat two weeks prior.

Having been there before, I knew the routine pretty well. I enjoyed my coffee right after sitting down. I had my iPod touch and used the time to bring certain things up to date. When I finished I went to the buffet and filled

185

my plate. When I returned the waiter poured a glass of red wine. I enjoyed the ambiance and slowly consumed my food. I had no idea how the encounter would conclude but having paid for the brunch, I wanted to be sure I had time to enjoy most if not all of it.

Right on time, the love birds fluttered in through the door. As I had expected, the head waiter was coming in my direction and they were flying in behind him. They laughed and chatted amiably as they approached, arm in arm, up to the table next to mine. Both noticed me at the same time. Their wings drooped, they came to a sudden stop and darkness and confusion descended over their aspects. They stood staring at me as I looked up at them. The waiter leading them in looked about in confusion thinking somehow he had done something to incur their displeasure. I let their discomfiture at their discovery linger by betraying no trace of emotion as I looked up at them. Time seemed to stand still. Tick tock, tick tock. My feelings were those of joy at having so squarely exposed their deceit.

They managed to crawl into their chairs and the waiter fled the scene looking for cover. We sat there in cloying silence. I would be damned if I was going to interrupt the exquisite pleasure of the moment by saying anything. Tick tock, tick tock.

Jenny sat in her seat, looking at the place setting in front of her. She then summonsed up the nerve to look over at me, saw me looking back at her, pushed her chair back, rose from her seat and without so much as a 'how do you do' walked unsteadily out of the room. Tom sat there. Emboldened, I left my place carrying my wine glass and joined him, taking Jenny's seat.

I could tell from his eyes he didn't know what to feel or think. When I caught his eye I said, "Tom, there's an old song. I think its title is: 'How long has this been going on?'"

He said nothing but looked at me, down at the table and then at me again. I went on, "Your playmate, recently departed, has a Facebook page. She puts up photographs of herself and her friends. One was of you and her. When I saw it, I knew that you were seeing her as long ago as the spring. I figured that was shortly after we got back to Boston after you got out of prison. I don't remember you mentioning her being on the visitors' list. How did you hook up so   soon?"

I couldn't resist that little dig. While Tom languished in prison for his fourteen months for keeping fraudulent accounts, his faithful mutt Kota dutifully wagged her tail every day, attempting to cheer him up. I didn't want him to forget what a sap I was.

He still said nothing but was now looking at me more than he had previously. I was viciously calm, "I couldn't figure out why you could never get a job but now it's quite clear. You weren't going to get many job offers when you confined your searching to Jenny's bed. You set me up Tom to make me think I was responsible for our marriage crumbling while all the time you had left it months earlier. How could you have done it to me, Tom?"

I waited. I wanted him to deny it. I wanted him to tell me I was mistaken and that he only took up with Jenny after we had split up. His silence was confirming my worst fears. All those thoughts I chased away about how Tom had been using and betraying me for month after month were true. He offered no explanation. He

187

gave no denial.   He affirmed the truth of everything I said.

"Why if you didn't want me didn't you just say so? Or were you keeping me as some sort of insurance policy in case your new adventure with Jenny didn't work out? Don't you know what you did to me Tom, or is it you just don't give a shit?"

He desperately wanted to leave, but somehow could not pull himself out of the seat. I waited for a response. He no longer looked at me.   He was looking around as if expecting somehow a brave knight on a giant white steed would come galloping through the door to plunge a lance into my heart to rescue him from his peril. I could tell what I had said struck home. I stopped talking. I wondered where Jenny had gone

Suddenly, I started to get a little anxious and my victorious assault seemed less than brilliant. I had a sour taste in my mouth that didn't come from the wine or the food but from fear. I feared if he got up and walked away then my only bit of revenge against him would have been these few words I just threw at him. What a shallow victory that would have been! I wanted more than that now that I knew the truth. I was putting Tom's name on my list right after that of Roger's. Tom, too, had to be utterly destroyed, probably even more so than Roger, because he put me into Roger's slimy hands based on the lie that I was doing it for someone who loved me.   What could be worst than demanding your wife sacrificing her virtue and vows to save the marriage while all the time you have no interest in saving it yourself? Not only that, to want to walk away from your wife and blame her infidelity for the dissolution of your marriage and burden her with the life-long guilt that had she acted otherwise the marriage might have been saved.

I knew I had to change tactics and become magnanimous and highly disingenuous. A woman scorned belongs in hell if she let's her fury show. I had been scorned. Although the fury caused the roiling of my soul, I fought to keep it well hidden within me. Tom would pay for his treachery but not quite now because he was second in line. He too would have to be destroyed but in due time. But first, like with all the others I had to lure him into my web.

I began to dissemble, "You know Tom, don't take it so hard. You know, like – it's no big deal. Don't feel bad. I understand. Things happen, as they say, you know that."

He looked at me surprised at the change of tone in my voice. I continued in a controlled conciliating manner, "You know, I know you guys weren't doing what you did because you wanted to hurt me. You don't know how bad I feel that you happened to run into me like this. You know, what's over is over. It'd be real bad if we let this destroy the little we have left. Look, go get Jenny. Tell her I'm fine. I still want to be good with you guys."

He looked at me confused. He didn't trust he wasn't bringing Jenny back into a trap. I looked him square in the eye and said: "Tom, I really mean that. I want to be your friend. I want to be Jenny's friend. I know what happened but as I said, it's in the past and we mustn't look back, only forward."

I got up. As I walked past him I put my hand on his shoulder and said in a soft voice, "Tom, go get Jenny. I'm almost done and I'll be leaving shortly. Don't let your day be ruined by this."

I went back to my table with my wine glass. The food that I had left had gotten cold. I signaled to the waiter and asked him to bring me some fresh coffee and some of the small Danish deserts that were on the table. He did this and I indulged. A few minutes later Tom and Jenny walked back into the room. Jenny eyed me apprehensively. I smiled at her and gave her a little wave. They sat back down. They didn't talk.

I finished up quickly, got up, and walked over to Jenny. She looked at me not knowing what to expect. I smiled and said, "You look fabulous, Jenny. It's so good seeing you. Thanks for making me a friend on the computer thing. I have to say that seeing you again it's clear why Tom dumped me. Enjoy your brunch."

I walked past her and touched her shoulder as a sign of forgiveness, at least that's what it was supposed to be. She reacted as if I had stuck a needle into her. I left and peace returned to the brunch at the Seaport Hotel.

I went for a long walk along the Boston waterfront. I marveled at my ability to control my emotions and to act in a deceptive manner. I wondered if the term Machiavellian would fit the course I had begun to follow in my life. I'd heard the term mentioned by Roger who would tell his lawyers they had to become more like that in their dealings with people Roger was trying to take advantage of. I knew what the term intended to connote: one who keeps his or her true motives hidden while deceiving or manipulating the other person.

But Machiavelli entitled his book 'The Prince.' He was addressing it to people of power. He suggested the best way they could keep their power was by keeping their followers happy and sometimes to do this it required some intrigue. I could see that term applying to people like Roger who had lots of power. I didn't have any. I reasoned it could not apply to me since the concept of power was inherent in it. If it didn't apply to me, was there a term that did. I first came up with 'sneaky smart' but upon reflection it left a lot out; I then decided that I liked indomitable. It properly reflected my mindset at that time. I thought nothing would stop me from pursuing my goal.

I reviewed what had happened that morning at brunch. I berated myself for not having planned out my encounter with Tom and Jenny a little better. I should have thought through the encounter by saying if A happens then I'll do B; or if A happens then I'll do C. I was lucky that I caught myself. I now decided that I had to make it up to both of them and befriend them in the same manner as I was doing with Roger. I had to remove any suspicion from their minds other than I was fully accepting of their relationship and felt no discomfort with it having gone on behind my back while I was married to Tom.

I also had to come up with a way to torture Tom for what he had done. I did not want to think of that just yet. It may have interfered with my plans for Roger.

Jenny also deserved my attention. Strangely, I didn't feel any great animosity against her and I tried to differentiate her from Tom and Roger. I said to myself, "She was in no relationship with me so why should I be angry with her." When I settled in to agree with that thought a little voice would whisper "Other than she was one of your closest friends." I told myself she didn't breach any trust or confidence and

191

then the little voice would say, "Other than sleeping with your husband." I said to myself, "I never thought that if another gal stole my man I should be mad at the gal," but the little voice said, "Sure Dakota, you can think that when it's never happened, but what about now. Stop fooling yourself; you're ready to explode."

I was ready to explode. The explosion came in private and evinced itself by my leaning against a post behind the Federal Courthouse overlooking the harbor experiencing a sudden pouring of tears from my eyes. Even the indomitable Dakota was still a woman. The betrayal bit deep into me and really, really hurt. I was mad at myself for having had that man as my man in the first place, a man who thought so little of me that he flew away at the first new flower that enticed him.

I suppose what made me lean to giving Jenny a pass was her reaction when she saw me. There was no braggadocio in her aspect, just a feeling of great embarrassment. She knew she had done me wrong. She felt bad about it. No gloating that she had my Tom just a sense of betrayal of one who used to be her friend. It was so intense that she had to flee. Yeah, she never should have done it but as I said she didn't breach any obligation she was under to me. That makes all the difference in the world when deciding who to get revenge against. Aim at the one who let you down, not the one who got what you wanted but you couldn't keep.

Yes, I thought, that's one way to look at it, but isn't there also another side of it? Jenny was desirable and beautiful and could have any man she desired. Tom's not such a stud that she just had to have him above all others. Maybe she did go after him and lured him away into the easy

192

life of lying in her bed waiting for her to come home rather than looking for a job to help support us for a sinister reason. Maybe there was something deep down inside her that made her want to out shine me by stealing my husband and by giving him the luxuries he wanted that I couldn't provide. Best friends, yes, we were that, but I have to admit, Naria, we competed pretty hard to outdo each other.

Perhaps in her mind it was a perfect turnabout. I dropped her friendship when I went topsy-turvy over Tom. Maybe she resented him taking me from her. We never think that we may be causing great hurt when we leave our close friends in platonic relationships and go off with an exclusive one in a sexual relationship. Was Jenny's revenge to take him from me as he did me from her? Maybe she left the table because she realized she reached so low to find Tom and was embarrassed I saw her poor taste.

I had two sides to my feelings for Jenny as you can see. I wanted to give her a pass but that little voice wanted me to put her on the list right after Tom. I decided she may have been as deserving as Roger or Tom to be on the list but I may have a need for some friend down the road and why not forgive her and try to resurrect what you'd destroyed.

A few days later I went through the message part of Facebook to contact Jenny again. I asked her to meet for lunch. She finally assented. It was nice as far as it goes. It wasn't like it once was. It was going to be hard to take it from where it was into a real friendship. So much water had gone under the bridge since we were close. Like a stream split in two by jutting land, we had gone our separate ways and have been now carried off into different and distant lands.

I assuaged her guilt. I told her horrid stories about Roger. I hoped to incorporate her into my plan of setting him up. She'd be another person out there who would back up my story. I intended to try to get closer to her but I didn't really know if she had the same desire. I kept thinking as I sat in the taxi going back to my condo, "You can't go home again to your youth." Jenny was part of my youth. But I knew I had to keep working at it.

I had always been in contact with Tom as I told you. It was a formal thing as part of our agreement and one best described as chilly. I tried to warm it up a bit, since I needed to bring Tom up to room temperature before I put him in the oven. I had no idea how I would get back at him but wanted to maintain my relationship since it is really difficult to attack a person who is wary and on guard. It's when the guard is dropped that the punch lands best.

Things with Roger were the same. I was to be there at his beck and call whenever the urge arose in him. It could be at any time. First thing in the morning, during his coffee break, after being out with the boys at night doing business; you get the idea. I was tempted to put a sign up in the condo: "Dakota's: Open for Business 24/7". I never did, but that was in my mind whenever Roger came in.

He was blissfully ignorant of any plan I had in my mind to bring him down. That was only natural. What had the wretch to fear from the wench? With all the power and pelf he'd surrounded himself with and exercised ruthlessly what threat could a harebrained lass be who for all he could see spent most of her spare time

194

after servicing him looking for split ends or reading Hollywood-type or supermarket tabloid magazines.

I wrote how I used to think of Elvis when Roger forced himself on me but those days had long past. Now I was intent on planning Roger's downfall. I studied him to determine whether he had any patterns of behavior that I could anticipate and fit my plan into. Most times there was sort of a pattern but not one that provided me the opening I sought. After we finished in the bedroom, he'd hang around for a couple of hours and have a drink or two and try to steer the conversation back into the bedroom seeking for me to talk about how good he was and how lucky I was to have him. Except, and this was a big exception, when he had appointments to meet people or business matters to attend to, he'd leave right after we finished. I would never know what was going to happen until it actually took place.

The more I paid attention it became clear that the only time available to me would be when he came over at the end of the work day for a quick uplift. When that happened he'd always stay around for a couple of drinks and then head to his suburban home to spend time with his wife and kids. He never scheduled business meetings on those nights nor would he take on any social engagements at night unless he included me in them so I would know of those beforehand. I settled upon the after-work time as being the most propitious time for carrying out the plan.

Things were rapidly falling into place. I'd stacked away enough money now, my New York place was secure, and people who could help me were being properly primed to act as I hoped they would. I had worked hard on Alison, my

195

lawyer, by playing into her preconceived hatred for men. I had manage to install Roger at the top of her list that I began to worry that given the right chance she'd stick a dagger in his heart and deprive me of my opportunity to torture him.

I had kept Roger enamored of me but I knew with a guy like him it was going to wane soon. Jenny and I had not become much friendlier; .we were far from being friends. I felt bad about this and wanted to bring her closer. I thought about it and recognized we avoided talking about her and Tom.

I thought it might have been because of this that she showed a hesitance to let down her guard with me. One day I told her, "Jenny, I know there's this big elephant in the room when we get together. It's Tom. I'm sorry for bringing him up, but if I don't, I won't be able to chase him away. Believe me; I do not hold you one bit responsible for anything that happened between Tom and me. Nor am I interested in knowing what happened between Tom and you in the past or in the present. I hope we never have to discuss him and we don't let it come in between us as individuals and as friends."

You want to know something, what I'd like to believe is that was probably the sincerest thing I said during that period of time. But truthfully, it may have been another big lie. Yet it was good I said it, whether it reflected my true feelings or not, because the ice between us seemed to melt and we started to get along better. I should mention that as Jenny and I seemed to get better, she seemed to be drifting away from Tom, especially after I all but told her she was welcome to him because I didn't want him.

This was just another example that it is not just men but also women; I guess it's something in human nature that once having achieved the long sought after goal one immediately looks for another goal to go after. It's the essence of sport. In golf one always wants a hole-in-one but when she gets it, she wants another one. It seems a person is always chasing after something and even if she achieves she wants it again, and again. Think of the Red Sox fans. Year after year all they ever wanted for 85 or so years was a world championship. They finally got it. Were they satisfied? No, they wanted the championship the next year.

I figured Jenny's drift away from Tom after I told her she could have him I figured came from her desire to have one up on me. As I said she'd tried to do that throughout our friendship – she was always trying best me, as I was trying to best her. We were so close that we had an almost sibling type rivalry. Maybe she just carried it too far with Tom. That day seeing me at brunch she realized it. All I know is that it seemed to me she was seeing a lot less of him but because that was a forbidden subject between us, I could only surmise that they were less involved as they had been from little things I picked up.

What were they? Well Tom was Tom. Maybe I thought he was having a tough time with Jenny because as the weeks went by our pro forma daily talks became a little less formal. Tom was warming up to me more. I smiled to myself thinking I was right after all about him wanting an insurance policy.

New York was still good. I'd succeeded in renting the place and beginning to establish an identity under my new name. More and more people knew CC who lived on East 73rd Street. I

197

was trying to figure out how to give Patricia Cofer back her name but that was down the list of things to do. I was extremely careful using her identification. I never used it if there was any chance at all that would cause a report to be sent to the IRS.

As for my money situation, I had plenty to live for a few years if I maintained a modest life style which more and more seemed to become me. I mentioned I disliked all the new toys and found comfort in books and reading. I didn't want many friends but the one's I seemed to find were nice. I decided some day I would look up my old friend Naria. I'd have liked to have some of our discussions again.

I don't want to say that I proceeded head on with my plans to destroy Roger without some regrets. One thing I knew, I'd probably never have a family of my own if I went through with this. What decent guy would ever want to marry a whore? That thought always bothered me because I knew to take Roger down I had to publicly besmirch my own character.

Any time I'd seem to falter in my resolve Roger would buttress me up by demanding that I do something that upset me. Oh, I should mention in case there is some confusion, Roger never was into child pornography nor did he use any foreign implements on me. Those were just tales I told to my lawyer, Alison, and perhaps Jenny, to get them to believe Roger was some sort of ogre.

The next step was to get the implements I needed to carry out the plan. One of them was a club like the night sticks that the cops carry. I drove down to Providence, RI, and went into a police supply store to get one. I asked if they sold any of those clubs police men carry. The man said, "What, a Paddy whacker?" I thought he said, "Paddy wagon." I said, "No, I don't want a Paddy wagon." He said, "I said Paddy whacker. A Billy club? – is that what you want?" I nodded. He went into the back and came out with what I figure I needed. He said, "The cops don't carry these any more, so we've got a few left over. This what you want?" I said it was. He said, "Then call it by the right name, it's a Paddy whacker." I took it and quickly left the store.

So I went home with my Paddy whacker. I remember thinking it was a strange name as was the name Paddy wagon. The Irish must have kept the cops real busy in the early days. I suppose now it wouldn't be politically correct to name a club or a police wagon after an ethnic group.

Having driven home with the club, I knew my part in this destruction of Roger was not going to be easy. I comforted myself by thinking that I wouldn't really appreciate things if I got them too easily. I knew there was going to be a lot of pain.

I'm pretty proud of what I did next. Let me digress a moment. There's an old Clint Eastwood movie where he plays Detective Callahan. This is the movie where he says near the end to the killer, "Do you feel lucky, punk!" Earlier in the movie Callahan is dogging the footsteps of the punk. The punk doesn't like it since with Callahan so close on his heels, he can't commit his crimes. The punk figures that if he claims that Callahan beat him up, then Callahan would be told to stay away from him. The punk arranges for some big vicious looking guy to beat him up. He then says to the media Callahan did it. Callahan's bosses tell him to stay away from the punk. The punk commits more crimes until Callahan catches up with him.

Well, I couldn't do what the punk did, you know, have someone else beat me up because it would leave a trail back to me. My resolve was to do everything by myself. So if I was going to be beaten up, I had to do it myself. I did not look forward to doing this but to carry out my plan I had to. Here's why I'm proud of myself.

I really have no mechanical skills. But using a small wooden box, I was able to construct a little torture device. The small end of the club I fastened to the bottom of the box so it was held fast in one place but the other end of the club, the striking end, could be moved back and forth. I then got one of those things that stretch called bungee cords, those rope type things that you use to hold the cover of a trash barrel so the raccoons can't get in it or to hold car trunks down with some tension when you stuff them too much. I fixed it so that I could push the business side of the club against the tension and let it go so that it would come back toward me very fast and hard. I practiced with it quite a bit before I began using it on myself.

I used it a few times on my upper and lower arms. I found that I bruised quite easily. But that was good because the pain was not so intense and the bruises would remain there for a while. Old bruises are good bruises when you're setting up the idea that you've been subject to beatings over a period of time.

My penultimate self beating before the show was when I let the bat hit me pretty good on the bone over my left eye. It was a stinging hit that did not hurt as much as it stunned me. I felt a quick, sharp pain. I put my hand to it and it felt wet. I went to the mirror and saw the skin had been broken a little under the eyebrow and a small amount of blood was coming out. I sensed a tingling feeling in the eye but didn't think I had accomplished too much. I was going to do it again but decided to wait a couple of days. I unassembled my devilish device and put it away. What was great about it was that when it was broken down into component parts there was no way you could ever figure out what it was used for.

Roger had been over earlier. He was leaving town that night for a few days and had no plans to come back. After putting the machine away, I settled into the couch with a good book I hid in my room, I forget what I was reading at the time but it wasn't any of that trash stuff I read when Roger was around. Sitting there I kept rubbing my eye. It didn't hurt as much as it seemed to bother my vision and irritate.

After an hour or so I got up and went to the bathroom to look at it. When I did, the area around my eye had swelled up and looked a little dark. That pleased me. I couldn't read any longer because the eye was getting watery so I went to bed.

When I woke up in the morning I found that I could not open my left eye. I went to the bathroom and from that little hit the whole area around my left eye was black and blue and so swollen that my eye could not open. I should have put ice on it right away. Rather than doing that, I called my lawyer, got dressed, and headed to her office. I no longer had to wait and walked past the receptionist right into her office. When she saw me, she burst into tears, "What happened?" she asked.

"He got mad at me." I said. "He kicked me."

"Oh, my God," she exclaimed, "that's awful. That's awful." She rushed around the desk to look at it more closely. She then went back to her desk and took out her digital camera. "I have to take photographs of this."

She took photographs, tried to console me, and again tried to persuade me to go to court. I told her I wanted to give him one more chance saying maybe when he kicked at me he didn't mean to hurt me like he did. I left her telling her I was going to go get medical treatment but not before seeing Jenny for coffee so that I could also horrify her. I paraded around that morning with the big black and blue mark on my face so my neighbors could see me. Later, I put ice on my eye.

When Roger saw it several days later it still looked awful. I told him that I had hit it on the edge of a cabinet door that I had left open. He was very kind and solicitous and could not do enough for me. He did have a good side to him when he wanted to show it.

SUNDAY MORNING: COFFEE AND SCONE

It is rainy today. That didn't stop me from going out and getting a raison and nut scone. I love scones especially those that I get up the street here on 3rd Avenue. It's perfect to have a rainy Sunday to tell about the how I undertook to bring about Roger's downfall. The only drawback is that after I finish this scone here, I'll be sad I didn't get a second one so I better eat it slowly. Sometimes I do splurge and get two but then I hate myself afterwards.

All was in place. My support was propped up and ready to fly into action when called. My plan was set. All I needed was the right time to carry it out. I wasn't anxious about it. I had thought it through and it seemed fool proof. I was pleased I had arrived at this point keeping my own counsel. No one had any idea what I was thinking or participated in my plan. None could appear out of the wood work to undermine my claim as to what I said happened.

As with all guys like Roger who think with their thing there was a finite time within which he'd be pleased with me. He'd at some point in the offing want to trade me in for a new model. The only indication I had that the exchange point was coming, probably a little sooner than I anticipated, was when he started to talk about people doing other stuff than we normally did. He wondered what excitement people found in bondage or inflicting pain during these encounters. He talked about how he'd read of people being tied to the posts of their beds and finding it heightened and prolonged the pleasure of their actions. It gave me an idea that I'll mention in a second or two but what I believe is that stuff spoke of sadistic people who lived only for sex and had exhausted their capacity for normal activity so they upped the ante. I didn't say that to him but his newly found fascination with it told me that to stay on this gravy train I'd soon have to satisfy his incipient desires for a deeper plunge into depravity or I'd be tossed off.

It was a gravy train only in the sense I had plenty of material comfort, it was fetid putrid smelling air tight box car when it came to spiritual and emotional feelings. I had steeled my feelings to everything I'd been doing. Even so there were those times when I stood on the balcony in my condo in the high rise building and a fleeting thought came to me that it would be best to step off and fall the ten plus floor to bring an end to all I was involved with. When that happened, I'd feel a shiver, rush inside, close the door and have a great wave of tiredness come over me. I'd crawl onto the couch and cover myself with my throw blanket and remain limp and groggy.

That fleeting thought seemed to be an alien voice that urged me to jump. It was not like I was thinking it but someone inside my mind who was suggesting it. It scared me to think that a persuasive voice could come out of the blue and secretly urge me to do things I had no intention of doing. That is what must happen to people who appear to be fine but suddenly kill themselves. It's not so much they consciously wanted to do it; they were compelled to do it by the voice in the mind.

More and more as I lived as Roger's toy I found that my nights could only pass if I'd ingested sleeping pills and that my days became tolerable with happy pills. Had I not had my projects to keep my mind occupied, if all I had to do was to sit around to be ready for Roger, I'm sure that alien voice would have altered the situation more dramatically. I was sure what was happening was unique to me because I so hated what I had become. Maybe it was as far back as then that I began to hate the person in the mirror. It's hard to believe it was that long ago.

I can see from this vantage point looking back that there were many thoughts that motivated me at the time I acted. I had to have been a little anxious thinking that Roger might be ready for a change. I probably did not understand myself that I may also have been ready for a change. It had not been a conscious recognition but subconsciously I was probably in a full rebellion at the idea of continuing to exist in the squalid mud of Roger's embrace.

There's no doubt that within each human there is different wiring. How it gets there is a wonder, but it was probably necessary to exist if the race was to survive in its formative days. Some people are rigid in their belief and stick to them through thick and thin; others go with the wind and adjust themselves to which ever is prevailing at the moment. I know this because for me what I was doing was repulsive yet there were so many women who seemed to do it without a second thought. There are people among us who are saints; and others who are bad to the bone. How then can the saint be singled out for praise or the evil person condemned if each is pre-wired to act a certain way?

There are many who can do what I was doing without a second thought. I saw them every time I went out socializing with Roger.

My actions to secure the comforts of life were tainted because Roger still stuck to his wife;

these others who had successfully used their womanly wares and wiles to convince their new squeeze to throw out the old and put on the new, as if life was really nothing more than a New Year's Eve party, were accepted without qualm. I was considered a live-in whore, they were, by the more euphemistic description, trophy wives. Trophies proudly paraded by those men who believe they were awarded to them because of their merit. Merit? Should a man be acclaimed for having abandoned a woman who bore his children and sacrificed during his early days of struggle for some spring time chick whose sole merit is her youth, looks and willingness?

I recognized that form mattered over substance. Suppose I had Roger drop his wife and marry me. The new form of our relationship would be approved by society; yet the substance of my action, destroying his intact family, merited no approval. There is no doubt that the wealthy decide what we accept or reject in society. What is good for them must be what is good for us so it is emulated when not enforced upon us.

During all this time as I was waiting for the proper time, I had continued to bruise my arms and sides with my diabolic machine so I looked like I had received beating in the past. I found no pleasure in doing this. It was painful but necessary.

The big event took place like this. Roger came over about five-thirty. We sat around and talked a bit. He told me he had to go back to the office by 7:30 for a meeting at 8:00 with some of his people who were opposing a group trying to unionize one of his plants. This wasn't exactly the night I was waiting for because I wanted him to go home to his wife, but I was primed and

206

figured it would be just as good. We could have our sex, he'd have to leave, and I would have the time to be set him up. He was having a glass of bourbon which he enjoyed after work, anticipating his hour or so of bed fun, when I got up and went into our room. I came back out with some rope I had purchased but kept it hidden behind my back.

"Rog. Remember a week or so ago, you were talking about doing things a little different?"

He looked up inquisitively. "What about, Dakota?"

"You know, to pick things up a bit, to have a little more excitement when we do it."

His interest quickly perked up when he figured out what I was talking about. "Yeah, yeah, I remember."

"I thought maybe this time we might try something different."

"What do you mean?"

"Voila!" I said bringing the ropes from around my back and holding them up. "Tonight is bondage night!"

He jumped out of the chair and rushed over to me with this greasy smile on his face. "You're kidding — I thought you didn't like this stuff — you never said — wow — that's great, that's really great."

"I was thinking," I said moving close to him and throwing my arms over his shoulders while still holding the ropes, "you tie me up today, just for a bit and we see how it is, and if we like it, I'll tie you up next."

He was already getting excited so I had to back off a little bit. I wanted the encounter to last for a while. I had to have certain things happen to insure the success of the plan. I wanted there to be rope burn marks around my wrists and ankles so I could allege that he tied me down while he beat me; I needed to have his DNA all over me both inside and out, and I needed to inflict some type of wound on him to show that I had tried to defend myself.

I convinced him that we should rehearse before we got into the actual happening by telling him that if I didn't like doing it, that way it could be a big back-off by me and I'd ruin the evening. I asked him to tie me up with my clothes on and let me be alone for a bit to see if I could get comfortable being bound to the bed. He tied me to the posts and went back to his bourbon. I spent the next few minutes pulling and twisting my wrists, raising bright red rope burns and actually a little blood. It was more difficult with my ankles because I couldn't twist them, but I was able to have some redness rise in the skin.

I called Roger back and had him untie me. I said I really like being tired up but I was thinking that it'd be better if we took it one step at a time and saw what it was like just with my ankles tied. I'd keep my arms free this time but next time we'd reverse it and keep my feet free, and if that worked out we'd then go for the total tied down.

He was so excited, I knew he'd go along with anything. He just wanted to get going as much as I wanted to stall. I knew I needed to keep my arms free because as I said, I was going to claw into his chest, shoulders and arms with my nails to show I had defended myself. I planned to blame my feet being tied for my actions scratching him by saying the heightened pleasure threw me out of control, as Roger believed happened with this bondage stuff, and also tell him that he'd might as well suffer with a little pain to start getting into the new way we were going to do this in the future.

Oh, and I should mention that as soon as Roger came in, I gave him one of those pills that made him last a little longer and heightened his pleasure. I needed to use that extra time and his total involvement with himself for the purpose of scratching him to bring out his blood and to get his skin scrapings under my finger nails. I would insist those scrapings be done when I got to the hospital.

I have to admit I did give Roger a great send off. I don't think he ever enjoyed himself as much with anyone as he did with me that night. I pulled out all stops to make it a most memorable time. I didn't want him to forget it. With my feet tied and the length of time we spent, I also got my ankles pretty rope-burned. He had scratches on his shoulders, chest, arms, and even a bite mark on his upper right arm that made him scream and almost screwed up the whole plan since I bit him harder than I intended and brought him back to momentary sanity but only for a few seconds until his passion took over again, but that was enough of a pause to throw a scare into me. I had managed to bring blood from some of the scratches and I made sure the blood got onto the sheets.

When we finished and the cold chill of everyday life pushed back into the room, he was a little angry at what I had done to him. I apologized for getting carried away and attributed it to the bondage. That calmed him for a moment until he went into the bathroom and saw the mess I had inflicted on his body. He came back into the room, "Look at me. I look like I was in a fight with an alley cat. What the hell did you do?" He stomped back into the bathroom.

The good thing was he was in a rush since he had to get to his office. He quickly cleaned up. I went out to the couch and examined my ankle and wrist wounds and was pleased at my state, especially when I saw I had bled from the ankles and knew that would be on the bed sheets. I tried not to do anything that would diminish the appearance of the wounds. Of course, I left the ropes still tied on the bed.

He came out dressed, but still in a sour mood. "You'll have to control yourself better, Dakota. You're too wild. Too violent."

"I thought you liked that."

"Not like what you do. I'll talk more about it with you. I've got to go now, but I'm telling you, I'm not that happy." I said to myself 'screw you!' I thought he was very happy during the activity but when the thrill was gone he's ready to turn on me.

I couldn't resist. I said, "Don't worry, Roger. It won't happen again."

He stopped, tossed one of his dirty looks at me, and then walked out the door. I had no time to lose. I first buttoned up the shirt I had been wearing and then tore it so that the buttons flew off. I took my bra and stretched it so the pins bent a little. I took my panties and put one foot on it and jerked them hard and they tore a bit at the elastic. I threw them on the floor.

I put on a pair of latex gloves like the doctors wear and started to assemble my devious device for inflicting wounds. The club – I fondly thought of as Mr. Paddy Whacker – I had shown to Roger a couple of week ago, letting him handle it. I told him I bought it to protect myself against an intruder into the place. After he

210

handled it a bit, swinging it in the air, pretending to defend himself against the intruder I spoke about, he put it down. I let it sit there until after he left and picked it up and put it away in such a way I'd preserve his fingerprints on it.

Quickly the machine was assembled and I started to beat my arms, with a couple of hits near my breast; I was not going to hit them because of the Dostoevsky story I read about how a judge hit his side and got cancer which convinced me any blow to my breast would be fatal, and on my ribs. I then turned it to my face until I had some blood trickling from it and I lay down on my pillow and turned my head into it, getting the blood on it. It was excruciatingly painful, especially the blows to my mouth when I could feel my teeth stabbing into my lips. I was afraid of breaking my teeth. When I thought I couldn't take anymore, I doubled up on the power of the blows by pushing Paddy Whacker deeper into the elastic, which made it come back with even more intense force.

I was losing my ability to function because the pain seemed to have been putting me into some type of shock so that I could stand it. I had really hurt myself and I knew I'd look a bloody mess to anyone who saw me. I left Paddy on the floor, disassembled the device, put shoes on it and put it in the closet. I took out my cell phone and pressed the speed dial number for Alison. She answered.

"Alison, it's me, he tried to kill me — I said no and he tied me down and beat me up — I think he's coming back to kill me — what should I do?

"Are you all right?"

211

"No — I think I've been unconscious — he beat me over and over and then raped me — he tied me to bed and raped me — it was horrid. Oh, Alison, what can I do — he's coming back to kill me."

I hung up. I called Jeannie and asked her to come and help me. I told her I was leaving the condo because I thought he would come back. I asked her to call Alison and gave her the number. Jeannie was in a total panic.

I put on a bath-robe and left the condo and went across the hall to the door of some people who I'd been friendly with over time. I banged on it. I heard someone approaching it so I stood back so the person looking through the scope thing in the door would see it was me. I knew people are very fearful about opening their doors. The door quickly swung open and the man with a stunned look in his face said, "Oh my God, what happened to you."

I said, "I was raped — call the police — let me in and lock the door —
He's coming back to kill me!"

He brought me in, closed the door and the die had been cast. I hoped I had done it in such a way that it would achieve the maximum of publicity so that Roger could not squelch it. I waited for the sound of the sirens and the rush in by the police. The man in the condo did the initial talking for me. I kept saying I was raped. I did not tell them by whom. I was being rushed to the hospital when Alison arrived on the scene with Jenny. I knew then I was in safe hands. She'd oversee everything. She insured that the evidence taken at the hospital was properly gathered and preserved. The DNA evidence from the hospital would show that Roger was the one who had penetrated me and the one whom I had scratched.

Alison steamed ahead making sure the incriminatory evidence from the condo was preserved. The search warrant would allow the cops to take photographs of the ropes used to tie me down, and of the torn or stretched clothing that I had worn strewed about the floor as if by a wild animal with the club lying next to them, and of the sheets showing the blood stains. Fingerprints taken from the club would show Roger's fingerprints, the sheets with the fresh blood from both Roger and me on them.

Alison was in charge. She'd make sure the police also took scrapings from under my fingernails. She was the one who identified for the police the person who had attacked me. She was the only one who could have done this because the name Roger Hunt made the detectives stop in fear of their jobs. The sergeant also had to talk to the lieutenant who spoke to the captain who called the chief. The chief rushed to the scene to talk to Alison along with a captain and two lieutenants.

After introductions, and Jenny told me this because she was present, the chief said to Alison, "You'll have to leave the scene."

Alison smiled and said, "I'm sorry chief, but this is my client's condominium and she gave me permission to be here."

"This is a crime scene. You'll have to vacate it."

"Not before you do your job and gather all the evidence."

"Listen. Ma'am, I don't know who you are but . . . "

"I'm Alison Huntingmen, chief, I'm sure you've seen me on Fox News and other local

213

channels – in fact, I'm a little surprised the local media hasn't arrived yet. I've already called them. I've also called the state police and they're on their way also."

The last thing the chief wanted was to take her on. He knew of her reputation. He had to consider his future and it was best not to clash with her. He turned to one of the lieutenants. "Have we gotten the evidence?"

"I think so chief. The guys from the photo lab have taken the photographs and the forensic guys have been all through the room."

He turned to Alison, "We've done what you wanted. So I suggest you leave."

"If you've gotten all the evidence, chief, then there's no necessity I leave, is there."

"It's up to you. Stay if you want."

"By the way chief, I don't think you've got all the evidence, there's a big piece still missing. Ah, here's Bob Kramer from Channel Five and Spencer Fields from the Globe. Come in gentlemen, I was just asking the chief why he's not gathering all the evidence in this case. He seems reluctant to do this. Perhaps you guys can find out what's going on."

"Look guys," the chief said, "I don't know what she's talking about, we've already gathered the evidence." He turned to his underlings and said "Isn't that so?" They all nodded indicated their agreement.

"I don't think so chief," Alison piped in. "The rapist, Roger Hunt, has not been arrested. I don't understand why not. I'm sure he'll have the evidence on his body which will support the victims claim."

"That so chief," Kramer asked. "You haven't arrested the suspect. Can I ask why?"

214

Spencer added, "Yes, chief, I'm sure our readers would like to know what's going on."

Jenny said that Alison really knew how to pull the right strings to get things done and to ensure they were done properly.

There's an old ditty that comes to my mind that goes, "Who takes care of the caretaker's daughter while the caretaker's busy taking care?"
Whenever I thought of it, I always thought of the daughter as being the police. I had this deep down belief that if someone is not watching the police, then they are apt to run amok.

That was why Alison was worth her weight in gold. She was the type of caretaker we all needed. Not only did she have the cojones to stand up to the cops and other official who might want to kowtow to Roger but she had the wherewithal to ensure that if they even thought of it everyone would know about it. Her initial job, with the help of the press — and by the way without the press to hold people accountable, which it seems more and more unwilling to do lately, we'd have no rights at all — was to ensure the cops did what they were supposed to do. If she didn't do it, Roger would have made sure that they did what he wanted them to do and no one would have heard of my case.

Roger was duly arrested and photographed, not only by the Quincy cops but by the state cops who tend to be less intimidated by power. Alison had contacted the Attorney General who assigned state police to oversee everything and they relieved the Quincy cops of all the evidence, to their great displeasure. Alison convinced the AG to do it because she had already documented Roger's ties to the local police department which made it impossible for

215

them to be objective in a case where he was the felon.

There were so many things that the local cops could do to make a case get messed up. They could lose evidence or photographs. Their record keeping system was structured so that this could easily happen. They could fail to do what they were supposed to do. They could drag things out or speed things up depending on their whim of the moment. They could not show up on the day of trial or show up without the evidence. Their tricks were endless. I heard once that in the middle of a trial a prosecutor sat stunned when he found out they had given the defense lawyer police reports the prosecutor did not have so that they could help out their friend who was on trial. There was no doubt in my mind that they needed a very good caretaker and I had found one.

After Roger was processed at the police station, the chief apologized to him for having been forced to take his picture and fingerprints. Roger's wrists never felt the cold steel handcuffs; his ears never heard the steel hitting the steel of a cell door being shut on him. His lawyers flocked to the police station and would have succeeded in preventing the cops from taking photographs of him if the state cops had not come on the scene.

A lot of people think of the state cops as some sort of goons because they seem to wear blinders doing their jobs, they brook no nonsense, they fail to tolerate fools and do it with an attitude that says, 'Come on, try me' as if they're itching to pull out their batons and play a tune on your head. But it is sometimes necessary for an orderly society to have these so called goons so that the people have a chance. In

216

Massachusetts the state cops despite their reputation for thuggish behavior have been corrupt that I heard. I can't imagine how difficult it must be for a victim to get justice in some places when going up against an influential person and no part of the establishment is free from taint.

I was at the Brigham and Women's hospital in Boston. Alison intervened to prevent them carting me off to the local hospital in Quincy to insure the rape testing was done by persons skilled in that area as they are at the Brigham. I was interviewed by both Quincy and State Police and forensic teams from both departments did what they were supposed to do. I looked like I had been hit by a train. My wrists and ankles were bloody and swollen and the photographs showing all of this came out well. There was no doubt in anyone's mind that I had been through a very bad beating.

I was in a lot of pain since I really overdid it to myself. I had bruised coming out all over my body. The doctors duly noted each one of them. The only thing that brought me any comfort was the thought of Roger who was for one of the first times in his life telling the total truth about something and no one believed him. That was the only thing that brought a smile to my face, and doing that when no one was around really hurt me.

The morning papers had the story as did the television news. The court house was wall-to-wall with reporters who were anxious to get photographs of Roger at his arrangement. They were to be disappointed. The prosecutor and the judge agreed that it was not necessary for Roger to appear. The case was continued for a month for a conference. Roger's power was already

217

being felt. To the press's inquiry of the DA whether it was usual for a person charged with a serious rape not to have to appear at his arraignment, the DA said he cannot comment on the matter because it was under investigation. I thought to myself, "They're investigating how they can make it go away."

I recall those days like they were yesterday. I was in the hospital about a week. When I got out I took a taxi to my condo. I rode up in the elevator, got out, and put my key in the door. It didn't open. The lock had been changed. I had been evicted.

Speaking of that, it's time I evict myself from this table and say good bye to Naria. I still have another life and I've got to get ready to go to the Lincoln Center today for a performance of Swan Lake by the American Ballet Company.

TUESDAY: AFTER LUNCH

I can't believe I haven't talked to you in two days, Naria. Looking back I see that's the longest period we haven't talked since I first started. When I think of sitting down with you I'm always mindful of an experience I had at one of those New York parties Tom and I used to throw. I met this man and after a few introductory remarks, he maneuvered me onto a couch where the two of us sat for over an hour during which time I didn't say a peep. As the hostess, I tried not to be rude, even though I should not have been cornered in my couch, and patiently listened to him as he told me boring story after boring story about himself that he believed quite interesting. Seriously, I swear, I had not uttered more than ten words to him during the whole hour or so I sat there.

I finally extricated myself from his grasp. The rest of the night as I engaged with one guest after the other I kept a wary eye on him as a river boat pilot looks out for snags on the river. I succeeded in getting through the night without being snared again. As the guests were leaving at four or so in the morning, oh to be young again and live in the days of hangovers, he came up to me and said, "I just want to tell you, you are the greatest conversationalist I have ever met. I don't think I enjoyed talking with anyone as much as I have talking to you tonight."

He left singing my praises. He thought I was great because I let him talk without interrupting him. To him, an ideal conversation is a monologue. I'm telling you this, Naria, because for the first time I have a sliver of an understanding of what he meant. Since I've been talking to you, I have to admit that you, Naria, are also a great conversationalist.

When I started with you today, I went back and reviewed some of the material I told you about last weekend. I was thinking as I did this how important it is to have the right attorney. The closer your attorney is to a junk yard dog, the better off you are. You know the old saw: "It's not the dog in the fight but the fight in the dog." That's what you want in your lawyer.

Alison had the fight, especially if it was well-watered with green and red: red rage and green money. The red inspired her; the green kept her inspiration and attention. There was no doubt in her mind that as much as she got great satisfaction from fighting for women and children who may be sexually abused, she still had to pay her own bills and keep up the style of living she'd become accustomed to. She was at her best when you made things good for her monetarily.

When I realized I had been locked out, I called Alison. I went for coffee and when I came back a locksmith handed me a key to get back into the condo. I heard later from Alison that she passed the word to Roger through his attorneys that the headline in the Boston Herald was going to be something along the line of: "Magnate Rapes Victim Again."

I heard later from others that Roger was out-of-his-mind mad about the whole matter. When he set his dogs loose, they started to think of how to hurt me. The first thing was to lock me out. They had no idea of how that would look in the media. Roger decided that his dogs needed a leash and put it on them himself. He ordered that nothing was to be done on this case unless he cleared it first.

I had no idea what a pain in the ass this case was going to become. I should have known it would be one but I didn't expect it to come from almost all sides. While I was in the hospital for a week or so after the attack, the detectives interviewed me over and over as did the DA's assistant who was going to handle the case, Nick Adams, and the victim witness people assigned to his office. I'd been telling so many people about how Roger attacked me that I was beginning to believe it myself.

Adams told me that Roger's attorneys wanted to interview me. I asked him if I had to be interviewed by them. He said it was up to me. So I said I didn't want to talk to them. All I wanted was to don the identity of Patricia Cofer in New York where I could climb onto my love seat, put my feet up, and get lost in a book.

After I got back into the condo, I called Alison to thank her for her help. I asked her if I could come to the office for a brief visit. She said she was busy but would put a few minutes aside for me whenever I got there.

She was keeping close watch over the case for me. I wanted to find out from her what was happening and what was expected of me so that I could plan my getaway. I got to say this. I was lucky because I could do this. I needed someone on my side who would take care of my interests. Alison was not only protecting me from Roger's attorneys and investigators, but she was also protecting me from the people who were supposed to be protecting me, the prosecutors and the cops.

Maybe it was just me because I was going up against Roger, but when I thought of the way the prosecutor Nick Adams kept questioning me I could almost believe he thought I had raped Roger, which I did in a sense but I shouldn't have been treated like I did. And as far as the cops were concerned, it seemed to me they had no problem at all with Roger's actions especially since I was a whore. It seemed in their minds that whores were supposed to be beaten up every once in a while.

Alison also got restraining orders keeping Roger and anyone on his behalf away from me. The last time I was with her when she visited me at the hospital she told me she planned to go to the DAs office to discuss the case with him. She greeted me with a warm smile when I came in, the smile we all give to the envelope that comes with money in it.

"How you doing, Dakota," she asked. "You look a lot better than when I last saw you."

She was right. Much of the damage I inflicted on myself had disappeared and with the right make-up I could hide the rest of it pretty well. "I'm feeling good, Alison, the nightmares seem to be less intense." I'd read somewhere that after such an attack as I pretended I suffered a woman would experience intense nightmares.

"That's good. Time is a good curative."

"I know you're busy but I was just wondering, you know, ah — can you tell me what happens next on the case? Did you talk to the DA?

"Yeah, I did. I told you before I'm pushing him to put it into the grand jury and to get an indictment. That's the usual way things are done. He won't commit to doing that but is talking about doing a probable cause hearing."

"Is that what is usually done?"

"Sometimes, it depends on the case, but in your type case it should not be necessary. It's pretty clear what happened."

"Why is he talking about — what did you say the name of that hearing is called?"

"A probable cause hearing"

"Why is he going to do one of those? Did he say? What does that mean — is that unusual?"

"Yes, and that's what got me worried. This type case should go directly to a grand jury. A probable cause case is a hearing before a judge who decides if Roger committed the rape – if he does he sends it to the grand jury – where there's no doubt as here, I don't understand why the DA isn't going to the grand jury right off the bat."

'You know he and Roger are social friends."

"Are you sure?"

"Of course, the DA's got a lot of money from Roger and he's been over the condo several times with him and out of the yacht too. Yes, they're good friends."

"I guess that explains it. He's doing Roger a favor."

"Is that right, can you do something about it?"

"I suppose I could try to get another prosecutor's office to take over the case but that'd only delay it a bit but it probably won't change the decision to go for a probable cause hearing. All the DAs cover for one another so none of them would do otherwise. No, I won't do that right now but I will let the DA know what I know about his relationship. That'll scare him a little and make him less likely to try to make the case against Roger go away."

"I thought we were relying on the media for that?"

"We are but the media's not going to be against a probable cause hearing because it will give it a good news day covering the hearing"

"Will I have to testify at that hearing?"

"You'll probably be the only witness."

"I don't understand why the DA would want to do this?"

"If the DA is trying to help out Roger what it does is gives Roger's lawyers an opportunity to question you before the real trial and they can use any contradictions to impeach you when you testify at that trial."

"Are you saying I'll have to testify twice?"

"Yes. If the DA has a probable cause hearing you'll have to testify there and again at trial."

"That's a downer. I thought I'd only have to testify once."

"Unfortunately for you, that's how it's going to work out."

"Is there any benefit to me in having a probable cause hearing?

"A little," Alison replied. "You'll have a chance to first testify in an easier type court room environment with no jury so you'll go through it once, that helps. Oh, yeah, I guess the other benefit is that if you die your testimony will be admissible at Roger's trial."

"I don't see it that way."

"What do you mean?"

"How's my dying a benefit to me."

"In a sense you're right. I don't suppose it'll make a difference to you then."

"But what did you mean? How can my testimony be used if I'm dead?"

"A defendant's had a right to cross-examine and confront the witness against him. If he is able to do it once, he can't complain if he doesn't get a second shot at the person if the person is dead or otherwise incapacitated from testifying."

"But how do I testify if I'm dead?"

"When you testify at the probable cause hearing they'll make a transcript, a recording, of your testimony. That will be read to the jury at the trial."

"It's hardly the same thing — you know as effective as me standing there and telling what happened — the jury doesn't see me."

"You're right – but the alternative is worse – no testimony at all."

"I see – it's something, I guess."

"Look at it this way; you'll be able to rest in peace knowing Roger will have to hear your testimony from beyond the grave."

"You know, I just thought of something I never even thought of this before. What's happens if Roger kills me before I testify?"

"You mean if you die?"

"No, if Roger kills me, or has me killed."

"If you die before any hearing there will be no case against Roger. You're the only witness to the rape."

"So if he kills me he wins?"

Alison seemed surprised by my statement. "You're not serious, are you?"

"Very! You don't know Roger. He's a thug in nice clothes. He wouldn't think twice of doing it."

I almost said, "If I'd realized that I probably wouldn't have pulled the stunt setting him up." But half way through the sentence I caught myself. I said, "If I'd realized that I wouldn't – you know – I wouldn't have gone to the police."

Alison didn't pick up on anything. She said, "You had no choice after what he did to you. He almost killed you."

"I know — but now I'm afraid he will." I replied, as the doubts about what I had done started to permeate my thinking. It was not so much that I regretted it; and not so much that my life may now be in danger, but more because I was so proud of my planning and thought myself quite clever. I saw that I never even considered this eventuality. I wondered how many other things there were that I did not take into account in making my plan.

That's not to say I wasn't becoming very concerned for my well being – that is my life. I was. For the first time I considered my mortality and how easily I could be killed. I didn't want to die. I wanted to live. I though of how easily Roger could get someone to arrange for my killing. I had to be double, no triple careful. I was decidedly uneasy. "Thank God I have New York," I thought.

Trying to keep my spirits up, Alison said, "Don't think like that. He wouldn't dare."

"He would. That's what Roger does. If he knows by killing me his case ends then I'm dead."

"I can assure you, Dakota, those things don't happen."

"Listen Alison, I've lived with Roger for a while now. I've seen how he operates. I've even heard him tell his lawyers to get rid of people and to do whatever it takes. He was talking to them about some people trying to organize some workers in one of his companies in Colombia – you know South America Colombia. A few days

226

later the lawyers said the problem had been resolved. I don't know what happened but I bet, if you check, you'll find some union organizers down there have disappeared or been killed. And that, Alison, was just about a tiny sliver of his empire. Look what I've done. I've struck at his whole empire – him."

"I'll see if I can get you some protection."

"That won't do me any good. For all I know the protection will be provided by Roger's thugs."

Uncharacteristically, my Rottweiler had lost her bark. This also unnerved me. My morning was turning into a visit to the dentist's office. I had to figure out what to do next myself since Alison seemed to be momentarily empty of suggestions or solutions. I knew Roger would kill me if he could. But if I could somehow forestall it, perhaps I could get through to the probable cause hearing and at least gain a little deterrence by my testimony. I said to Alison.

"Alison, let me see if I got this straight. It's not in Roger's interest to kill me after I testify at the probable cause hearing, is that right?"

"I'm telling you, Dakota, he won't try to kill you."

"Alison, answer my question – once I testify Roger can't make the case disappear by killing me, is that right?"

"Yes, your probable cause testimony can be used at trial."

"So what I can see, Roger has to kill me before the probable cause hearing if he's going to do it."

"From his point of view, that would be the best time."

I was really scared at this point. I couldn't walk away from what I had done because the DA could force me to testify and I'd already caused some damage to Roger's reputation with the news reports of the rape. I felt strongly that the only way I'd get some protection was to get my testimony on record. I had to buy time until that date. I figured if I gave Roger some hope I was backing down, then he might hold off on killing me. Maybe if it looked like he could buy me off he would prefer to that than wiping me out.

"Look, Alison, I want this to go away. I want you to see how much money Roger will pay to have me refuse to testify."

"I can't do that, Dakota. I won't be part to compromising your case like that. It's against everything I believe. Roger's a pervert. You can't just think of yourself. Think of all those other women and those little children in the porn videos who are depending on you."

"Alison, do you want me dead?"

She didn't answer.

I got up. "All right, fine. Don't help me but I'll get a lawyer who will. It's not that I don't appreciate what you've done for me, Alison, but for me this is a life or death situation."

I knew that lawyers were greedy. I learned this in part listening to Alison talk about other cases, some she'd been involved in where the victims decided not to testify, and others she knew about. She was particularly incensed by what happened in Michael Jackson's case and the Bryant case, whoever that was. They paid off their victims to shut up and the lawyers got a bundle of money for themselves. I always thought Alison's ire at these deals was because the money the lawyers had put in their pocket.

228

Now she was watching me planning to walk out and possibly put a great deal of money in another lawyer's pocket. She knew other lawyers would be stumbling over themselves to take my case. It is too much to expect anyone standing on the cusp of a big money day to forego it for the sake of principle. I expected she'd drop her principles like a hot potato not to have to live with the idea some other lawyer had filled his pockets with money that rightfully belonged to her.

"Wait a minute, Dakota. If that's what you want. That's what I'll do. But I'll tell you, I think you are making a mistake."

I thanked her and said I'd be in touch. I can't say I wasn't worried. Rather than taking the T home, I hopped in a taxi. I called Alison. "Alison, listen, I don't know how you do this but somehow get the word back to Roger that he'd better not kill me — you know tell him it'll look bad for him or his company or something like that if I all of a sudden I end up dead or disappear — you know what I mean."

She indicated she'd do what she could. I then thought to myself, "It won't look half as bad for them as it will for me if I'm dead." I'll tell you, I was really petrified at this time. How could I have ever thought I could take on Roger and come out alive? I was like a speck of dust to him and I could just imagine his sheer intense anger knowing what I had done to him and that there was no way out of my trap I set for him. I mean, no way but one which was killing me.

When I reached the condo, I pulled the curtains and adjusted the light timers so that it looked like I was living there. I activated the silent alarm system that was in the apartment by calling the alarm company and asking them to do this. It was part of every condo in the building but you had to agree to pay a monthly fee to make it operational. I'd never felt a need for it until now. When I came back, I knew I'd sleep better knowing I had that protection.

I then took the elevator down to the parking garage. I walked out through the back entrance of the building to where I could grab a taxi. I took the taxi to the North Quincy T stop. I took the T to Harvard Square. Got out of the station and took a cab back to the bus stop at South Station where I grabbed a bus to New York. I had made arrangements with Alison that I'd stay in touch with her by calling her.

I felt please with myself that I had prepared for living a new life in New York. I never thought I'd need the place as a matter of life and death but it sure felt like that then. When I got to my New York place I breathed a sigh of relief. I knew I was safe for the present.

I decided to keep in touch of what was happening in the Boston area by going on the internet at a public wireless place and read the Boston Globe and Herald and the Patriot Ledger out of Quincy. These had been the newspapers that covered the story of Roger raping me with front page coverage and editorials questioning him remaining as CEO of Hunt Enterprises. There was a story in the Globe of a planned emergency board of directors meeting to consider suspending him.

The morning of the third day after I was in New York, I went to Starbucks. I had bought an Apple iPad which was easy to carry and easy to operate in getting on the net and reading the news. I logged onto the Herald and read on the fifth page of its newspaper the following headline: *Rape Victim's Condo Violated.* The article read: *"Two men were arrested inside the condominium in Quincy last night and charged with burglary. The men identified as Patrick O'Byrne and Kevin Dwyer were discovered by Quincy police inside the condominium where it is alleged that CEO Roger Hunt had recently violently raped a young woman. Detective Chargers of the Quincy police said "Not only was a woman violated in the condo but now the condo itself has been violated. The men were held without bail at the Quincy police station and will be arraigned in the District Court in the morning."*

When I read that I was beside myself. I left the Starbucks and went back to my apartment. What did it mean, I wondered, that two men had broken into my condo? Most importantly, I wanted to know who they were. I was sorely tempted to reach out for Alison or someone else in the area to find out more, but because it was so paramount in my mind to keep my New York location protected, I didn't do it. I knew that later that day there be a more complete report on the matter in the Patriot Ledger. I tried to read a book that morning to get my mind off it. It was impossible. I set out for Central Park and walked around the reservoir again and again to calm down and help the time go past.

That afternoon I went back to Starbucks and again got on line. I went to the Patriot Ledger web site. I don't have a copy of the story but I read it over and over and it went something like this:

"It was a little over two weeks ago that it was alleged that a woman was viciously raped and beaten by the CEO of Hunt Industries, Roger Hunt, in a condominium at Marina Bay. Last night when the Quincy Police responded to a

silent alarm at that location they found exiting the condominium two men, Patrick O'Byrne and Kevin Dwyer. These men were arraigned in the Quincy Court this morning and were held in twenty-five thousand dollars cash bail. Assistant District Attorney, Timothy Spillaine, asked that the men be held without bail pending their proper identification. The attorneys for the defendants, Alison Hunting and Julie Oterini argued that they be released on their own personal recognizance suggesting there was no reason to question their identities. Judge Eliot Sluzman said he'd normally grant the defendants request but since the prosecutor questioned their identification he set the cash bail as noted and continued the case for a week when he'd review the bail.

Both men were identified by their Irish passports that showed they had arrived in the country two days prior to their arrest. According to Quincy police both remained silent except to give their names and home addresses which were in Dublin. Neither could provide any address here in America which raised suspicions. Assistant District Attorney Spillane suggested to the court that some suspect the men may not be Irish as they spoke with Middle Eastern accents. Judge Sluzman said he supposed there were people with Irish passports who spoke with a brogue, without a brogue, and with accents from many areas. He was not going to hold someone without bail based on that assertion alone but he would, as indicated, put a bail on them sufficient to hold them. He said at the end of the week he would reduce the bail to personal if the prosecutors did not come up with more information. It is not known if the attorneys for the defendants will appeal the bail."

I didn't know what to really think after reading that. One of the great difficulties I had, and I still have, is that I had no one to bounce this problem off of. I had to figure it out by myself. Even though earlier I had great confidence in my ability to do this, when I realized that I never considered that my plan to destroy Roger may end up with him planning to do the same to me, I had lost a lot of my cockiness.

Obviously two things really bothered me. The first was that my attorney, Alison Hunting represented one of the men. The other was that two days after coming to the country these men are in my condominium. I knew that there were millions of condominiums they could choose from so why are they in mine so soon after coming here. Did they come here to go to mine? That was a scary thought.

Aside from what to think, I was really frightened. If I had been at the condo, and I probably would have been if I did not have this New York hideout, I'd probably be dead. This all reinforced in me the awareness that I would only be safe in New York if I made sure I made no more missteps. I could do nothing with the people back in the Boston area that would indicate I was in New York. That meant I could not call back to the Boston area from New York City on my cell phone because that could be traced back to there. I had to assume that Google phone could also be traced back to a specific geographical zone. I was certain now that if Roger brought two people in with Irish passports to kill me, he had the ability and determination to track down the location from where I made a cell call. To stay safe, I assumed that there were people who had immediate information to the location of any cell tower where my calls originated. That meant I had to go away from New York to make my calls.

To calm my nerves and protect my hideaway, I flew out to San Francisco where I planned to stay for a week or so. When I got there, I called back to Alison knowing when they got the information on my phone they'd see I was calling from the West Coast. The first words out of her mouth were: "Where've you been?"

I responded, "I told you I'd call you to keep in touch."

"I know you did but I have to see you. Can you come to my office? I have to see you!"

"What about?"

"It's best we don't discuss it over the telephone."

"I can't come there for a few days. I'm out of town."

"Where are you?"

I changed the subject, "Has anything happened while I was gone?"

"I've got to talk with you in person."

"I'm not close to Boston, Alison. Can you tell me whether you talked to Roger's people – are they willing to deal?"

"That's what I want to talk to you about and I can't do it over the telephone – can you make arrangements to see me."

"Fine, I'll make arrangements but what about the DA? Did you talk with him? Is there still going to be a probably cause hearing?"

"I'll tell you about that when I see you."

"Why can't you talk about that over the telephone?"

"Look, Dakota! I don't see any sense in giving it to you piecemeal. It's all part of one big picture. You know that. It all has to come together in one neat package. Do you understand?"

"Frankly, Alison, no. You're not telling me anything."

"I'm doing what is best for you, Dakota. That's what you wanted me to do – now what is best is that you come and see me."

"So there's nothing that happened that you feel you should tell me about? Nothing has changed of any importance that I should know. I mean – look Alison, I told you Roger's out to kill me and I'm out here sort of hiding – has anything happened that I should be aware of. You know what I mean?"

"Nothing, Dakota, nothing at all. Look if you don't want to come here, let's set up a place to meet. I'll come to you, that's more than fair."

"Sure, Alison. Let me get back to you."

That was about how the call went. All Alison wanted to do was to locate me. She told me nothing, not even about the break into my condo. That scared me. She knew Roger was out to kill me. That should have been the first words out of her mouth. I was convinced she had gone over to the enemy. I was cut off from everyone. Then I thought of Nick Adams, the assistant DA who was handling the case. I'd call him. He didn't seem to be the type that Roger could reach, but I didn't know anything anymore. It was not too long ago I believed Alison was my champion through thick and thin but now I wondered whether she was part of the team plotting my demise.

I called Adams through the main number for the DA's office. It was all I had. It took a while to get through to him and I had to say my name over and over again to different voices who asked who was calling. I was thinking of hanging up, and probably would have if I had another choice, when Adams came on the telephone.

"Hello?"

"Mr. Nick Adams."

"Right here."

"Mr. Adams, this is . . . . "

"Is this Dakota?

"Yes."

"Dakota, I'm glad you called. I've been trying to reach out for you."

"Mr. Adams, before we go on and in case I forget, can you give me a number I can reach you at without going through a hundred people?"

"Sure, Dakota." He gave me his private office number and his cell. I didn't know what to make of his quick willingness to do this.

"Use those numbers to stay in touch with me, how about you, can you give me your numbers?"

"No, I'm moving about so it's best I call you."

"Have it your way but you've got to stay in touch, as I said I've been trying to reach you for a couple of days now.

"Did you call my lawyer, Alison Hunting?"

"I didn't think she represented you."

"Why do you say that?"

"When I first wanted to reach out to you, I called her as she had asked me. She told me she no longer represented you and did not know who was doing it. I assumed that you let her go and got someone else. Did you?"

"No, not yet – can I deal directly with you if I don't."

"Absolutely!"

"So why were you looking for me?"

"I want to sit down with you and go over the case before the probable cause hearing."

"I thought it was going to the grand jury?"

"I did too but my boss told me he wanted a probable cause hearing done so that's what I've got to do."

"Did he tell you why?"

"No. You don't understand, Dakota. He's the boss. He doesn't have to explain things to me. It's his call."

"Can you be honest with me?"

"I'll try."

"Is it unusual in a case like mine to have a probable cause hearing?"

"Honestly, yes, but don't read too much into it. Look Dakota, don't start looking behind what's happening. It's unusual but fully consistent with the way the system operates. And don't, please, think for any minute that I'm personally not one-hundred percent behind you. You've got to trust me if we're going to be successful."

"Mr. Adams, can I ask you something?"

"Absolutely!"

I thought Mr. Adams liked his 'absolutelys." I asked him the question that was for me was the only way I could test his commitment to me. "Has anything happened to my case that I should be aware of since we last talked."

"Yes, we've got some of the forensic reports back which back up your story. That's good news. The people who lived next to you in the condo also back you up. Other than that – you know, the case is coming along as it should."

"Nothing else."

"No, and as I said, we just have to go over your testimony again before the probable cause hearing."

"When's the hearing?"

"The tenth of next month, it's a Wednesday."

"Is that a definite date?"

"Absolutely!"

"Can it be continued to another time?"

"Unlikely!"

"I've heard these cases are always continued."

"Not yours, Dakota. You've put Mr. Big on the hot seat and he wants to get off as soon as he can. Roger Hunt's attorneys are pushing for this date and have told me they will oppose any continuances. They've even filed a motion for the assignment of a special judge to hear it. I don't think it'll be continued. That's why I need to talk to you."

"What happens if I don't show up?"

"What makes you say that?"

"I'm just wondering."

"You have to show up. I'll have to subpoena you. I'm not going to let you walk away from this, Dakota. After what he did to you, I'll have you held as a material witness to make sure you show up."

"But suppose you can't find me and I don't show up on the tenth."

"The case against Roger Hunt will be dismissed. But I can still bring you in to the grand jury and get an indictment."

"Suppose your boss won't let you?"

"Why would he do that?"

"He's a friend of Roger Hunt. I've been with him when he's been with Roger. I don't think he wants to do this."

238

"Let me tell you Dakota, you're wrong. He's not trying this case. I am. I've never met Mr. Hunt. I can assure you. this case will be tried like any other case."

"I wish I could believe you Mr. Adams but I don't. That's why I might not show up."

"Then I'm going to have to bring you in."

"Don't waste your time, you can't find me."

"Look, Dakota, I know you must have your reasons for wanting Roger Hunt to get away with raping you but you do have an obligation to the people . . ."

"An obligation to what, Mr. Adams? To be killed by Roger! I don't think so!"

"What are you talking about? Has he threatened you?"

"Hasn't he?"

"What do you mean?"

"What is it you're hiding from me?"

"I don't understand, I'm not hiding – oh, I see. You've heard about the break-in to your condo, is that it?"

"Why didn't you tell me about it?"

"I didn't think it had anything to do with you, personally. It was a couple of guys committing a break-in, that's all."

"Of all the condos in the world, why did they choose mine?"

"How do I know? Why do any burglars choose any house? I wish we knew that, Dakota. Burglaries happen all the time. We don't attribute anything special to one over another."

"Maybe you should."

"Tell me why – in your case it is different."

"Come on Mr. Adams – if you . . ."

"Call me Nick; it may help to break the ice between us."

"All right, Nick – have you looked into the break at all?"

"No – it's being handled by Timmy Spillane in the District Court. He's fully capable of handling it."

"So you don't think it impacts my case at all."

"I haven't to this point."

"You don't find it suspicious that two guys fly into the United States from Ireland and of all things decide to break into my apartment. These are not your normal burglary guys – they came here for a purpose. From what I read they didn't even have U.S. addresses and you weren't sure of their identities. Did you find out who they are?

"I can't answer that, Dakota. I haven't given a second thought to the case."

"Can you do that for me? See if you can find out who they are and why they went to my condo or anything you can about them. I'd sure rest easier if I knew more about them."

"I'll get right on it. Call me back in an hour or so and I'll ease your fears."

I felt much better after that. I initially thought he had a sinister purpose in not telling me about the break-in to my condo but realized that for him it was just another break-in that had no bearing on my case. I wasn't totally at ease because I could see he did not appreciate the threat Roger presented to me. But at least I had a feeling that Roger could not buy him off.

I did call him back but right now I'm tired, Naria so I'll tell you what happens when I see you again.

WEDNESDAY MORNING: BACK FROM A WALK

Here I am back again as promised. Too bad you can't go out and enjoy the weather. Today is just another beautiful day outside. Well Naria, looking back I see that I told you I'd tell you what happened when I called DA Adams back.

Nick, I'll call him Nick since that's what I began to call him after the first call, answered the phone. He told me about the men who broke into my condo. Both had put up bail and were let out of jail; their passports were forgeries; and no one knew who the men were or where they were although there was a chance they could find out because they did have their fingerprints. Everyone agreed they were not Irish. Neither of their lawyers could give any assistance as to their whereabouts even though they were instrumental in posting the bail.

I think that was the last thing I wanted to hear. Two guys had flown into the U.S. with fake passports and of all the things they could have done, they decided to break into my apartment. Even I knew that their visit to my condo was not for other than very sinister purposes.

I'll try to remember the conversation I had with Nick after he told me that.

I said, "What does that tell you?"

"That there is something suspicious about what happened."

"Suspicious, Nick? It's as plain as the walls around you. These were hired assassins. Why were they breaking into my condo? It wasn't to steal anything money. They had enough money behind them to hire two big time

241

lawyers and to put up twenty-five thousand dollars bail each. So what was it Nick. It wasn't to get a good night sleep since they could afford to sleep anywhere. There's only one explanation, they wanted to see me. Isn't it nice that these unknown men came all the way across the ocean with fake passports just to pay a visit to me? Now tell me Nick, who has the type of money to pay for something like this and who would benefit greatly from it. Or, are you afraid to face it."

Funny, when I said that the chill I felt when I first heard this was heightened. Was it that no one seemed to be putting two and two together or was it everyone was in on the plot? I didn't know what was happening. I began to realize how insignificant I was in the run of things especially when weighed against a bag of gold. Roger with his skillions of dollars was like the United States Government, which could kill anyone at anytime it wished. The United States had its War on Terror; Roger his war on Dakota. I thought to myself I wouldn't be surprised if he didn't have access to CIA drones that could follow me from the skies and kill me. The headline would read: "Accidental Drone Firing" The story would be about this poor woman who was killed while walking in Central Park when a drone encountered an unusual electronic disturbance field which caused one of its missiles to accidentally fire. The article would note that the Government hired the security branch of Hunt Enterprises to investigate the unfortunate malfunction.

I think I did get the seriousness of my position across to Nick.

He said, "I'm beginning to understand you, Dakota. I can't deny you make sense when I look at this from your perspective. It's just, how do I say it, it's just we can understand how a man like Roger Hunt can succumb to passion and carry out a rape but we find it extremely difficult to believe that a man in his position would involve himself in a calculated murder. We don't seem to want to let our thoughts go in that direction for all it implies. We've look upon Roger Hunt as a man who has everything in the world; we've never considered to what extent he will go to hold on to it."

He went on for a few more sentences in the same vein then he asked, "I think I'm going to have to line up some protection for you."

I replied, "Nick. I don't want that. All I want is for you to be on my side. All I want is for you to understand Roger Hunt is out to kill me and he can do it in such a way it'll never be traced back to him. Understand that and you'll understand why things have to be done my way. I'm truly fighting for my life. If you don't want my death to be on your hands here is what you have to do. Go to court on the 10th prepared to go forward. Don't ever tell anyone you've talked to me. If I'm alive, I'll show up. Just be prepared to try it on that day. It's the only way I can be sure I'm not killed. Do that for me, Nick. Oh, and have some extra police you trust in the court that day in case they want to take me out there. Remember, Roger does not want me to testify."

He seemed to understand. I only hoped he did. I'd not be talking to him again until the 10th because after I returned to New York, I did not plan to use my cell phone again. I'd use CC's which meant I'd not be in contact with anyone from Boston.

I was tired after talking to Nick, but I figured he was on my side which was a relief. I

243

lay down and shut my eyes for a bit since I still had some more calls to make. I wanted to be sure I was not making any mistakes in my calculations. As I told you, I was less sure of myself now.

When I called Alison back, my paranoia increased as well as my belief that she was working with Roger in tracking me down. I wasn't sure but I did not think I mentioned to her that I was in California when I last talked with her. We had hardly exchanged greetings when I recall the conversation went like: "I have to get together with you, Dakota. It's very important. I'll fly out to California to meet with you."

I wanted to ask, "How did you know I was in California?" I didn't because I knew this would make her realize I knew her game. I played Suzy the Sap and went along with her.

"Sure that'd be great."

"All right, fine. I'll make the arrangements."

"Look I'm at the Mark Hopkins – when you arrive here give your name and they'll tell you what room I'm in since I'm moving to a lower floor. When do you think you'll be here?"

"I don't know, I'll have to make arrangements."

"Well let me know. Send me a message what flight you'll be on so I'll make sure I'm at the hotel when you get in. I'm not going to sit around my hotel all day waiting for you, you know. There's a lot to do out here."

When I hung up I picked up the telephone again and called down to the lobby. I asked them what was their procedure was when someone came in and asked for my room number. They said they would not give it out without my

244

permission but would ring my room. I asked them if rather than doing that, if they'd call my cell number since I was planning to go to another room and then to lunch. They took down my number.

I quickly packed up my stuff and put on one of my disguises and left my room. I went down to through the lobby of the hotel feeling comfortable in my disguise but worried; irrationally I think now, that Roger would have his people already moving in on me. I remained in that state for a while until I caught myself and calmed down. I convinced myself there was no way he could get people to the hotel that quickly.

I took a taxi to the airport. There, I suddenly decided to purchase a plane ticket to Boston. The plane was not going to leave for another four hours which was good because it game me time to call others and to have the people think I was still in San Francisco.

I called Jenny through her main office number. I assumed that any number I dialed would be known to Roger. I didn't know whether all my calls were being recorded. I could see Roger having the cell phone company working for him but I hoped the NSA was not. By calling her main number, no one would know who I was talking to unless the line was wiretapped.

I asked her what was going on. She asked me if I were all right and immediately told me that my condo had been broken into and that the two men were arrested. I asked her what she thought of it. She said she didn't want to scare me but she thought they were after me and were probably sent there by Roger. Jenny who knew nothing about law or police work came up with that conclusion and none of the cops seemed to be able to do it.

I told her I was scared. I said that I believed Roger wanted to kill me. I said I was on the West Coast. She said I should go to the police. I told her Roger has long tentacles and can get me anywhere so I had to keep moving around. I asked her if she would put me up if I showed up at her house unannounced some night. She said she would. I said: "I hope you won't be too uncomfortable with me being around you and Tom."

"Tommy!" She said. "Don't make me laugh."

"What do you mean?"

"You want to know — good, I've been wanting to tell you this since we had our little set-to — I know it didn't look like it to you but Tommy and I weren't lovers. I couldn't explain it to you — you made me agree not to talk about it — remember. There was a little infatuation by me early on with Tommy but mostly it was innocent shit — early on he came on to me pretty good and we might have slept together twice — but that was it — I stopped when I caught myself — after that we went out but only as friends, no physical contact except holding hands or stuff like that — no sex stuff. You know just a couple of times early on but to tell you the truth I liked Tommy as friend — not in bed. You thought Tommy lived with me. He never did. I wouldn't let him — he stayed at his uncle's in Quincy, which he hated — he kept trying to move in with me, which I wouldn't have — when you saw us at the brunch, we were pretty much washed up and even our friendship was on the rocks — I was getting real tired of him — that's why I ran out of the room when I saw you — I was horrified to think of what you thought of me and at the time it was not true — if I'd been in love with him and was sleeping

246

with him you should have known that I wouldn't have run but would have stuck it in your face, you know me."

To say I never expected this was an understatement. To say I had great difficulty believing a word she said was not. While she spun such a fairy tale at me I was questioning even more how I was seeing things. I had missed completely the idea that Roger would try to kill me. Did I miss that my best friend would lie to me about undermining me? Why did I tell her I didn't want to talk about it? What a fool I was. I needed to look her in the face to discuss this, then I could tell if she was lying or not.

She went on, "And when you saw that picture on Facebook of me and Tommy – did you notice it was the only one taken at that party and all the other parties I had lots of photographs – I had taken all those down. Tommy must have put that back up without me knowing – you don't think I'd have made you my friend and given you access to my page if I'd known I had a picture of me and Tommy there, do you?"

She was trying hard to convince me. I think I said she was shrewd and calculated every move. I should have realized she knows every picture in her Facebook and who is in each one.

"But that's neither here nor there," she added. "It's something I wanted to get out. You gave me the chance when you asked if your coming here would interfere with me and Tommy. Tommy and I had sex twice, if that, because the second time I think I stopped it. I was not responsible for Tommy and you parting. Tommy was, or you were. I don't know what went on in your life. I do know Tommy was running around with a half of dozen women, it wasn't my bed he was looking for work from. He

247

just had no desire to look for work. Anyway, I have nothing to do with him anymore although he called me a few days ago. Are you sitting down?"

I had no idea what to expect. She's now asking me if I'm sitting down when I was about prostrate on the floor with all she had been throwing at me. I told her I was.

"Well Tommy calls me and tells me he's got a job and a nice place to live. The apartment goes with the job. It's over where you used to have your condo. Pretty good deal for your ex."

"I can't believe it. He finally got off his ass and found one."

"Oh, it's not like that. It found him. Hunt Enterprises reached out for him and gave it to him. He's involved in their internal security. He's working for Roger and like you, living in one of his places."

She was right. It was good I was sitting down.

"Jenny, you'll be next."

"Come on Dakota – you know me – I'd kill myself before I ever had anything to do with that guy after what he did to you."

"Thanks Jenny."

"Oh, got to get back to work, Dakota, but to answer your question, my door is always open to you."

"Thanks, hey, ah Jenny – you don't have to have a number for Tom, do you, that's if he has a phone?

"They also gave him a cell phone. Hang on, I'll get it."

I got the number and hung up thinking, "Wow Tom's really a bastard. Not only was he trying to break up our marriage and making me think I was at fault, he was screwing with Jenny probably much more than I thought and with others."

It was a short time after that I received a text message from Alison. "Must cancel plans for a day or 2. Will keep U posted." I pretty much expected that as I did the call I received from Michael at Mark Hopkins just before I was scheduled to board the flight. "There are two delivery men at the desk who have a package for you. They say it is necessary for them to personally deliver the package to you and to witness your signature. Should I let them up?"

"Have you given them my room number?"

"No, ma'am."

"Michael – don't give them my number under any circumstance. Tell them I'm busy and I'd appreciate it if they could come back tomorrow."

He told me he would do that. Amazingly, it took Roger only about four to six hours to put people into my hotel. It was like he had people all over the country standing by to do his bidding.

I made one last call before getting on the plane. It was to Tom. When he answered his cell, I said, "Hey, Tom, it's Dakota. Remember me?"

"Hi Kota, how you doing?"

"Pretty good Tom, and you?"

"Good, Kota."

"Jenny tells me you're working."

"Yeah. I got a job at your old place."

"What you doing?"

"Some sort of security stuff, you know like watching to make sure people aren't walking off with stuff – it's just temporary – I'm going into one of their financial division soon handling some accounts."

249

"Tom, I understand you got some new digs."

"Yeah, I do Kota – pretty nice too – at the Marina in Quincy – you know where that is don't you?"

"Yeah, Tom, I do. I have a place over there myself."

"You do? I didn't know that, Kota."

"You should have, I'm sure I mentioned it to you."

"Maybe, Kota, I don't know, you know, maybe you did but it didn't register."

"Hey, listen Tom, any chance I can bunk in with you sometime if I have to?"

"No questions asked and nothing demanded, Kota, would love to have you. But you said you had your own place here."

"I heard something happened there so it's sort of creepy right now."

"I hear you."

"Thanks, Tom. I'll be in touch."

Why did I call Tom, you're probably wondering. Well, as I told you earlier, after I took care of Roger I planned to do in Tom. I didn't know how exactly. Early on I had an idea how to get Roger. But I figured how I could best get back at Tom would eventually come to me. So as you've heard me say Naria, it's best not to show your hand before you play it. Or, as someone else said in a different context, "Keep your friends close but your enemies closer."

On the flight I was able to get some sleep, but not much. I wasn't too bothered by that because with a little luck I hoped to be back in my New York hideaway later in the day. I could rest as much as I wanted then. I probably would have had more sleep if I didn't keep thinking of the conversation I had with Jenny. My mind was in turmoil because of that call.

I couldn't figure out what that was all about. Why when I'm calling her from the West Coast does she suddenly go on with that long explanation? Yeah, I told her early on I didn't want to talk about it but what about all those other times we were together before I pulled my big act. If she'd unloaded that story on me earlier it would have made it a lot easier to get by her involvement with Tom if that's all it was. Why did she let it linger in my mind that Tom had spent all his time with her if he didn't?

I thought over what she said. It was what I wanted to hear, you know, that there really wasn't anything more than a couple of slip ups on her part and that it was other women who led Tom astray and not her. That would make reconciliation with her easy – I could understand a night or two of bad judgment. I tried to compare what she said with what I knew myself, not what I had guessed had happened.

She said when I saw them at the brunch they were pretty much washed up. She didn't know I had seen them the week before. They were far from washed up at that point. They were practically making out in the room with all their touches and kissing. If that was washed up, what the hell would they have been doing if they weren't, rolling around on the buffet table?

Even the second time they came in arm in arm like love birds as if they had just come down from a love nest in the hotel. What else did she say, I tried to recall. Yes, the Facebook remark. How does that make sense? How would Tom have access to her Facebook to put up that picture on her Facebook if he had been living at his uncle's in Quincy and never lived with her? I didn't know for sure but didn't the person who owned the Facebook page control what could be put on it?

I began to believe Jenny had just spun a big lie to me. When she said if she'd been in love with him she'd have stayed at the table and stuck it in my face, there's no way she'd have done that. Jenny wasn't an in your face type, I knew that about her. If on the other hand they had been washed up, she would have stayed at the table and not run. She ran because she was embarrassed.

Maybe, I thought, she deliberately put the Facebook picture up of her and Tom. She didn't have to make me her friend. When she did she must have known, even if her involvement in Tom was only on two occasions, it would have been best not to disclose it. I told you how Jenny was shrewd and knew what she was doing at all times. She'd have never let me accidentally discover the picture.

But what's her game now? Why is she lying to me about her past involvement with Tom, if she is? Why now? But what did she gain about deliberately letting me know about her and Tom on Facebook, if she did.

You can understand why I got little sleep. I had great trust in Jenny before we talked but now I was confused. Had Roger also reached out to her? It certainly would be in his interest to do so. But Jenny said she hated him and she made tons of money working for Putnam. Nothing made sense except thinking all this meant they'd be no sleep on the plane trip.

I got to a downtown Boston Starbuck's off School Street about 7:15. I went into it, got my morning coffee and sat at the counter with the iPad I was carrying. I went on to Google voice

252

and sent a text message to Alison: "If I call to your office, what time will you be in?" A few minutes later she replied, "Anytime after 8."

I left Starbuck's after finishing my coffee. I assumed none of Roger's dogs would be running around the streets of Boston looking for me having left my scent in San Francisco. I planned to hold the room out there a couple of more days before calling them and canceling it. For the moment I assumed that Boston would be fine since I could not use a disguise going in to see Alison.

I arrived there about 8:10 or so. Knowing how they operated, I knew that Charlie, the receptionist, would not be in. I could walk right in on Alison which I did.

She was bent over the desk and was lifting a coffee up to her mouth when I entered. She froze in that position for a second and then put the cup down. I notice her hand was shaking as she did.

In the bubbliest voice I could put on I chimed, "Well here you are, Alison, just as you said."

The normal voluble and loud legal bark meister had lost her pep as well as her voice. I pulled up the chair I usually sat in.

"So, Alison. I understand you no longer represent me. In fact, you now represent Roger Hunt and have become a spy for him directing his hit men toward me. Isn't there something in the legal ethics, you lawyers do have some ethics, I believe, that say that's a no – no?"

She still didn't know what to say. I had fired a full salvo at her, and not a puff came back at me.

I waited as she stared dumbfounded at me. "So what's going on? What is it you want to tell me?"

"You've got it all wrong," she said with an utter lack of conviction.

"Exactly what have I got wrong?"

"What I'm doing I have a full legal right to do," she said recovering herself somewhat and reaching in her bag of legal bullshit to find something to start pulling herself off the floor and fling at me. "I've had a relationship with you. When I decided to terminated it which is my right I did my best to notify you. I was unable to do that and that's all I'm required to do."

"Fine, you can say that but don't think for one second I don't know what you really did. But you said you had something to tell me and wanted to meet with me, was that it?"

"I wanted to explain to you Dakota, for your sake, and this was done at your suggestion. You wanted to negotiate with Roger Hunt a deal to see if he was willing to pay you off for what he says is he never did and you would in turn ask the charges against him be dropped. I decided that it would be best that I not represent you in that endeavor. When I decided that, I tried to notify you to tell you that was my decision. You may remember I advised against you doing it."

She paused to study me to see my reaction. Seeing none she continued, "But I also decided that because of my prior relationship with you, I may be able to work with you in coming up with a resolution of the matter. I therefore went to Roger Hunt and proposed that he retain me to represent him in his dealings with you which he has done. I wanted to meet you to tell you that I no longer represented you but I represent Roger Hunt. I think because I know the issue so well, I can put together a deal that will satisfy both of you."

"Sounds noble, Alison."

"What did you say?"

"What you just said really moves me – skipping the legalese what you said is Roger is paying you work a deal with me – and you want me to accept you are doing it in my best interest, is that it."

"That's a fair summary, yes."

"Do you always do that?"

"What?"

"Work against your master."

"I'm not working against him if I get the deal that is in his interest, and in your interest."

"Can you do that?" I inquired.

"Do what?"

"Serve two masters."

"I can do my best."

"Isn't there something wrong with that?"

"No, not if both sides know who I'm representing and there is no confusion there."

"But what you did in our case, Alison, is you have taken me into your confidence, learned my desires and fears, and then changed sides to use what you've learned from me against me."

"Believe me, nothing you said to me will be learned by Roger nor will it be taken into consideration in my dealings with you."

"You're going to erase things for your mind?"

"No, but I'm going to act as if I never heard them."

"All right, Alison, what are you offering?"

"I've got these papers here that I want you to sign. I'll let you look at them. If there are any questions, I'll be glad to explain."

"Before I look at them, can I ask you a question?"

"Of course."

"Who were the two guys who broke into my condominium?"

"I wish I knew. I only knew them by the names they gave the authorities. Nothing more."

"Did you have any conversations with them?"

"You know I can't disclose those."

"Who paid you to represent them?"

"I'm not at liberty to disclose that."

"You put up the money for their bail; where did you get it from?"

"That also comes in the attorney-client privilege."

"Can you tell me what they were doing in my condominium?"

"I didn't discuss that with them and if I did . . . ."

"I know, the attorney client privilege prevents you. But you know, Alison that I know why they were there. You know I know who paid them to go there. You know that Roger sent them to kill me. And let's keep one thing straight, Alison. I didn't ask you to go to Roger to make a deal just for money, I asked you to make sure he didn't kill me. Let me ask you this, you told Roger where I was staying in San Francisco, didn't you."

"You got it all wrong Dakota."

"Did you tell Roger that I was in San Francisco?"

"Of course, he was interested in the status of our negotiations so I told him I'd been able to speak to you."

"You know, of course, that he sent a couple of thugs over to my hotel to make a visit to me, didn't you."

"I knew no such thing."

"Are you telling me, Alison, all this stuff you have done sits fine with you – you know the reason I asked you to negotiate with Roger was because I feared for my life. You then become one of Roger's lawyers and represent the people who came to my condo to kill me and even after that knowing full well he's trying to kill me give him my address in San Francisco. Do you expect me to think you don't know what you are doing? How many dollars is he paying you to help him exterminate me? I can't believe money means so much to you that you'd become complicit in my murder."

"I don't think he's anyway involved in trying to kill you."

"Well, you have to live with yourself Alison – now what are you proposing that you are doing on my behalf."

She reached for the papers and handed me copies. "If you read these you'll understand it fully but I'll explain. You will retract all charges against Roger; admit that he never raped or otherwise attacked you, that in your confusion after the attack on you by a stranger, you wrongly identified Roger and having done that you were afraid to admit your mistake. Your statement is set out in the document. Roger will agree not to sue you or in any way take any action against you, and that means, Alison, any action."

"You mean, like trying to kill me."

"Any action at all."

"Can we add that he agrees neither he nor anyone on his behalf will attempt to kill or hurt me? You know be a little more specific."

"I think that is covered by the words "any action."

"Is that about it?"

"Well, there's also the money part."

"What's that?"

"Hunt Enterprises, as the owner of the condominium where the attack occurred, will pay you as damages for your suffering the sum of five hundred thousand dollars, for its failure to properly ensure your safety from the stranger who attacked you."

"That's a nice start but it'd be better if they made it a nice round figure like one million dollars, you know, one million for each time they sent people out to kill me which means it would be at least two million now."

"Aside from the money, Dakota, what about the rest of it?"

"It sounds all right to me but I'll have to run it by my attorney."

"You have an attorney?"

"Of course, when I learned you no longer represented me, I went out and got another attorney."

"When did you learn I wasn't . . ."

"When the DA told me you withdrew."

"So who's representing you now?"

"Ha! She's a nice lawyer but if I told you, you'd scurry to Roger with the information and he'd steal her away from me. So let's call her Attorney X."

"Then have her look at it. You'll see it says what I said it said. And get back to me, the sooner the better."

'You'll see if you can spice up the stew."

258

"I'll talk to Roger Hunt about it."

"When I come back you'll have a better answer, I hope."

"I will but I don't think it will be going up much higher than it is at – but I'll explain your position to him.

"One final thing, now tell me the truth on this if you know how. If I don't show up for the probable cause hearing what will happen?"

"The case against Roger will be dismissed."

"But it can come back again, can't it?"

"Yes, of course. It can always be filed again or brought before the grand jury."

"Here's what I'm thinking – if like I don't show up, I drop out of sight – I'm asking you this because you always said the DAs should force people to testify – I'm thinking if I signed the papers you wanted me to sign, the DA could force me to testify anyway – you said the newspapers would keep the pressure on him in this case – but if I don't show up and let a little time pass and the pressure goes down and I sign those papers – you know like I sign them and do a video showing that it's really me signing them and I admit on the video I panicked, got confused and named Roger and then I was afraid to take it back because the cops would be mad or charge me with lying to them – wouldn't it be better for Roger – you know if we do all this after the charges are dropped."

"That's something I would discuss with my client."

"And, you know if I did that, maybe that would make Roger willing to throw in some extra dough when he saw the video clearing him of everything."

259

As you can tell Naria, I was desperately trying to chase away murder incorporated until after the probable cause hearing. I figured after I said my peace to Alison and showed her that I knew she was a greedy unethical bitch who'd set up another to be killed if the money was right then I'd do whatever I could to make them think I was going along with clearing Roger and all I was interested in was the money, you know. I wanted Roger to think he'd be exonerated and it was best to call off the dogs because my statement and writings clearing him would restore his former status, a lot more than killing me which would leave the scent of a rapist on him even though he wouldn't go to jail.

I left it that I was going to the condo in Quincy for a couple of days since my attorney was out of town. When I said that, Alison gave me a strange look, sort of like a smirk. She must have known that if I went there I'd be in for a big surprise.

I went on to tell her that when my attorney got back I'd meet with her and if the papers were all right I'd bring them back. I suggested to Alison that Roger is better off if I live and when I don't show up for the probable cause hearing he'll be well on his way to getting his reputation back. I said, "You've done a good job for your client. I shook her hand and left with the papers. You see how bad I had become! I could shake the hands of a person who was aiding a conspiracy to kill me."

I'm sure Roger knew about the whole thing by the time I hit the street. I walked to Park Street and took the T to South Station. I got on the first commuter train that was pulling out and got off at the next stop, Copley just as the train was pulling out. No one else got out like that so I felt comfortable I wasn't being followed. I waited for a train that went out to Route 128 which I also got off of. I closely watched whoever else got off and no one seemed to be suspicious. I hung around until the place cleared. I bought a ticket for a later train to Penn Station. I then went up the escalator and walked across to the other side of the tracks.

I should mention I was on the platform when my cell phone rang. It was the front door clerk in my hotel in San Francisco. He said he hoped he didn't wake me but there were two men at the desk with a package for me. I looked at my watch it was before seven on the West Coast. I told him that I was feeling ill and they should come back tomorrow.

I took the next train back to Copley and then hopped on a New York bound train. I walked from Penn Station across to Third Street and took the underground up to 68th and walked to my apartment. I was dog tired. I was finally home and I could get some rest. It was now time for a full scale blackout. No communications at all. I didn't plan to leave New York or to surface again until the Fifth, five days before the probable cause.

THURSDAY EVENING: AFTER DINNER

I won't be bothering you too much, Naria. I'm a little tired tonight but I figured I'd try to get a little conversation going with you before I went to bed. I have a confession to make. I haven't been totally honest with you.

You remember how I began writing. I said my story was too sad to be told. I've gotten over that mostly. I'm telling it to you. You may recall I was concerned that if I told it to anyone else that person would feel compelled to tell other persons, or even be under some type of legal obligation to reveal what I'm telling you. But with you, I knew it would never go beyond you.

However, what made me able to tell it to you was to deceive you a little bit, probably something I could not have done had I been talking to another person. Now don't get upset at me. I trust you fully. I know you would never tell my secrets. But I had to consider what if someone came along and forced you to reveal what you knew. You know, like, suppose someone broke into this apartment and found where you stay when I'm not around, picked you up, opened the covers, and saw our conversation. That would be pretty bad for me.

I wouldn't blame you if it happened. I knew if someone else got a hold of you, you'd have no choice but to reveal what I discussed with you. So that's what caused my little deception.

I've done changed some of the names of the people and places I've told you about. I haven't changed their positions. What I mean is — like — I said Roger is a CEO, but his name isn't Roger. The company isn't Hunt Industries.

262

My name isn't Dakota. My husband's name wasn't Tom. But what transpired between me and my ex-husband is absolutely true. Everything that occurred between me and Roger that I write about is entirely true as are what happened between me and Jenny and my lawyer, Alison.

The relationship with New Hampshire, Boston, and other places are fudged a little. Other places I mentioned are also, like I may have been in LA rather than San Francisco, things like that. Everything I've said about New York is totally true.

They used to say at the beginning of a movie, I don't know if they do anymore, but they'd say "This story is true, only the names have been changed to protect the innocent." I can't say that's the case here. I should say, "The names have been changed to protect my privacy." I couldn't say "to protect the innocence" because some would think Roger or Tom were innocent.

Maybe in one sense they were – the man-made law sense, you know, they didn't do what the law, the law made by men, charged them with doing. But they did other things, worse than the man-made law, that justified any punishment they received. Man-made laws don't protect women who are out working hard while her husband is sleeping in another woman's bed. They don't protecting women from philandering bosses who use them, abuse them and refuse them any help when the moment ends. I know you'd say they're not crimes. But that's my point, Naria, they're not because men made the laws for themselves not for us. If we made the laws maybe they would be crimes. Isn't a woman raped when she provides her youthful comforts to her husband, gives birth to his children,

263

nourishes them from her body, raises them, often times while working herself, when her husband walks away from her and then fights her in court to deprive her of a decent living? Is that not worse than what Alison said about one night of non consensual sex taken by her husband against her which she said is called rape?

Our society is based on laws made by men and interpreted by men who wore the black robes of the judiciary. When have women ever made the laws? Maybe until we do we're entitled to interpret them our own way and to use them to our benefit like men have done for all time.

I hope you don't mind this mild deception, Naria. I'm sure you understand it's really something I had to do. If you could I know you'd tell me you have no doubt that I did the right thing. Now I'll go on.

During the time when I returned to New York and the 5th of the next month, I had a wonderful time escaping from all that had gone on. I stayed away from the internet. I had no idea what was going on back in Boston. I spent most of the time in the library, book stores, coffee shops, and my apartment. There were so many things I wanted to read about and you know what is perfect, when I read I had no limits on me. What I mean is I could read all night long if I wanted because I did not have to get up in the morning. I had pure freedom to do what I wanted when I wanted. I often thought I was in a dream and someday I'd wake up and it would be gone.

There were times I wished that back when Tom walked out I just walked out also and came back to New York and set up here and resumed life in the slow lane. The closer I came to the 5th, the more I was tempted not to go back.

264

Oh, I so much wanted to go on with this dream life.

But unfortunately, as I've said, I've got this part of me that keeps me from resting when I feel I can undo an injustice. Not to return would mean all the abuse I took from Roger and all the violations he inflicted on me – not even considering all the abuse he caused other women and how he wrecked their lives – would go unpunished. He'd go on using his position to exploit women and would do so with impunity.

I know I was taught as part of my religion that an important aspect of life is not to seek revenge. One is to turn the other cheek. But aren't we also taught to love our neighbor which means we have to look out for their well being. If a bastard like Roger runs amok victimizing one woman after another, how is it not a sacred duty to stop him from continuing to hurt women if one can? So whenever I wanted to shrink from getting back at Roger, I would cast it in terms of a moral obligation for me to go forward.

I had problems with the 'means to justify the end' enigma. You know, can one use evil means to bring about a good result; or must one stay with good means knowing an evil result will occur. Much of that comes down to the definition of good or evil. With Roger, I made up the whole rape and assault which some would say was wrong. The end result may be that I end Roger's reign of terror over women. That is something that is right. If I did nothing, his evil would go on and on. So maybe it is a weighing of evil and good. You can do little evils to bring about a big good.

Even then, what some consider little evils, others may not. Lying, for instance. Some say you can never lie. Others say lies are justifiable at times. We all know the Anne Frank issue – is lying to Nazis permissible to save her life? Is there any doubt that such lies that served to protect her were good? Or, do we limit the evil in lies to when they contravene man-made laws like perjury or lying to FBI agents? How is it a woman can go to prison if she lies to an FBI agent about a stock transaction but a man isn't punished if he lies to his wife about his destructive actions damaging her well-being? What is more important, preserving the integrity of the stock market or of our families?

I did consider these things. My makeup made me. Rationalizing like I did, I fully justified what I was doing to myself. That's all I felt was necessary. I did not want to justify my actions to any one other than me.

But knowing I was fighting for my life, that my actual life was on the line is really what buttressed me up and propelled me forward during these times when I wanted to stay in the lap of luxury in my apartment and put aside the travails of life. If Roger had not set about to kill me, perhaps I would have been less motivated to return to Boston. But because he wanted me dead, I knew my only hope of not being hunted down and killed by Roger's goons was to struggle on.

The desire to live made me put down my books and set out for Boston on the train. I had donned my newest disguise, that of an old woman with grey hair, a slumped over posture, pasty worn out skin with thick eye glasses, a housekeeper's dress and a cane to set out for Boston on the train. My destination was the Brookside House which was a short walking distance from the Quincy courthouse. This was a type of lodging house where you took rooms for a more extended period than you would at a motel. It was similar to a motel but more modest, the type of place an old person would be content to stay for a time. I had a small room and a kitchen. I could keep some snacks and do some cooking.

I arrived there late at night on the 5th and checked in, paying cash, quipping that I didn't like them credit cards paraphernalia. I paid them for a week in advance and said that just about ate up all my money. I chatted away saying that I was in town to see some of my grand kids.

On the morning of the 6th I went over to the courthouse. I went in and sat around the corridors. I'll tell you it is a real horrible place with everything being conducted inside this big building with very little day light coming in and out. I went in and out about a half dozen times that day smiling imbecile-like at everyone getting them used to seeing me. I'd sit in the courtrooms and listen to the cases, again trying to become more of a fixture than a person. I passed unnoticed by everyone after a couple of hours. Who pays attention to an old person slumped down on the bench outside the courtroom leaning on her cane? I did the same thing on the morning of the 7th, 8th, and 9th.

By then I was as noticed by the courthouse people as the wind that came in when the door was opened. I'd waddle through the metal detector accompanied by sympathetic smiles the young bestow on the harmless old eccentrics who like to pass the mornings in the courthouse looking for trials because their TVs are broken.

When the 10th came I was at the court house early. I noticed there was a different type

267

of person hanging around. It seemed they were some type of special guard type people. They're the new people we have in America developed by those above-the-law companies like that one that used to be called Blackwater, and then called Xe, that provide comfort and protection to the rich. These are our über alles Americans – the creations of corporate America drawn from people taught to kill in our wars who operate not according to man-made laws that apply to most but under special corporate-made laws that provided special exceptions from the former.

Some stood right behind the court officers who were doing the screening at the front door suspiciously eying each person who entered. I passed on into the courthouse without a second glance. I heard one court officer say, "She's here all the time." I went over to the list to examine it being a little apprehensive that the case might not be scheduled. But there it was, Commonwealth v. Roger Hunt, Court room 24. I went upstairs and sat on a bench outside the courtroom. After some other people entered, I went in and took a seat. Every once in a while some special guard type person would look in or a court officer would pass through. No one noticed me. The court room filled slowly up. There were at least a half dozen press people who came in strutting around their importance soon to be followed by the ubiquitous television camera.

I was sitting about three rows back, off to the side. A little commotion occurred when Roger came in surrounded by his retinue of dark-suited lawyers. Roger tried to look his arrogant self but I could see he was less than happy to be in a situation where he was not in charge. I was hoping the judge and prosecutor had not yet been put on his payroll. He had six or so lawyers. It was hard to tell. After he came in with some of them, others came in drips and dabs. Maybe they all weren't lawyers but they went up to the lawyers, spoke with them, and then either took a seat or left the room again. There were also the special guard type people milling around casting hard looks at everyone in the courtroom.

As I expected, Alison arrived and happily gathered herself into the middle of the lawyers that crawled around where Roger was seated and joined with them in vying to find favor in his sight or a perhaps a blessing from his smile. Then I saw the assistant DA Nick Adams come in. He scanned the courtroom; I assume he was checking to see if I had arrived. Some of Roger's lawyers sped over to Nick and he spoke briefly with them. They quickly scurried back to Roger to report with smiles on their faces. This seemed to make Roger relax a bit but he still looked uncomfortable.

I think by now he figured out that I wasn't a push-over and had become his Achilles heel. Look at the position he found himself in being forced to rub shoulders with all these little people, the type of people he believed he had risen above. How humiliated he must have felt looking at them continually gawking at him. I'm sure in his wildest dreams he could not have anticipated a woman would put him in this position. He had to know every endearing word I said to him was a lie. I hoped he painfully regretted every pleasurable moment he seized from me. I knew that in the future he wouldn't be telling other women of the lustful times he had with me as he used to tell me of the ones he had with others.

I hoped any remembrance of me tore into his soul and made him nauseous. I liked to think that in his future exploitations of women, if he had any, he'd never be able to fully trust any of them. He'd have to think if that little know-nothing broad without a thought in her numbskull head could do this to him, what would prevent any other woman from doing it.

Watching him I wondered what we would say if we ran into each other again. All I could picture was Roger erupting in rage thrusting himself forward at me, arms extended, open handed reaching to put both hands around my neck. That would have been the extent of our conversation. I'm sure knowing Roger, he's repeated that scenario in his mind dozens of times.

At nine o'clock sharp the judge came into the court behind a court officer who said we should all stand. He then recited something else and told us to be seated. The judge said to the woman in front of him, "Call the case."

Unnoticed, I started to slip off my disguise. The woman said, "This is a probable cause hearing of Commonwealth vs. Roger Hunt. Nicholas Adams is appearing for the Commonwealth, Paul Warring and others for the defendant. The defendant, Roger Hunt is in court. Please stand to be recognized by the court."

Roger stood up. Along with him every one of his attorneys also stood for some strange reason I could not get.

She said: "Thank you, you may be seated." They all sat down together.

The judge spoke up, "Is the Commonwealth ready for this hearing."

Nick stood up and said, "I expect I will be. I am waiting for my witness to appear."

Paul Warring stood up, "May I address the court?" When the judge indicated his assent, Warring said, "If it please the court, this matter is scheduled for nine o'clock, I would expect the Commonwealth would be prepared to proceed at that time. Mr. Adams has advised counsel he has not heard from his witness for several weeks and is himself unsure of whether his witness will appear. I don't see anything that will be gained by delay. I suggest the court dismiss the charges against Mr. Hunt since the Commonwealth is not prepared to proceed."

The judge said, "Mr. Adams, how long do you suggest we wait for your witness?"

"A reasonable time, your honor."

"Do you have any reason to believe you witness will be here."

"Yes, your honor, she said she would be here. Could I ask the court officer to step out of the court room and see if she is in the building?"

Saying that, Nick looked around again. I stood up as he did and waved at him. He stared at me for a second without figuring out who I was and then a big smile passed across his face. "That's all right, your honor, I see my witness is in the court room. The Commonwealth's ready to proceed. I call her to the stand."

All of Roger's lawyers jumped up and looked around. Roger sat still, facing straight ahead. As I was the only one in the audience standing up, they stared angrily at me. Alison, likewise standing, was chattering away to the man next to her and pointing at me.

"Ladies, Gentlemen, please sit down. Will the witness please step forward and be sworn. I passed over all the legs and laps separating me

271

from the aisle. When I reached it went forward to where the woman was standing. She asked me to raise my right hand and swore me in. I felt fine. I wasn't nervous at all. I looked at the judge. He was busy writing in a black note book. I looked at Roger. He was the picture of hatefulness. He glared back at me. Our eyes locked for a couple of seconds. I guess it was obvious. His lawyer jumped up, "Your honor, I'd ask the court to instruct the witness to stop trying to intimidate Mr. Hunt."

The judge being taken by surprised looked up confused. "What was that Mr. Warring? What did you say?"

"It is obvious that the witness is trying to intimidate Mr. Hunt by staring at him. I ask she be directed to stop doing that."

Still a little confused the judge said, "Yes, yes, no staring in the court room, the witness is so instructed."

Warring sat down please that he had stuck the first blow. I kept staring at Roger and he back at me. Warring tugged at the sleeve of his suit jacket trying to get his attention and I assume a pat on his head. My attention was drawn away from Roger by Nick Adams who was standing off to my left who began to ask me questions.

Although it was an excruciating day, I found a lot of pleasure in being able to sit so close to Roger telling a made-up story that he was unable to do anything about. I could tell lie after lie right in his face — look at each of the photographs taken of me showing my bloody dreadful self-inflicted wounds and hesitantly say, "Yes, Mr. Hunt did that to me." I was jumping with joy inside and each time I identified him as having caused one of my wounds I looked at him and saw his look of scorn and hate as he thought it was unbelievable that this was happening to him. Can you imagine how glorious it is to be able to do something like that to an evil person? I felt I was following one of the greatest of all teachings — "Do unto others as they would have done to you." Roger was evil personified and here he was getting back a full dose of his own medicine.

Nick Adams asked me questions for about an hour. Then Roger's lawyer, Seymour Warring rose. He started asking me questions in a quiet voice, then a louder voice, then a very loud voice, then an angry voice, then a threatening voice, and then a supplicating voice, and he went on and on, over, under and around every little bit of my testimony. We took a half hour lunch at 1:00. We resumed again. At 4:00 Warring seemed to be tiring a bit. In a sense I felt sorry for him.

My story was simple. It wasn't a case of misidentification. I was Roger's whore, so I knew who he was. It wasn't a case of consent. I had the burn marks to show he tied me up, the beating marks about my face and body, and the old bruises along with a picture of my eyes being shut a few weeks earlier. There was not question I was penetrated. Nor was there a question of who had done the penetration. If ever there was an open and shut case this was it. The blood on the bed, identified by DNA belonged to two people, Roger and I. The semen belonged to Roger. At 6:30, when Warring finally conceded by saying no more question, there was only one of two conclusions that could be reached. I was beaten and raped by Roger or I had some kind of consensual sadomasochistic sex with Roger, beaten myself up, and then staggered out seeking help. Everyone knew the latter was an impossible conclusion.   Things like that don't happen.

When Warring sat down, the judge said that I could leave the stand.   I walked over toward Nick and took a seat that he offered to me at his counsel's table. The judge said as the TV cameras rolled, "Gentlemen, ladies, normally at this point I would ask for counsel to argue. But it is late. I've spent a full day, more than a full day, listening to the testimony of one witness. The standard that I have to decide is based upon the testimony. Is it probable the events set forth in the complaints happened and if it is probable, which is a low standard, that the case should be bound over to the grand jury.   Given the standard and the lateness of the hour, I find that argument by counsel is not necessary because I have had the opportunity to have a thorough hearing and listen to as comprehensive cross-examination as I've ever had the pleasure of hearing. My compliments to you Mr. Warring. However, I must find, despite your fine efforts to convince me of some other happening, Mr. Warring, that probable cause exists that Mr. Hunt did commit the crimes as alleged."   He went on to continue the same bail on Roger and he left the bench.

Stunned silence would best describe the courtroom at that moment. I couldn't see Roger's face because Nick was blocking my view. When Nick moved and I looked over, I could not see through the wall of glum attorneys that surrounded him. I felt good. I had purchased an insurance policy. My testimony was recorded for all time. The death sentence over my head had to be lifted. I'm sure Roger knew that it made no sense to kill me because even with the sterile

274

testimony of a transcript the photographs and physical evidence would destroy him.

Roger knew that now his only hope was to keep me alive and do whatever he could to have me tell the truth. This was to be something Roger would find quite unique. He had spent most of his life having his lawyers find people who would lie for him. Now he had to see if he could have a witness tell the truth. I was sure that although Roger despised me, he had to accept that I had become a formidable opponent. He had to know all his lawyers, money and power were useless to him if he could not get me to tell the truth. For the first time in many years Roger was feeling how it is to be on the bottom dependent upon someone else.

I stood watching as Roger and his crowd moved out of the courtroom. Alison had lingered behind. I walked over to her. I said, "You didn't do such a good job for your client."

She stared at me with as much contempt as Roger.

"I hope you remind him to call back his war dogs. If he kills me, he kills himself. You know that."

She didn't say anything. She had lost her bite and bark.

I went on, "Tell him I know, because you told me, my testimony is on record and will live after me. Tell him I'm still ready to deal. But the price has to be right."

She got her voice back, "I'll pass on the message."

"Remember, Alison, only my recantation can save him from a long bit in jail and give him back his reputation. With my death he loses everything. See what you can do for me. I'll be in touch."

She repeated herself, "I'll let him know."

I couldn't resist, "I hope your double-cross was worth it to you Alison. Knowing Roger like I do, I don't think he's going to be throwing many golden nuggets your way. I don't suppose you'd think of coming back to me."

I left her standing there, puzzling over my remarks. I walked out of the courtroom past some of the special guard type goons who had been standing around all day. They couldn't figure out how they missed me. Roger won't be too happy paying them either. I wondered what they would have done if they did spot me before I testified. Would they have been bold enough to drag me out of the courthouse or try to kill me among all the courthouse people. They lived by the rules of the rich and powerful. Under those special rules they may have been able to do those things, drag me out and take me to one of their black hole places where they take other people. Who could stop them?

But things were different now. I felt like I had a protective coat of armor over me. The goons stared menacingly but impotently at me. I walked over to the Brookside House where I had been saying. I walked past the front desk. The clerk did not recognize me since I looked nothing like the old woman. He probably assumed that I was visiting someone. I didn't know if I had been followed.

I walked down the long corridor to my room and before entering it looked down the corridors. No one was there. Once inside my room I packed up the few things I had. I made soup. I originally planned to leave right away. But I was bone tired. The day was exhilarating but exhausting. I thought about my situation. I felt protected but I wasn't sure. I imagined if I

276

had been followed the clerk at the desk would not be able to help who ever inquired about me. All he could say is that I wasn't staying there, that I had probably come there to visit someone, or else walked in the front and out the back, as some people do especially in inclement weather. I realized I was safer there than any place else outside of New York at that moment. As I said I was real tired. I looked at my bed and decided to stay there for the night. I felt happy. I was safe for a while and I could now go on to part two of my plan.

I'll stop now, Naria. I'm tired.

FRIDAY: AFTERNOON

I got out very early the next morning and returned to New York after undergoing the usual round-about route. I knew I had the probable cause testimony insurance but I didn't know if the word had gone out to all of Roger's troops that the "kill her" signal had be taken down. I figured when the special goons got together that next day they'd understand how I suddenly materialized in the courtroom. That would bring them back to the Brookside House to see if the "old woman" was living there. It was best not to be around. I did not know how well I would stand up under the enhanced interrogation techniques devised by the Cheney gang.

That day after I returned I gave some serious thought to my status. I recognized when I entered into my journey I began with what would be generous if I said it was extreme naïveté. Much that had transpired had been put together with strong determination but lots of luck. The biggest piece of luck was my urge to escape and have a hideaway. If I had not done that, when I learned that my life was in jeopardy I don't know what I would have done or whether I'd have survived. Certainly had I not have my East 73rd Street hideaway and stayed in my condo those two travelers from across the Atlantic would have completed their work.

After being back a few days, I took the train down to DC. Except for school excursions I'd never been there. It's really a nice place. I stayed several days sightseeing. I'd have to say my favorite spot is on the walkway at Maya Lin's Vietnam Veterans Memorial where I descend down and slowly climb up walking by over fifty-eight thousand names of those who died who shouted out to me to remember the waste of war: young people, many forced to serve, in a fruitless endeavor manufactured by politicians and generals for other than noble ends.

While in DC I called back to Nick Adams to see what was going on. He said I did well at the probable cause hearing. He told me that the case would be going to the grand jury a week from Monday. I'd have to testify. He wanted to meet me at his office but I convinced him that wasn't necessary. It wasn't hard. He asked me for a number he could call me at. I told him I'd call him. We made arrangements for me to meet him outside the grand jury room.

I called Alison. She asked me to drop by and see her, or she'd come to see me. She said she didn't like to talk over the phone but she had some paperwork she wanted to discuss with me. I told her I would as soon as I had the chance. She said it was extremely urgent that I do it as soon as I could. I sensed desperation in her voice. She was far from bossy but talking more like a supplicant. I wondered what happened between her and Roger. Did she sell him something on which she couldn't deliver? Unlike last time, she asked for no information on my whereabouts.

I was going to call Jenny to see if I could stay at her place when I went there to testify but changed my mind. I was still up in the air with her. I had difficulty figuring out whether her protestations of innocence were an act or not. It they were an act, I couldn't understand what she was going to gain out of it. Why didn't she leave it like it was? We had agreed not to talk about Tom and I could believe what I wanted to about it. Not understanding why she brought it up like she did bothered me.

That left Tom. Writing this, I can see what happened to me how I plunged headlong into my plan for vengeance against Roger and then took upon myself the Joan of Arc aura of vanquishing evil. I didn't hear voices from God as she did but there were the imagined accumulated cries of all my women ancestors who had gotten the rotten end of the stick of life who inspired me to take on Roger for them and all women.

It's that brook no injustice attitude that I'm stuck with. I saw how it had spun out of control. I was well on the way to putting Roger out of action for a long time. I didn't know at that point how much longer his company would keep him as CEO – I knew how much that meant to him and if he lost it he'd be crushed since that gave him his identity. Was that why Alison pushed me for an early meeting?

I had to try to weigh the consequences of delay in meeting Alison with the events happening to Roger. If Roger lost his position, then what would that mean for me. I wanted that to happen to him, didn't I? I wanted to destroy him, but the more and more I thought about it I realized that in doing it he'd probably have me destroyed. Had I so intermingled my fate with Roger that if I bring about his downfall I'll bring about my own? I would have accomplished a noble thing in destroying that pig but did I want to do it at the cost of my life? These were the things I was pondering at that time.

That admiral who said, "Damn the torpedoes, full steam ahead," made exactly that calculation. He was willing to lose his life rather than see his naval group not go forward into danger. I know early on I had said that same thing, but that wasn't in the face of a death sentence. One can be very brave on the couch at home. I found that I was wavering a bit. Did I like life too much? Isn't it ironic that when I started this I was talking about how I could not go on much longer because of the wreck I made out of my life but back then when it seemed my life was in danger I so much wanted to protect it. What a frail, feckless, fickle female I am.

When I was wondering if I should take my foot of the neck of the snake Roger how could I know if he would slither off into the brush happy to be free again or whether he would twirl around and bite me with his venomous fangs. I rued my indecision and weakness in thinking these things. I had to keep reminding myself of my outrage at Roger's actions while thinking that if I had to remind myself of my outraged, I wasn't really in that state.

I was confused. I was on the cusp of attaining my goal and doubts were sneaking in. The frustration was I did not want to admit to myself that the doubts were born out of fear. But looking back, where else could they have come from? I had rationalized that my actions were justified. If so, wherefrom the uncertainty?

There was one thing of which I had no doubt; Tom put me in this position. He was the true villain. He had me agree to be a whore so that I could blackmail Roger and get us money all the time he was planning on throwing it in my face. He had left me behind by sleeping with Jenny, or others, but he couldn't leave me in peace. He wanted to destroy my soul. If Tom did not propose I take the road to damnation and bite the apple of adultery, I never would have followed it if I had not been wildly in love with him. He used my love and twisted it. I had the

281

innocence of a child. He turned me into a hard hearted conniving vixen. I had been having second thoughts about Roger without understanding why other than my craving to live, I had none about Tom.

But I had an idea how to destroy Roger. It was, as I've told you and you've seen, quite simple and foolproof. I used his lust against him. I had him in my web. As long as I was willing to accept the pain of a beating, he was dead meat even though he was a powerful and ruthless.

Tom should have been easier than Roger because he had no power and little courage. But having done Roger, my options on Tom were limited. I obviously couldn't pull the rape scam with him. That was something a person could only do once no matter what. Aside from that, I knew I could never beat myself again as I did then. It wasn't but two or three weeks after I did it that I was amazed I had the ability to do it. It seems we humans can sometimes do some physical feats only once. When time comes to do it we carry it off with aplomb. Looking back we have no idea how we did it and if asked to do it again we never could. That was how I looked at the night that I accused Roger of raping me.

I deliberately had not thought of what action I would take against Tom until I finished with Roger. I had disciplined myself to think of carrying out only one vengeful act at a time. There were things I knew I couldn't do. I wanted nothing to do with having to testify in court. I wanted not to be involved in a situation where I could be accused of a crime. Yes, girls, I did give thought to taking Tom's magic wand away from him. I suppose if laws were woman-made, that would be and effective penalty. But under the laws as they exist, doing that would make me subject to the criminal laws, and unlike with homicide where one can sometimes argue it was justified, there was no defense of justified castration.

It was good that I had time. With Roger the clock was ticking because I was in a situation where I was being used, abused and manhandled. Even though he didn't abuse me every day it was possible that he could so I could never escape except when he left town and I found refuge in the City. It hung over me like Damocles sword. I was never free. It weighed on my mind every waking hour of every day. My self esteem was in the gutter. I yearned to be clean, to take like a twenty four hour hot shower and wash all traces of sordidness from me. I didn't want anymore balcony experiences picturing myself splattered over the sidewalk. So it was imperative that I end it with Roger and I having had a plan to do it, I did.

Tom was not in my life. He had taken from me what he selfishly wanted and also what I wanted from life. But I had no compulsion to rush to destroy him. That was fortunate because the strictures I had placed on myself my options were severely limited. Not having planned a way to do it, I feared there may be no way to taking Tom down. I thought perhaps I was in the situation of every other happily married woman who had her husband suddenly walk out on her. Most of them appeared to accept it. They went on silently lamenting their fate and eking out their existence tearing at their insides and probably wondering what they did wrong when the answer was nothing except to have grown a little older.

If only I could have done that. If only I just walked away and let bygones be bygones.

But I couldn't. That thing I have in me wouldn't let me do it. Sometimes we're doomed to be what we've been programmed to be from all times. From the moment of conception certain things are fixed forever – the sins and the wins of all our ancestors get mixed together. Our destiny is well set before we take our first breath. Mine was when I got that gene from that young woman who left her young child with a neighbor, secreted a dagger in the folds of her skirt, and plunged it in the heart of the overlord who had hung her husband for stealing a loaf of bread.

I should have walked away, but I couldn't. Tom had to pay for his treachery. To extract that payment, I had to be close to him, not in the way we used to be, I could never go back to the sexual stuff with him. At the time I was planning this I had no desire to know any other man after experiencing the two decrepit ones who had known and used me other than as a friend and or a buddy, if that.

I called Nick Adams the Monday before grand jury using a Google number and hoping it couldn't be traced. He begged me to come to his office on the Friday before. He said it was absolutely imperative that I do. I agreed to meet him at 4:30 on that day. That meant I'd be in the Boston area from Friday evening until Monday afternoon. I'd need a place to sleep for three nights.

I hadn't been back to my condo for a long while. I did not feel comfortable staying there. I planned to ask Tom if I could stay with him and if not, I'd suck it up and ask Jenny. I called Tom on his cell phone. He said no problem. He had a spare bedroom but I was always welcome to climb in with him – fat chance – it'd be good to see me again and we'd be able to catch up. You know, except for the hints of abusing me, all that stuff that makes a phone call pleasant and the expected arrival comfortable.

There was one hitch. He may not be there until late Friday night, if at all, because he was planning a day trip to a casino in Connecticut and sometimes he'd end up spending the night there. But I could make myself at home and he'd catch up with me sometime on Saturday. He said he'd overnight a key and the information about the alarm and other stuff I'd have to know when I got there Friday. I told him I'd be traveling but if he could get it to Nick Adams at the DA's office that would be great. I mentioned I could get another place for Friday but he insisted on having me stay there. So I agreed; I'd do it.

I traveled light Friday morning. I had all my stuff in my condo so even though I still had no desire to stay there overnight, I figured I could shoot in there during the day and pick up whatever I needed. Plus I remember that I had some clothes there I wanted to retrieve.

I got on the Acela Express at Penn Station. The trip was quick. The warm sun coming through the window and the mesmerizing sound of the iron wheels speeding over the tracks lulled me off to sleep.

When I got to the DA's office, Nick's secretary came down to take me through the reception area. She said he was tied up for a few minutes with some other people in his office. She took me to a small conference room and asked me to wait there.

I refused her offer of tea or coffee. The room was not that big. It'd fit no more than six people. The furniture was government issued: hard black plastic chairs with chrome metal legs, a brown Formica topped table with shiny chrome metal legs, and green steel bookcases.

I hate sitting down in an empty room with nothing to do but to stare at the walls. So I perused the books. Most books were legal type treatises that had accumulated years of dust a testament to the computer's use for legal research. A few seemed not to be of that genre. I was attracted to one that had an interesting title significantly at variance with the other books, *"Missing Beauty"* I picked it up and sat down with it. I wondered what it was doing in a DA's office. I read the inside flap. It explained that it involved a case that the Norfolk DA's office prosecuted many years earlier. I hadn't quite finished reading the flaps when Nick came in.

We went over what the grand jury would be about. It'd only be Nick asking me questions. Roger's lawyers would not be there. The jurors could ask me questions but he didn't think they'd be many, if any. He handed me a transcript of my testimony at the probable cause hearing and asked me to read it over the weekend. He said that it was important that I do it so I'd "minimize any contradictions in my testimony" and "refresh my recollection" so that during trial any attempt "to impeach me" by referring to "prior inconsistent statements" would be lessened. I was so struck by that legal jargon that I asked him to repeat what he said and I wrote down the words I put in quotes, that's how I still remember them.

Just before leaving, I asked him if I could borrow the *Missing Beauty* book. He said I could keep it if I wanted to since they were planning to clean out that room and use it as a room where kids could go when their parents who were victims or witnesses brought them to the office. I thanked him. Then as I was walking out and he said, "Dakota, I'm sorry. You can't keep the book. If I give it to you, I'll have to disclose it to defense counsel that I did and they'll make a big deal out of it saying I've given you something of value for your testimony. Let's say you can borrow it, but there's no due date." I said, fine. It made no difference to me. To tell the truth I had no idea why he was bothered about it and thought he'd have to tell anyone.

He also gave me an envelope that had been left there by Tom. In the taxi heading to Tom's condo, I opened the envelope. The key was there. It looked just like my condo key, but I guessed all the keys in that complex looked the same. I pulled out the paper with the information on it. I looked at the directions and then the address and the condo number. It took me a second or two for it to register. I realized that Tom was living in my condominium.

"How could he be?" I asked myself. "It must be a mistake." I tried to think it through. "Why would Tom have moved into my condo?" I realized it was probable Tom did not know it was mine. I never had him over there or gave him my address. All my communications with Tom had been over the cell phone. He's living in the condo without knowing that it was once mine.

I attempted to figure out when I was last there. It was when I got out of the hospital after meeting with Alison a week or so after the rape. I recalled that now. I was locked out; Alison got the locksmith, I got back in and then went to see her. After that I back there and fixed it up so it'd look like I was living there and I went to New York. Then there was the break-in after that. I'd not been there since.

Thinking of Alison made me think of our last meeting when I told her I was going over the condo and she gave me that strange look. She must have known, of course she knew, that I had been tossed out. She probably also knew that I never went there like I told her I planned to do when I left her. What she knew Roger knew.

What about Jenny? Did she know Tom was in my old place? I couldn't decide. I don't think she ever came there to visit me. What about the time of the rape? I wasn't sure. I leaned back in my seat, looked out the window at the passing scenery and thought how strange it was to be going back to spend some time in the condo where I once lived. I planned to stay with Tom so I would not have to stay in my condo but now to stay with him meant I'd have to stay there. I didn't know how I felt about that. It'd take time to process it. I knew I couldn't stay there that night since Tom said he may not be home. I'd have to get a hotel room. Whether I could stay there after that, I'd think about tomorrow.

I asked the cab driver to take me to the Four Seasons in Boston. I arrived there with my transcript, book, and decision about where I was going to stay the next night. I had a lovely dinner and was in my room for the night before seven. I had no desire to read the transcript thinking "who cares if they", then not remembering the words and taking out my paper to look at them I finished the thought, "impeach me with prior inconsistent statements." Nor had I a desire to watch television.

I picked up *Missing Beauty* and began to read. The author, Teresa Carpenter, wrote well, and I was quickly into the book. I was reading way into the wee hours and close to if not past the bar closing times in New York City. As I've mentioned, one of the joys of my life was not to be confined by arbitrary time limits in reading because I had nothing to compel me to get out of bed at a certain hour. I don't know what time I put the book down but when I did I knew how to bring about Tom's destruction. What a relief to have finally come up with a plan that fit within the limitations I had imposed on myself.

A major part of the plan was me keeping in touch with Tom and having access to his, my, condo. I still felt like the condo was mine and he was a usurper. When I registered at the hotel I vacillated between doing it for just Friday or for the whole weekend through Sunday. I told you how I had some deep reservations about returning to that condo. But any doubts I may have had about going back there I had to put aside. The plan required access to Tom and his condo.

I woke up shortly before noon. It was past check out time. I rang the desk and told them I was delayed. I then called Tom to see if we could have dinner that night. He had a date but said he'd definitely be staying at the condo after it. Knowing this, I told him I'd be there and added that due to complications I did not stay there Friday night. He didn't seem to care one way or the other.

After dinner in town, I took a taxi over to the condo. It was strange standing in front of the door with the key Tom had mailed to me. On a whim, I took my old key out of my pocket book to see if that would work. It did. I thought, "When Roger's company hired Tom and gave him my condo they didn't bother to change the locks, or, did they tell the locksmith to change them and

289

he just didn't bother but made a couple of more keys?"

When I went in there and looked around it was totally not me. Everything had been changed even the color of the wall paint. Nothing of me remained, absolutely nothing. They had come in and totally cleaned it out and wiped away any memory that remained of me. That felt strange being totally obliterated like that. I was sure all my clothes and other effects went down one of the company's giant incinerators. It was good I had become a minimalist living without all the fancy extras most Americans seem to need. I'd learned that material things just fence you in.

I think of the song that said "the best things in life are free." It's true to a great extent. Library books, water, fresh air (what's left of it), open parks, talks with friends, the joy of love, smiles from strangers, an unexpected politeness, a bird's song, the scent of flowers, that special unique feeling that comes on the perfect spring day, being left alone to think, a silent communication with your God (if you believe) or with yourself, there's so much that is free, and probably to the chagrin of the government untaxable, that with modest shelter and adequate food – give us this day our daily bread – one can lead a full life like that cowboy who only wanted to sit on his Cayuse underneath the starry skies.

I don't want you to think I was totally unaffected by the trashing of that part of my life represented by the things I owned in the condo. It was at a minimal uncomfortable seeing that everything had been removed and probably destroyed. I'm just saying that when I came face to face with what had happened, my life had gone off in another direction so that whatever hurt I felt from it I could handle easily. I'd later think when I was over the initial jolt that I was better off because any reminder of those days would be of things I'd best want to forget.

I didn't have much to do after I walked around the condo looking at all the changes that had been made. I'd finished the book and refused to read the transcript especially in that condo. There was no reading material of any other kind there. Tom was as unread as I was at one time, two typical college graduates of those days. I had three choices, watch TV, go to bed, or take a walk around the area. I turned on the TV. I went to TCM to see what movie was being shown. It was a Western so I shut it off. It was too early for bed so I went out for a walk over to the yacht basin. I walked around looking at the boats, stopped at one of the bars for a beer, and returned to the condo about 3 hours later.

I went to bed in the spare bedroom locking the door behind me. I didn't want Tom getting some crazy ideas like climbing into bed with me and trying to have one for old time's sake.

Lying there I knew I wouldn't fall asleep. I'd gotten up too late that day. Worse, I wanted to fall asleep and whenever I think about wanting to go to sleep I was guaranteed to be wide awake. In all my years I've never figured sleep out. You can't will yourself to sleep, at least I can't. I have to lie there and wait and try not to think. Then from somewhere in the room sleep seeps in and sneaks up on me and sends me off to who knows where. Except for dreams, and who can truly explain what causes them and their purpose – although a few times when I woke and recollected my dreams the Freudian idea of wish fulfillment was so obvious that I had no doubt for some of them he's right – but most times, at least for me, they're a confused jumble of thoughts, some with patterns and others without.   But beyond the dreams, what is happening when all is dark in the mind. Where am I? What is happening to my mind? How do I decide to wake up?   Why if I lie awake all night I'm not rested but if I sleep I am.   Why does prolonged lack of sleep produce disorientation in some and madness in others?

Sorry, Naria, I've run away from my tale. That night lying in the spare bedroom I didn't think those thoughts, all I thought about was when the hell I was going to go to sleep and the more I did the less likely it became. I heard Tom come in. He did come to my door and turn the handle. I tensed up a bit but he quickly went away to my relief. The last thing I remember before I fell asleep was thinking of the song Cheating Heart and saying the words in my mind "but sleep won't come the whole night through" but it did, and I awoke when I heard some knocking on the door.

I got out of bed and walked to the door and opened it. I was dressed sufficiently that I wouldn't be at all inviting. Tom said, "You going to sleep all morning?" I asked him the time. He said it was ten-thirty. I thought, "Hell, I've still got a good hour and a half more of sleep before I exhaust the morning."   Thinking it made me yearn to go back to bed. He spoke, "I'm heading out – I just wanted to tell you. I'll be back about three or four."

I was still a little groggy from sleep and responded with a sophisticated, "Oh! Thanks."

He said, "I'm meeting your buddy Jenny for lunch."

That chased the cobwebs away. "You're going for brunch?"

"Yeah, you know that. You met us there that time."

"I didn't know you – you guys still doing that?"

"Absolutely – when we do, we usually stay over Saturday night at the Seaport Hotel and then go down. Like it's you know real nice that way sliding down to such a great brunch after climbing out of the sack. But with you being here and everything, I thought, since I promised, I'd come here last night."

"That was bully of you, Tom!" I said facetiously thinking what a sensitive guy Tom was throwing all that in my face as if I was some guy sitting in a locker room with him.

"What?"

"Nothing."

"Oh!"

"Enjoy!"

"Yeah, thanks."

He left. I jumped back into bed. I was wide awake. I tried to go back to my conversation with Jenny. I remember thinking, "She said she was having nothing to do with Tom – yeah, and even in the past she said they did it twice, maybe not even that, maybe what she meant was twice a night – what in the hell does she think I'm supposed to think they are they doing in bed at the Seaport Saturday nights – playing Texas hold 'em?"

I was back to the puzzle of Jenny. Why does she feel a need to lie to me about her and Tom? Or is Tom lying to me for some reason trying to make me jealous of Jenny? Jenny knows I'm staying at Tom's, doesn't she know he'll tell me he's going to brunch with her. I really couldn't figure out what was going on with her and that worried me. Why? It is because she is a loose end and in my plans I did not like loose ends. I had to figure out what she was up to before I could have a fool proof plan. Or could I just ignore her and go on without figuring her out?

A RAINY SATURDAY MORNING: WITH COFFEE

I stayed in bed for a few more minutes trying to understand how to fit in what was happening with my plans. Jenny was a wild card. That meant I had to become closer to her than I wanted to do but I had to be very wary since she knew me very well. She denied any involvement with Tom yet she has had a significant one. I figured the first thing that was imperative to do was to find out whether she was using Tom in place of another type stimulator or whether she had real feelings for him. If the former, I could incorporate her into my plan; if the latter, then my plan might be weakened.

Obviously I was tempted to put on a disguise and study them at brunch. The urge to do that was thwarted by the desire to get under the covers and suck up a few more hours of slumber. I fell off to sleep.

Tom came back about three o'clock and immediately turned on the TV to watch some game or another. I had to get away from the noise and went out for a walk It was nice to be able to walk around again feeling somewhat protected. When I thought that, I remembered I had to meet up with Alison after the grand jury hearing the next day. Sunday night I went out to dinner with Tom. It was pleasant enough but we'd had traveled such different paths since the "out-of-the-big-bed" day that there was no way to even get close to recapturing what we once had. I felt I never knew the man. That bothered me a whole lot. How could it be that I was married to this man and so much in love with him but now I felt nothing, absolutely nothing? There was nothing there, a big emptiness. Our conversation stumbled along. I had nothing I really wanted to say to him. This experience was almost as bad as being in bed with Roger. I let him talk about his work which bored me to death. I suffered the boredom because I knew no matter what he said my feelings would have been the same, I was staring into a bottomless void, total emptiness.

I don't know what he felt. I looked in his eyes and saw two vacant spaces. I think I would have dozed off over my lobster if I didn't finally think of a subject I was interested in. I said, "How was your brunch with Jenny?"

"Good," he said.

"You're still seeing her a lot?

"No more than usual, well I don't know. . . "

"What do you mean?"

"I never saw her that much, only on the weekends when we'd do brunch. I don't see her during the weeks at all."

"You used to."

"Yeah, a while ago, when we . . . I don't want to go over that. That's in the past."

"So you just see her at these brunches and stay overnight with her the night before at the Seaport?"

"Sort of."

"That's a strange relationship."

"Yeah, I guess you could say that. But you know, that's between us, you know."

"I mean, you guys got any plans?"

"You know Jenny – she doesn't plan – lives for the moment – no, no plans, it's, to tell you the truth, Kota, the times I spend with her, and it's not every Saturday night, last night for instance, it wasn't that you were here that I didn't stay with her, it's she had other things to do, we've only stayed over at the Seaport once – I don't want you to think – you know there's more to it than there is."

Tom was walking back his story. I wondered did Jenny tell him to do this or was it the truth. How does one know these things? How do you penetrate a lie? Is that why on the tablet Moses carried down from Mount Sinai which forbid murder, adultery, theft, and coveting, all evils admittedly highly destructive of an orderly society, included the admonition not to bear false witness, that is to lie? How can I, how can anyone, decide anything if the truth is not known?

I saw that I wasn't getting anywhere there so I changed tact. "Tom, did you know I lived in the Marina area when I was shacking up with Roger?"

"Yeah, I think you mentioned it to me, or at least I heard it from Jenny or someone else."

"Do you know where I was living?"

"I wondered about that," he replied. "You know, when you asked me if you could stay over with me I wondered why you didn't stay in your own place. Why didn't you?"

When he said that I knew, if he was telling the truth, that he did not know he was in my condo. I didn't know what I'd gain by telling him that he was so I didn't, but I had to answer his question.

"I don't have it anymore."

"Oh, that's why."

Tom was naturally incurious. So we lapsed back into our forced conversation punctuated by a lot of silence. Whether Tom felt the same way I did, it's hard to tell. On the way back to the condo he put his arm over my shoulder. I gently took it off. Words weren't necessary. I guess guys can still want to get it on even after nothing is there. Maybe women do too to get through a tough night. But not me, I'd had enough of guys, at least at that moment to prefer aloneness to emotionless intrusion.

Grand jury on Monday was a walk in the park on a pleasant day. Softball questions were thrown at me, which I batted out of the park. I'd gotten to Nick Adams's office early that morning and spent some time talking to him. I told him I was living with Tom, who had taken over the apartment where I had been raped. I asked him if that would adversely affect the case. He seemed puzzled. He said something like perhaps it did because it could be argued that if you return to where it happened maybe it looks like you weren't sufficiently traumatized by it. I asked him what women who are raped in the bedrooms of their homes. What do they do after being raped never return to their homes? He got my point. I told him sometimes people have to suck it up and go where they'd prefer not to.

I also started to lay the ground work for my plan. I told him that the one problem I had with being there, which wasn't the truth, was that Tom worked for Roger. I shouldn't have had to remind him that Roger wanted to kill me at one point but just to be sure he remembered I did, especially since I had just felt the need to remind him that rape victims sometimes have to sleep in the bed where they were raped. To my surprise, he'd forgotten about the two guys with the fake passports. That slightly upset me until I realized how for most people unless a thing happens to or impacts them they don't remember too well what happened to another.

I said I didn't think Roger would use Tom to kill me especially now since it wasn't in his interest. Nick asked me why I was staying there if I had that fear. I answered I'd prefer to stay there than some other place by myself but I thought as long as it was in Roger's interest not to kill me, Tom wouldn't do it. Then I added, "Although he is fully capable of doing it if Roger told him to do so." Nick mumbled something to the effect that I'd better be careful.

Nick was as easy to lie to as it was easy for me to lie; I had to learn to lie to live, which is an excellent motivator. I knew I had nothing to fear from Tom. He ran away from even the thought of violence. He could never hurt anyone physically. But it didn't hurt my plan to instill in Nick the idea that he was capable of doing it.

When I finished with the grand jury I hurried over to see my old friend Alison. I was anxious to see what she thought was extremely urgent. I wondered if she ever figured out I was scamming her with all my tales about Roger's child porn stuff and his assault and rape of me. Or did she not care one way or the other, having as her main concern her desire for money and she'd been using the anti-child porn and pro-woman victim bit just as a way to get her grubby hands on as much as she could get. Maybe she didn't know herself why she did things. A lot of us drift along like that. I once did, but I couldn't anymore. Everything I did now was for a purpose.

In the short time I'd know her our positions had become reversed. At one time I depended upon her for help, now she was depending on me. We tossed the usual "how you beens" back and forth before she got down to business.

"Roger doesn't want to deal with you. He says he never laid a hand on you."

"Do you believe him," I asked.

"I'm just telling you what he said."

"I know that but do you believe him? Don't you think that's important?"

"Not particularly."

"If he never laid a hand on me how did he get all those scratches and bite mark? How did his DNA come from under my nails and from the blood on my sheets? Maybe you ought to tell your client that he might believe he never laid a hand on me but no one else believes it."

She had no answer and waited for me to finish. "If I could go on," she said.

"Sure, since you won't answer my questions."

"Roger nevertheless is willing to make a deal with you. If you tell the truth about what happened, he is willing to consider authorizing the expenditure of company money to the sum of two million dollars to settle any suit you may bring against him."

"Four!"

"Four?"

"Four million and it's a deal." Then I threw in something I knew would strike at her greedy soul. "I'm sure the lawyer I hire will want a million to file the suit so that will leave me with three – that's what I want."

The thought that some other lawyer would come in and file a pre-determined suit that would take no more than a few hours work and walk away with a million had to kill her. She had to know that could have been her if she played her cards right. She lost a cool million out the window because she shifted sides for a quick pay day of a handful of thousands. I knew she had to be thinking how she could insinuate herself into being the lawyer in the suit.

"I'll give him the figure. I don't know if he'll buy it."

"Alison, don't give me that. I'm going down cheap. Money means nothing to Roger. I'm sure he's paying you real well to represent him." I knew I shouldn't have said that but I couldn't resist. I knew Roger was a cheap bastard who would be squeezing Alison for every penny. I'd seen him do it to all the lawyers who represented him.

She didn't respond.

"Here's what I want, I went on. I want you to tell Roger four million. I want you to tell him, now write this down, I know the money means nothing to him, I forgive him for the rape on the night he is charged and I don't want any money for that, are you writing, but I want it for all the other times he raped me and the other women at the office."

When she finished writing she looked up. "You saying there were other rapes?"

"He'll understand what I mean when you tell him."

"I'll get the message to him."

"Also tell him, I've told the DA he wants to kill me and if I'm found dead after this deal goes through the DA will know who did it."

"You still think he wants to kill you?"

"Yeah, I do, and you know another thing Alison, if I were you I'd not be too sure he wouldn't want to kill you. You know too much. Roger likes a clean plate."

She almost fell out of her seat when I said that. I thought she never considered her own life may be in jeopardy. I went on, "You know about him sending those dudes into my place in Quincy and you tipped him off about where I was in San Francisco. He probably did a lot of other shit

301

against me that I'm unaware of that you know about. But Roger knows that you know a lot of things that can sink him. I'm sure he's probably just playing out the string on you until you bring home the bacon."

From the look on her face, I thought I was going to have to resuscitate her. Every word I said seemed to hit the mark. Maybe unlike what I had just thought, she had figured this out before by herself and hearing it from another came as a double shock. She didn't respond but just looked at me. I couldn't believe this was the reaction of the woman who I thought of as a bull dog. Again it showed lawyers can be tough when giving advice to people about what to do under threat but when they get themselves in that position they realize all the good words they use to buck up others were really very empty.

I broke her spell by saying, "So you'll let me know Alison. You have my cell number."

"Yeah, I will," she said, her face full of fear.

I never thought I'd say this but I felt sorry for her. I wanted to go up to her and give her a hug and try to reassure her that everything was all right. Poor Alison had gone from dismay at losing a million dollar fee to a realization that she might lose her life. She wasn't having a good day. But despite these feelings, I could not resist playing with her.

Without meaning it and without a second thought I said, "You know Alison, one last thing, can you recommend an attorney who would bring the case?"

She replied, "I thought you had an attorney."

I remembered I'd told her that before. "Yes, I did, but I got rid of her. I didn't like her style the way I used to like yours so I got rid of her."

"Oh," she said.

"You couldn't represent me in the suit, could you?" I was really torturing the poor woman with that question. I was going beyond what I felt I should have done even though I did owe Alison some grief for dropping me as a client. But to have her sit there and wonder if she could just reach out and clasp in her little greedy hands a million dollars had to torment her.

"I'd have to clear that with Roger," she said. "You'd want me?"

"Of course," I said. Then using her words, "You know more about the case than anyone else so it'd be easy for me, I wouldn't have to try to bring another lawyer up to speed."

"I'll let you know," she said.

I then told her I was going to the West Coast for a week or so and when I got back I'd call her.

She was most considerate of me as I left walking me out to the elevator and chatting friendly with me all the way. I played along. You see how rotten to the core I had become. I had no intention of ever settling with Roger. I just wanted to torture him. Now I was also torturing poor Alison. I just hoped Roger would not go after her when he realized he was being strung along.

I hopped on the T and went over to Copley Square. I went into the library and took out a few novels. I'd heard of this Irish writer and a Spanish writer, well to be correct I should say a Catalan writer, who I wanted to read. I went back to the condo, settled myself in and picked up a book. I wanted to get some space before I

303

visited Jenny. I had to find out whose side she was on.

After reading most of the afternoon, I walked over to the local watering hole and got a beer. I looked out over the water. I thought of my plan and my conversations with people to see how they fit in. I had a sense something was not complete. I remembered saying to Alison I had to go to the West Coast. I saw how that would fit into my plans. I'd go there and rent a place where I could live, at least make people believe I lived there. Then if there was any question where I was saying when I wasn't in Boston, that's where they'd believe I was. I knew they'd be a full out search for me after I pulled my stunt on Tom so I figured that was what I had to do next.

The next couple of days I hung around reading my books and thinking about how to execute my plan. I read in the newspaper that Roger had been to court for his arraignment and had said he was not guilty.

I left for San Diego after that. I rented a nice apartment up near La Jolla for a year. Furnished it up sparsely, but enough to make it comfortable for someone to live in. I installed a telephone I made some calls back to Tom, Alison and Nick and made enough nuisance of myself with my neighbors each time I was there that people would be able to identify me as the one who live there. I'd be back there a half a dozen or even more times before I pulled my caper.

When I returned after my first trip, I wanted to speak with Jenny to see how she fit into my plans. I still had the OK to stay with Tom. That was important. I made plans for dinner with Jenny for the next night after I got in. Aside from reading, before going off to meet

Jenny, I made a trip over to Nick Adams, he had left me a message he wanted to talk to me.

Nick said he'd just got a notice from the court about the case. He said that Roger's lawyers were pushing for a quick trial which I had read. I asked him what that meant. He replied that normally it takes about six months but in my case because all the reports and tests had been done and already given to Roger's attorney and there had already been a probable cause hearing there really was no real reason for a delay. The judge set the trial date for six weeks from the time I was sitting there. A special judge had been assigned and Nick was sure the case would be tried on that date.

I told him I thought cases were always delayed. Nick said the reason this was happening so quickly was also because he did not object to it. His boss told him to get it to trial as quickly as possible.

"I thought you were in charge of the case, and not your boss," I said.

"I am," Nick replied. "I'm in charge of it except for things like that."

"Why didn't you tell him you wanted more time?" I asked worrying that I might not have enough time to complete my plans.

"I did," Nick said. "He asked me why and I really had no reason because I had all the evidence already. So he told me to get it to trial quickly."

"So what does that mean for me?"

"It's good. It'll get the case over sooner. It's probably best not to drag it out."

"But it seems to me – you said Roger's attorneys wanted it tried quickly – you're going along with what they want. Why do they want it done quickly?"

"From what they said, the board of directors of Roger's company has withheld any decision on Roger's status as CEO until after the trial if the trial is held quickly – other than that because of all the bad publicity they're going to remove him."

"I don't understand. What you're saying is your boss told you to do it so that you can help Roger. You said you'd never do anything like that. How can I trust you now?"

Nick was flabbergasted. I knew what he did was next to nothing but I wanted to pin him against the wall with suspicion. I want to make him think I thought he had double-crossed me. It'd make it that much easier for him to fall into my trap again.

He pleaded for my understanding, "It's nothing what I've done. It doesn't affect your case."

I wouldn't let him off the floor. "It does. You know it does. It means your boss is working to help Roger and so are you." Then seeing him dumbfounded I pushed it to the next level, "I could be killed by Tom for all you'd care and nothing would be done about it. Oh, I feel so alone. No one wants to help me."

"It's not like that Dakota, really. You're making too much out of it."

"Promise me one thing, Nick. All I want is one thing. If I'm killed by Tom, you won't let him or Roger get away with it even if your boss tells you to do nothing about it."

"Dakota, that'd never happened. You're not going to be killed by anyone."

"Just promise me, Nick, that's all I want, your promise that you'll do your job."

'All I can tell you . . . "

"Promise me Nick."

"Yes, Dakota, I promise."

"I just hope you're a man of your word Nick. I say that because Tom keeps pressing me to say Roger did nothing to me. He keeps saying if I don't change my story quickly, I'll be sorry. And, I don't know if I told you," knowing full well I did, "Tom can be very violent."

"Look Dakota, let me put you up somewhere. We've got funds for that. I'll ask the DA."

"No, I don't trust you, or your boss, or your cops."

"You have to Dakota. I'll guarantee you you'll be safe."

"No, no, no, Nick, after what you've done already. Your guarantee's only as good as your boss's and he's a friend of Roger's. No I'll go to my place in San Diego." I then blurted out, "Oh! I didn't mean that."

"Didn't mean what?"

"I didn't want you to know I had a place to live there. I didn't want anyone to know. That's my hideaway where I go to get away. Promise me another thing Nick, you'll never tell anyone about it. I should not have mentioned it."

This time he quickly answered he promised. I ended by saying I'd stay in contact with him everyday on his cell. I told him he was the only one I trusted. I'd keep him informed about where I was at all times and he was not to tell anyone else. He agreed to go along with that. "Every day, Nick, every day until the trial."

I got up to go. I walked to the door. I then pulled the coup d'grace. I turned, looked at him for two or three seconds putting on a very stern look without saying a word, then said in a soft voice, "Nick, if I ever don't call, I'm dead." I

307

turned away from him. I couldn't stop myself from grinning. I left his office.

I met Jenny at the new restaurant that had opened on the waterfront, the Green Lantern. We chatted amiably for a while like old friends have the ability to do. It was so different from the time with Tom. How is it that meeting an old friend it feels like you've left her a couple of days before in the middle of a conversation and pick right up on it again but when meeting with an ex-spouse it feels like its been forever since you've seen him, wish it was longer and seems like you have nothing to really talk about. Maybe that's only me.

Jenny told me pretty much the story Tom did. They don't see each other during the week, but once in a while they shack up in Boston and have the brunch the next day. It was only once in a while and as she told it she'd have me believe it was only once. My trust in her was sinking with every word she said.

She went on to say that what she told me before was true. They'd only slept together once or twice and as far as she was concerned there was nothing between them. All that possibly remained was that she loved the brunch at the Seaport, went there every Sunday, and some Sundays she liked to wake up in that hotel and go downstairs to the brunch and on one or two times, apparently the two times I just happened to see her, she'd invite Tom or someone else to stay over with her.

She went on and on about how it was her one major faults or weakness. Like smoking, she knew it wasn't good for her but she didn't want to give it up. She laughed when I asked her if she had any plans with Tom. She said, "I said I had a weakness; I didn't say I was a dope.

Tommy means nothing more to me than a little Saturday night fling and to be absolutely honest with you Kota, I'm all through with him."

I thought to myself "I've heard this song before."

I asked her, "Has Tom ever been violent to you?"

"Tom?" she asked. "Tom, violent, you know the answer to that."

"I thought I did?" I returned.

"What do you mean?" she asked

"You know lately he's been saying strange things about what he'd like to do to me."

"Like what?"

"Between you and me, and to go no where else, Tom's been after me to sleep with him. You know with you and . . . . "

"Hey, Kota, I don't care if you do or not — it won't bother me."

"I'm not saying that, Jenny — what I was going to say is if you're sleeping with him and some others, I can't figure out why he's bothering me. I'd think he'd be satisfied."

"Are men ever satisfied?"

"What I know about men you could put in a, in a thimble. I don't know. All I do know is Tom's been after me and he said, and I didn't know what he meant, he said he'd get it one way or the other."

"That doesn't sound like Tommy."

"I know, of all persons I know that, I'm trying to figure out if he's changed, that's why I wondered about him and you."

"I told you about us. He doesn't have to threaten because what I give him satisfies him. What else can I tell you?"

"Nothing, I'm glad of that for you. I guess since I don't do what he wants, he figures he can scare me into giving it."

"That's not good, Dakota. Maybe it's not a good idea you living there."

That was a good answer that I wanted. Her concern for me was greater than her involvement with Tom.

"I'll see." Now I thought I'd plant another seed. I wanted to suggest that maybe Tom's attitude to me changed because of his working for Roger. "Do you know Roger Hunt?"

I didn't expect it to explode in my face, "Yes, I've been working for him lately."

"You're working for him?"

"Yes, he's paying me pretty well for some investment advice I give to him."

"You're not, how do I put it?"

"I told you I'm working for him. Whatever else I'm doing with him, if anything, is none of your business, Dakota."

"Do you work with Tom?"

"No, he's in another area."

"You know what Roger did to me?"

"He denies it."

"You believe him?"

'Look Dakota, you got your issues, don't make them mine, all right."

"No it's not all right, Jenny." I was getting angry which surprised me since I'd worked so hard to master my emotions. "What's with you? First, Tom and now Roger?"

"Roger!" She retorted. "You've got no claims on Roger."

She was right. She could have Roger all she wanted, if she wanted him. What the hell did I care about him? What was throwing me off? I didn't understand why I was so upset. I excused myself saying I had to go to the lady's room. I walked in there and leaned back against the door. "What did it mean that Jenny was sleeping with Roger?"

I went back to the table after a bit. When I sat down she said, "I'm glad you brought up Roger."

I looked straight at her. I was planning to avoid the subject since I didn't have my bearings on the correct course to proceed. But it looked like I was underway now.

"Why's that Jenny?"

"Look, Kota. I know this is a hard subject for you. It is for me. But when I met Roger and talked with him, I thought knowing you and now knowing him I could talk to you about it."

"I'm waiting. What is it you want to say?" Damn, I was boiling inside again, what was it with me? Calm down, I said, but my voice showed my emotions. I reached for my wine glass and took a big swallow.

"Roger wants to apologize to you. He wants to give you what you want; I guess you and your lawyer have worked it out. He says he knows your reasons for doing what you've done. He says; now don't get anymore upset, he says . . ."

"Who says I'm upset?" I yelled and leaned back in my chair and started demonstrating how upset I was by of all things starting to cry. I sat there with tears pouring down my eyes. I could feel the whole place staring at me having called attention to myself with my outburst. No one moved it seemed. I wanted to get up and run but I held myself there. When forever was over I said, "I'm sorry. I don't know why I did that."

I picked up my purse off the table and got up. I walked to the front door of the restaurant

311

got in a cab and went to Tom's. He wasn't in which was good. I hung around for a bit unsure of what to do. I got on the net and booked a 5:00 am flight to San Diego. I called a cab. I took it directly to the airport. I got there before midnight. I sat in the waiting area reading and trying to sleep for the rest of the night. I was sitting on the beach at noon time trying to put all the pieces together. Like with Humpty Dumpty, at that moment I didn't know if it was possible. My iPad alarm rang; I called Nick and told him I was still alive and fine.

I really wasn't. I wanted to get back to my New York place but I had to spend some time here in California and make as much noise as I could so people would know me, as I said. I spent three or four days there, I don't remember exactly, and flew to New York. If I was going to succeed in my plan, I needed time to think and prepare and I could really only do that in New York City. I needed two days there to get my head on straight. I called Nick using Google voice and told him I would not call for the next two days. I did not want to call anyone from New York.

A SCARY SUNDAY MORNING

I'm not sure what happened, Naria. It was a little unnerving. I was at Grace's at the counter ordering scones. I thought I heard someone say 'Kota?' I turned which I know I shouldn't have done. I'm so used to being called CC that the name Kota should not have registered with me at all but it did. Hearing it, as I said I turned. There were several people standing around and behind me but no one was looking at me, as far as I could tell because I caught myself quickly and turned back. I ordered the scone, paid for it at the check out, and hurried home.

I felt so good going out but so lousy coming back. I checked to see if anyone was following me but you know there are lots of people around all the time. Everyone seemed suspicious in my frightened mind. How could anyone have possibly known who I was after all these years? Walking back I thought of my disguise. I rushed out this morning because I felt so good. I hardly bothered to fix myself up thinking I'd be out and back quickly. I just thought of my coffee and scone.

When I came in I went to the mirror. Just what I feared! I've known deep inside that I've become sloppy in disguising myself lately. Today I hardly did anything. I didn't even wear the glasses or teeth. Oh my gosh, what a mistake.

Thinking of it now, the voice sounded like Jenny's but it may be nothing. Sitting here I'm not even sure I heard anything. Maybe I imagined all of it. I'm not Dakota or Kota anymore, what has it been, four, five years since I've heard that name. I've never had this happen before so why now. It couldn't possibly happen the one morning I'm really bad in disguising myself that someone who knew me from the past happened to be in Grace's. No, things don't happen like that.

Look at my writing, it's so shaky. I've got to calm down. You know what it must be, writing this yesterday about the time I sat down with Jenny, that terrible conversation I had with her and realizing she was involved with Roger, must have stayed with me. While I was at the counter ordering I may have been thinking back to that again and imagined her voice. That's what it must have been. It had to be that.

I've got to get away from this for a bit. I'm going to lie down.

SUNDAY AFTERNOON: AFTER RESTING

I'm back. I'm still a little unsettled but I've got to get my mind off it. I tried to read a bit but it didn't do much good. Somehow I don't feel like going out which is a bad sign. I don't remember feeling like that before, ever. I suppose I'll calm down in a bit. In the interim, I figure I'll go on with the story.

I faithfully called Nick everyday around noon time except for the two days I was in New York. Sometimes I spoke with him and other times I'd just leave a message. The trial was set for the fifteenth. I had two weeks before the time it was to start. I was spending the time in San Diego. I didn't think I'd get back to New York again until I executed my plan.

As you might expect, Alison was after me to call her. I did several times and we went back and forth over the language that was being used in the settlement. The money was all set. We had to figure out how it would be paid. She said the check would go to her and she'd distribute it out of her client's funds. I said, "You know Alison, as much as I trust you I don't. You did turn on me once. You're working for me today but tonight you could be back on Roger's team. We need another way."

I called Tom. I told him I needed to stay at his place until the trial. He said he'd get back to me. I figured he had to run it by Roger. He got back to me about fifteen or twenty minutes later and said it would be fine. I forget what excuse he used to explain why he couldn't give me an answer right away. It didn't matter to me. All I wanted was to stay in his condo up to the time of the trial. I went to California stayed a day or two and then flew back to Boston.

I went to see Nick to go over what would happen at the trial. He wanted me to be available first thing on Monday, the fifteenth. I didn't tell him anything about the deal I was working out with Alison. I told him I'd continue to do the routine calls everyday around noon. He wanted one more meeting on Friday the 12th. I agreed to meet him that morning. I kept a low profile that week other than going over to see Alison.

I started to draw blood from my body at this time. I'd take a little at a time and put it in a vial and I hid it in the refrigerator. I figured I'd like to draw about a pint over the week's period. Googling the subject, it appeared that wouldn't have a detrimental effect on me. I'd hope that using it strategically I would pull off the trick. I also pulled hair out of my head and kept it for later use.

Tom initially tried to hit on me but he finally got the message that he was heading to nowheresville and he left me alone for the most part. The 14th, Sunday, was the day I was going to do it. Tom usually watched football games at home then. He was deep into the football fantasy stuff so he was very intent on them.

I had two things left to do in the week and a half before the 14th that were important. I had to get in place the settlement deal with Alison. I knew she'd be getting jittery with the trial coming on so quickly that she'd want the deal put together right away. I had, as I said, no intention of making a deal so I had to string her along as much as I could. I wanted first of all to see if I could extract any more money out of Roger, not that I needed much but the more I had the happier it made me and the more irate Roger would be when he went down for the

316

count. Second I had to figure out a mechanism to delay making the deal public until the morning of the trial. Oh, yeah, there was a third thing. I wanted to meet again with Jenny. I really don't know why but I did.

I went to Alison's that Wednesday or Thursday, about ten or so days before the trial date. Everything runs together around this time so I might be off a bit. Actually, it is very much of a blur although some aspects of it are as clear as if they just happened. Alison was waiting for me with a stack of papers on her desk. She asked me to read them first. I did. It took a while. She said she would answer my questions at the end.

When I finished she asked me if they were fine. I said I had questions, first about the money, how it was to be paid, and next about the timing of my statement.

She said they were willing to do the money any way I wanted but obviously would not release any until the statement was made public and I publicly and openly vouched for it.

"What does that mean?" I asked.

"You will stand up in a public setting with the press there and will give out this statement, acknowledge you signed it, that it is the absolute truth, and you will answer questions."

"I can't just sign it and go away."

"No, it has to be as I said."

"Do you recommend I do this?"

"Positively!"

"Are your representing me or Roger?"

"You, you know that."

"Then tell me are there any down sides to me doing it."

"Not that I know of, you mean will Roger come after you like you once feared he was doing?

"Yeah, I suppose that's one of them."

"It's not worth it to him. To be frank, Dakota, he's just of a mind right now, and I say this as sincerely as I can, to put you out of his mind forever. He looks at you as a business deal gone sour. If he can get his name and reputation back, I'll swear to you that he's going to look at you as nothing more than biggest business mistake of his career which was as much his own fault as yours.. I don't know how to convince you of this because you have the belief he tried to have you killed. I'm not going to get into a discussion of that with you because trying to get you to change your mind about that would like be trying to change your mind about your religious beliefs. But believe me; he just wants to get on with his life. What can I say? Do I think you're totally safe, no doubt about it, none whatsoever."

"What about the DA?"

"You should know that answer yourself, Dakota."

"What do you mean?"

"You're the one who told me he was Roger's friend, didn't you?"

"Does he know about this?"

"Let me say this; when you recant you testimony, I'm sure he's not going to want to prosecute Roger."

"I'm not worried about Roger but it seems you are."

"What do you mean?"

"You've all but told me the DA knows of the deal and he's all right with it and Roger's going to get off."

318

"You can interpret it that way if you want."

"You know all about Roger but what about me?"

"You – you?"

"Have you talked to the DA about me?"

She looked back at me as if caught by surprise. I went on.

"You're now supposed to be my lawyer, did you forget? Have you made a deal with the DA for me – you know about the deal for Roger but what about me?"

She knew what I meant. She had tried to blow it by me. I had no doubt she'd never stopped representing Roger. I knew she'd never get the million out of the four million. She'd have to settle for a lot less but she wouldn't know that until Roger stuck it too her. Alison thought that by screwing me she'd gain favor in Roger's eyes. How little she knew a guy like Roger.

"You got to do that Alison; I want to know what's going to happen to me." I didn't have to go into it with her. She knew I was facing a perjury rap for having testified in the probable cause hearing under oath and now stating everything I said was a lie. Any lawyer worth her weight in salt representing someone would have had that upper most in her mind and have gone over it with me. I'd checked the law. I think it said perjury in a case like this was ten or twenty years in prison, I forget what at this time.

She remained quiet for a remarkably long time for her. I wondered if I didn't just cause the deal to go south. She knew they couldn't get an open guarantee from the DA not to prosecute me. She'd hoped I wouldn't know that. She was in a predicament. She had to report back to Roger and his lawyers to figure this out. That would take time. For me that was good, I needed time.

"So I assume you'll do that."

"I'll look into it," she said.

"Fine," I said. "Now, about the money. I'll come by Monday morning and pick up two hundred thousand in cash. That'll be the good faith down payment. After I sign the statement and all that other stuff, I'll want another 200 in cash and three cashier checks, two for a million each, and one for the 600 thousand. You can make your own arrangement for the remaining million."

"I'll let Roger know."

"Let me ask you another thing, Alison. I've been doing reading on this stuff that's how I knew I needed the DA's protection. But I'm also thinking this, it's what happened in the books I've read − it's you'll know the term something like jeopardy attaching, you've heard that?

"Yes, of course."

"That means that once the trial starts the DA has to prove his case or lose, doesn't it?"

"Yes."

"What if I take the stand at the trial and rather than going though all this signing here and standing up in public and being questioned which I don't like, why don't I deny anything happened when I'm testifying. Then Roger goes scot free, doesn't he?"

"He would but he doesn't want to do it that way, he wants the agreement up front."

"Isn't my way better? If the DA leaves his position, Nick Adams tells me he's going to be made a judge, the next DA can come in and go after Roger and force me to testify, you know that. Why not do it my way?"

"I told you, Roger doesn't trust you."

"It's not a question of trust, Alison. It's a question of life and death for me. You know I testified at the probable cause hearing to stay alive. When Roger sent those thugs after me to kill me I knew I had to do that. Now, I think I've seen the light and Roger's seen the light. Remember how I was scared when I learned from you I could be killed, since that time everything I've done is to make sure that doesn't happen. If I double-cross Roger, he's got nothing to lose by sending his gun men after me. If I could turn back the clock, I never would have reported being raped by Roger, but you're to blame for that. You kept encouraging me to go to the cops. You even protected me that night and had Roger arrested. I wonder if he knows that. Do me a favor; see if you can convince Roger that my way is better. Get me some protection from the DA and have the two hundred here Monday, I'll see you then."

I went on like that. I sensed from Alison's demeanor, especially when she had no answer why she didn't make a deal for me with the DA, that everything was being recorded or transmitted and that Roger was listening to everything that transpired. I wanted badly for Roger to go along with that deal of starting the trial and being exonerated during it. I knew him. He would react to it positively wanting to wrap it up once and for all and get on with his life.

He'd be shouting at his lawyers for not telling him about it and how if the DA became a judge he could be in jeopardy from another DA. I thought things were coming together pretty well.

It was over the weekend when I called Nick that he answered which was unusual on weekends.

"Oh, hi Nick, I didn't expect you."

321

"You all right, Dakota?"

"Yeah, fine. Just reporting in; I'm still alive."

"Glad to hear it."

"Dakota, the boss came in to me yesterday. He asked me what I'd do if you changed your testimony on the stand. It sort of caught me by surprise. Do you know what he's talking about?"

"No. I have no idea."

"I wonder why he asked me that."

"What did you tell him?"

"I pretty much said I'd talk to you to find out if you were planning to do it."

"What would you do if I did?"

"Are you serious?"

"No, I was just curious. I've no intention of doing it but what would you do if something like that happened?"

"I suppose I'd tell the witness about the perjury statute and warn her of the consequences and if she did tell a different story I'd indict her for perjury."

"Do people do things like that?"

"Like what?"

"Change their testimony."

"Not often, but sometimes on small things, but usually not on the big things."

"Well don't worry about me Nick; you know what I'm going to testify to."

"Thanks, Dakota, I'm wondering why the boss asked."

"So am I. If you find out let me know."

The Monday morning the week before the trial, I went to Alison's office. She had the package of money there for me. I took it. She said Roger would go along with the deal but he said that he expected I'd come through for him. I assured her I would. I asked her about what the DA had planned to do when I changed my testimony. She said she had no guarantee yet but felt comfortable about getting one. I told her I planned to meet with the DA around 9:00 the next Monday. I hope she had it by then.

"What if I can't get you something in writing by then?" she asked.

I should have said "too bad then I'll testify" or something like that. I knew though that would make Roger uneasy. He wanted guarantees, no loose ends. I said, "I'll take my chances. I'll come through with Roger, I expect him to come through for me. As you said, he wants to go on and forget this stuff. If I'm prosecuted this will go on and on and remind people of what Roger was accused of. If you don't have it in writing but tell me it's in the works, I'll go along with it. I also want to get on with my life, Alison. This isn't what I want to be doing any longer than I have to. Next Monday after I recant, I want to pick up my money and head west, or south, but somewhere out of here."

I went back to the apartment with the cash. I then took a taxi to the airport where I rented a car. I drove the car back to the condo and put the money in its trunk. I called Jenny and asked if we could have dinner that Thursday night. She said she'd call me back she had to check. I figured she'd have to clear it with Roger. She called back and said sure. We'd meet at 7 o'clock over at Dedham in the new restaurant that just opened, Blue Ice. Sometime during the week I asked Tom if I could borrow his car to go over there. He consented, I think there was a Thursday night game on he planned to watch.

Before leaving I drew some blood out of my arm and took some of the hair I had pulled out. I opened the trunk and put the hair and the blood in there spreading it around a bit but leaving the bulk in one area. I drove to Dedham. Jenny was there when I arrived. There wasn't much of a crowd and we were quickly seated.

We were friendly enough when we first sat down. Knowing her like I do, she believed she had the upper hand on me. I don't blame her after what happened the night at the Green Lantern. I finally dabbed my toe into the shark infested waters with, "You still seeing Roger?"

"I don't think that's any of your business, Kota."

"Probably not, but when I ran out on you last time you were telling me Roger wanted to do a deal with me. I thought if you were still going out with him you, you know, you could tell me if he still does."

"Trial's next Monday, isn't it Dakota?"

"Yes."

"You're going to take back everything you said about Roger raping you, is that right."

"That's my present intention," I answered.

"I can assure you, if you do, Roger will honor his commitment to you."

"He told you that?"

"Yes."

"So you're still seeing him."

"I said it was none of your business Dakota, and it isn't.

"Yeah, I guess so."

She then jumped right into the subject. "But I'll tell you something Dakota, you and I have totally different opinions about Roger. I could never believe he'd have hurt you like you said. I'd love you to tell me what really happened."

"You saw me in the hospital; Jenny and you believe that Roger would never hurt anyone."

"Funny, but now that I know him the answer is yes."

"You think I made the whole thing up?"

"About Roger beating you, of course."

"How did I get beaten up then, if Roger didn't do it?"

"That's something only you know Dakota."

Here she was, throwing the truth back into my face as if somehow she knew what had happened. What else could I say but, "Believe what you want, Jenny, I can't control how you think. I never could. I suppose too you don't believe Tom could be violent toward me."

"Tommy, I don't know as well as you want to think I know him. Tommy has a little bit of a wild side to him, unlike Roger who's under control all the time. I've never seen Tommy angry or violent but then every time I've been with him he's been quite happy. You must not be pleasing him."

"I've kept my distance from him and he doesn't like it. Has he ever mentioned it to you?"

"I don't see Tommy anymore. My brunches with Roger are at the Four Seasons now."

"So you are still seeing him?"

"I guess I let the cat out of the bag. Yes, I'm still seeing him. I didn't want to mention it, thinking I'd upset you, but I didn't want to lie to you. Yes, and something else, he's getting divorced and we plan to get married."

"Has he told his wife?"

"There you go again, Dakota. You never can think good of anyone. Always got to knock a person a bit, you know that."

We struggled through the rest of the meal. I drove back to the condo and put Tom's car in its usual spot.

Friday I met with Nick Adams. We went over a couple of things. I told him I'd keep calling him and see him on Monday at nine in the morning. He wanted to know how I felt about going through with it. I told him I'd never been more determined to do anything than that in my life. Leaving I said, "I'll be here Monday morning unless Tom stops me." He looked at me, nodded, and said, "Be sure to keep in touch."

That Saturday is gone from my memory. Sunday I got up early. I made breakfast for Tom, something I hadn't done since the "out-of-the-big-bed" day. I felt it had a nice symmetry to it. He got up around 11:00 and was pleasantly surprised. I told him not to make anything out of it, it's just sometimes old habits are hard to break. He said something about maybe there were others I still wanted to cling to. I let it pass.

I went into my room. I told him I was going to read and then go out for a while and do some shopping. I asked him if he needed anything. He said he was fine. He went to the refrigerator and said, "If you pick up a couple of six packs that'd be good." I told him I would. He went off into the den to watch the football games.

I had a pretty good quantity of blood I poured some on the pillow and matted some of my hair in it. Sprinkled some against the bed board as if it were splattered, put a good deal on the sheet so it would go into the mattress, made some droppings along the floor to the door. I put some on the butcher knife I had taken in the room with me.

326

I knew that Jenny and Roger would be off in dream land somewhere. I called her land line at her condo and left a message, "Jenny, I'm really scared, Tom's got a knife and he's threatening me with it. He wants me to change my mind. I don't know what to do. Can you help me?" My voice was sufficiently trained as you know to make it sound like I was really frightened. I called Alison's cell. It went to message, as I figured it would. She'd recognize my number and since she was trying to duck me, not wanting to tell me they had nothing in writing from the DA, I left her a message, "Alison, please call, I need your help!" It was ambiguous enough that she'd figure she could ignore it.

When all that was done I left all of Dakota's personal stuff in the room. I put a little blood on my cell phone and tossed it off to the side. My wallet and pocketbook containing all my identifications were left on the dresser where I normally kept them. I listened until I heard the TV announcer talking excitedly about an ongoing play. I had put on a disguise with the teeth, glasses and wig. I slipped out of the room, left the knife in the kitchen drawer, went out the door and down into the garage. I got in my car and drove back to the airport. I turned it in. I took the package out, took a taxi from the airport to South Station. I hopped on a train to New York City.

I never went back to Boston again. That was, what did I say, four or five years ago, maybe more. I stopped counting.

MONDAY MORNING — EARLY

The story made the New York Times. As best I could piece together from reading the Times and the Boston papers on the net, Nick Adams got worried sometime Sunday afternoon when I didn't call him. He reached out for me and my phone did not answer even though it rang. Jenny got home later that day in the early evening; she got my message and called Tom. He said I'd gone out earlier shopping and had not gotten back. He'd tell me that she called.

Monday morning when I didn't show Nick became quite concerned. He reported to the court that his main witness was missing. He requested a delay. He sent a couple of state troopers over to the condo to look for me. Somehow they tracked Tom down and he gave them permission to go into the apartment. They went into my room and saw all my identification stuff still there. One of them told the NY Times reporter that he immediately thought of the Chandra Levy case. They questioned Tom. He said I went out sometime Sunday and he had not seen me since. Based on what they saw they got a search warrant for the apartment and for Tom's car. They found my blood in both places in a sufficient amount that indicated I had been violently assaulted in the apartment and then put in the trunk of the car and taken someplace. Probably to a dumpster somewhere but maybe even dumped into the harbor.

Jenny had to come forward with her telephone call to her apartment as the state cops started to track the numbers. Alison also came under heavy criticism for her role in getting my message and doing nothing about it. It was obvious to everyone that I had been murdered

328

and carted off somewhere. Surveillance was put on my San Diego apartment and I never appeared there. Roger lost his position as CEO and eventually ended up pleading guilty to a crime he never committed. The DA could prove the case with the probable cause transcripts and all the other evidence after the court accepted the idea that I was never going to be able to come back and testify. Roger was told if he went to trial the DA was going to recommend life in prison but on a plea the recommendation would be ten to fifteen years. The judge sentenced him to seven to fifteen. He's probably getting out around this time.

Tom was eventually indicted for murder. The Commonwealth had experts who would testify with the large loss of blood I could never have survived. Others would testify about the obvious fact that I would not have left the apartment without taking my identification and that proved I was forced from the apartment. Tom's car had the blood in the trunk. And, of course, Tom admitted he was home all day so he put himself at the scene of the murder. It was not going to be open and shut but the DA thought he could get to the jury and if he did he'd convict Tom. Tom was sufficiently frightened by spending the rest of his life in jail for a crime he didn't commit, agreed to plead guilty to manslaughter. He received a nine to fifteen year sentence. He'll also be eligible to get out in a year or two.

To my surprise, Roger did divorce his wife but it was at her instigation. I guess she stuck it out with him until he could no longer provide her with the life style she wanted. After the divorce, Roger true to his word married Jenny in prison. I guess they let people do such things in

Massachusetts but I could never understand Jenny who was on the outside wanting to hitch her wagon to someone on the inside. All I could figure was that she'd be able to trust him since she'd know where he'd be sleeping at night.

Alison, I don't know what happened to her. I think she lost her gig on Fox news. She got a lot of bad press around the time and a lot of women's groups blamed her for not saving my life. But she got off easy for what she did as far as I was concerned.

For me, well you see it's difficult to have a real life once you've put a couple of innocent people in jail. The sweetness of the revenge soon soured when the hatred I had built up toward Tom and Roger lost its poignancy. The sad thing is I can never give back to them what they had lost. But I also have been unable to give myself what I most wanted, a life to go on with. I never figured that into my calculations.

I still hold my looks. I could date guys but don't. What can I tell them about myself when they asked me questions. It was fine for me to live as if I had just dropped out of the sky onto New York City but people you meet want to know something about you.

I couldn't talk about anything with people other than pure fantasy which meant, as I recognized, I couldn't ever have a serious relationship with anyone, or I should say with anyone I'd like to have such a relationship with. I never thought any of this through really thoroughly. I never considered the consequences of living without a past or having a past so abominable to every right thinking person that I am forever required to conceal it.

I was happy for a while with my peace and books, but like all things, books after all, are only books. Perhaps if they could smile at you they might fill some need. I knew I could go out and get a little dog or cat for company but I wasn't an animal person. I suppose when you come down to it, Roger and Tom aren't the only persons in prison. In a sense they are luckier than I am, they'll get out someday; I won't.

I think of what I miss most is the touch of another human. You know like to lean against someone and know that someone means something to me and me to him. Like to have someone put their arms around me or give me a hug, never mind a delicious kiss. Yes, a kiss, I do miss the kisses the kind of kisses I had with Tom when we first started out. I think I'd give up all of this for one nice long hug and the ability to snuggle up to someone and feel his warmth. I have to start over again but I'm trapped.

But I'm beginning to let myself get down again which I shouldn't do. Since I've started this talk with you, Naria, I have felt a lot better about myself. Maybe my trouble is New York City. Suppose I go out west somewhere. There must be some guy out there who'd take me no questions asked and who I could build a life with. Yes, perhaps that's it; the City is nice, it saved me and given me my life back but the life it has given me is no longer enough. I need more.

When I saw myself in the mirror this morning I realized that I'm still quite pretty and I've kept in good shape. I know coming up to my mid-thirties I'm pretty old so I'd better get going now since forty, the end of the line and old age, is just around the corner.

I just answered the phone. It was a woman's voice. She asked me to meet her at Starbucks over on Second Avenue. She wouldn't tell me what it was about but said it was in my interest that I do it. I don't know what to do. I guess I should go and meet her to see what it is all about. I wonder if it had anything to do with yesterday at Grace's.

I've got nothing to worry about. It's broad day light out. I'm in the middle of New York City. I think I'll take you along with me Naria. I've heard of cases where people are called out of their apartments and while they are gone the apartment is broken into. I'm not worried about that happening here, I don't have anything of value but I do have you and I've put so much time into you that I never want to have anything happen to you.

I'll tell you one thing, Naria, I don't like mysteries. I'll solve this in a few minutes although, I do feel my mouth getting a little dry. Sometimes I make a mountain out of a mole hill. Well, I'm dilly-dallying now so I better get going. We'll talk a little later because there are other things that happened I want to tell you about. But let me take you out now for some fresh air.

AFTER NOTE:

Dakota went to meet a woman at Starbucks. We know she was at Starbucks because she left this notebook there. I don't think it could have been there too long before I got there. I'm sure if she accidentally left it behind she would have returned during the hour I sat there. After all she took the notebook because she feared someone might break into her apartment after she left so she would have been highly conscious of protecting it.

I have to conclude that she deliberately left the notebook on the seat. She must have slipped it onto the seat, or even sat on it, when the person who arranged the meeting showed up. She had to have wanted to hide it from the person so I assume she recognized her. They must have talked and went outside and the notebook was left behind. I did ask the person at the counter if anything unusual had happened that morning and she said no. Something must have happened outside that prevented her from going back in to retrieve it. If that is the case, she may have been terminated with extreme prejudice.

On the other hand, she may have made up the whole thing about receiving a call to go to Starbucks. She may have decided to write that she did so that when the notebook was found some would assume she was somehow abducted as I just did. If we believe she was terminated then she could close this chapter on her life like she tried to do when she went to New York City. She could start a new life because people would think that she was dead. She could go west and no one would follow her. She would also get the

333

monkey of guilt off her back by disclosing her diabolical actions and hope that her victims could get some type of relief from the effects they suffered. This way also she'd feel more free believing they would no longer want to hunt her down and kill her. But that would have been very risky because the notebook could have easy been thrown into the trash.

I believe what she wrote actually happened. How she planned her acts and how the justice system responded in my opinion seems to be a realistic account, something that she could not make up unless she had been through it. If she made up the story, it would make no sense after all that work to leave it on a seat at Starbucks. At one time I thought this was a product of the writer's imagination. Now I'm convinced that if this is all imagination the author would have looked high and low for this notebook since she put so much effort into it. It's all so strange.

I've read the notebook cover to cover on several occasions looking for clues. I've given up trying to figure this out on my own. I hope my action in sharing it with others will allow me to get some type of closure. I almost rue the day I decided to go get coffee or even more to see the notebook and believe it was my job to protect it. That's all water over the dam now.

What's in Dakota's notebook is an example of what happens when a person makes a decision to try to gain from evil. Things spin out of control, the center doesn't hold. That's why I think of this as a tale of the fruit of the poisonous tree. That's the thread that runs through the story. Like Eve when she resolved to taste a little evil, or Pandora when she decided to peek into that box, Dakota entered into a world where there could be no good consequences. Although she accomplished all she set out to do in the end she found herself imprisoned by her success.

My overriding feeling is that the writer has paid the ultimate price. Could it have been Jenny who saw her at Grace's and then met her at Starbucks? Would she have willingly gone off with Jenny leaving her notebook behind? Or was that the only way she could cry out for help? Was Jenny in New York City with Roger? These are things I guess I'll never know unless someone comes forward.

All I hope is that someone reading the words in the notebook will recognize the situation set out there and use it to rectify the wrongs this woman had done. I also hope that Dakota, or whoever she is, is still alive. She got herself caught up in her own web of evil. She was right that she had a story that was too sad to be told. If she found her way west, I hope it is to a better life.

Reading over this just now I recalled something I had totally forgotten about. When I first picked up the notebook I looked inside it, saw the writing, and read some. While doing this I looked up. A woman, pretty, mid-thirties, dark hair, well-dressed, Mediterranean complexion of the stylish women in Barcelona or Rome, was standing just inside the door opening. She was looking straight at me. For a second I had a feeling she was coming over to claim it because I remember a sense of panic coming over me thinking I'd have to explain why I was reading her notebook. I looked down as I closed it and when I looked up again she was gone.

www.ingramcontent.com/pod-product-compliance
Lightning Source LLC
Chambersburg PA
CBHW070205260626
47160CB00002B/455